I Love You More

I Love You More

By Stacy Finz

LYRICAL PRESS
Kensington Publishing Corp.
www.kensingtonbooks.com

LYRICAL PRESS are published by

Kensington Publishing Corp.
119 West 40th Street
New York, NY 10018

All Kensington titles, imprints, and distributed lines are available at special quantity discounts for bulk purchases for sales promotion, premiums, fund-raising, educational, or institutional use.

Special book excerpts or customized printings can also be created to fit specific needs. For details, write or phone the office of the Kensington Sales Manager: Kensington Publishing Corp., 119 West 40th Street, New York, NY 10018. Attn. Sales Department. Phone: 1-800-221-2647.

Lyrical Press Books and Lyrical Press eBooks logo Reg. U.S. Pat. & TM Off.

First Electronic Edition: February 2024
ISBN: 978-1-5161-1121-3 (ebook)

First Print Edition: February 2024
ISBN: 978-1-5161-1122-0

Printed in the United States of America

To my sister Laura.

Acknowledgments

I would like to thank my editor, John Scognamiglio. His insight is always invaluable and working with him is a dream.

Thanks to Alex Nicolajsen for all the encouragement, cheerleading, and kind words over the years. I am so lucky to have you in my corner.

To my agent, Jill Marsal, who is the best first reader a writer can ask for. I couldn't do this without your guidance.

Thanks to the entire talented team at Kensington. It takes a village.

Above all, thanks to my husband, Jaxon, who makes everything possible.

"There is a distinct, awful pain that comes with loving someone more than they love you."

—Steve Maraboli

Tess

I can barely see the teleprompter, my vision is so blurry. And for a second, I fear my mascara is smudged. Then I realize I don't give a rat's ass, not about smudged mascara or my hair, or looking perky at the ass crack of four.

All I can think about is revenge.

My hands shake as I shuffle the papers in front of me, her voice still in my head.

"It's two in the goddamn morning, this better be important."

For a moment I thought I had the wrong number, then quickly realized I'd used automatic dial. It was Kit's private phone, the one reserved for family, the one reserved for me, his wife. "Who the hell is this?" I snapped.

There was a long pause, then, "Oh shit, I picked up the wrong phone," then a lot of background noise, then Kit. "Tess?"

An hour ago, I was a happily married woman, getting ready for work, calling to tell my husband I missed him and that I couldn't wait to see him tonight. Sure, it was early, too early, but I'd tried all night and he never picked up. I assumed he was partying after the team's big win and hadn't even gone to bed yet. And of course, there's the superstition—Lord knows Major League Baseball is full of them—that if I don't call him before he boards the team plane to wish him safe travels, something terrible will happen.

Ironically, something terrible did happen. To me.

I tell myself to focus on the broadcast. There's only a couple of hours left. Afterward, I can throw something, tear up Kit's clothes, sell his Gold Glove Award on eBay. But in the meantime...*Grin and bear it*.

We have a new set today. The NBC designers have been working on it for months. The *Good Morning New York* backdrop has been changed from yellow to bright orange and we no longer have chairs, just a curved white couch that's supposed to make it look like you're in our living room instead of a studio in Manhattan. The table is Lucite, so we actually have to wear something presentable from the waist down, not our pajama bottoms.

The massive arrangement of fresh flowers is a nice touch, and under ordinary circumstances I would appreciate how the orange hue of the lilies is a perfect match to the backdrop.

I'm sure some high-paid consultant told station executives that we could up our ratings if the set looked more like a high-end hotel lobby than an actual newsroom. Next week, they'll hire another consultant who will tell them train cars are trending and the set will be reconstructed to look like *Murder on the Orient Express.*

Roy is at the weather map. Another hot and sticky day in New York.

The biggest thing I miss about San Francisco, besides my family of course, is the cool, foggy summers. Here, I have to scrape off my makeup and reapply new as soon as I get from the car to Rockefeller Plaza. If it wasn't for the fact that someone might recognize me—even at the ass crack of four—I would show up sans makeup and turn my face over to Cindy, my stylist.

While we go to a package on how to make the most of the city during a staycation, I check my phone. Kit has been calling nonstop, even though he knows I'm on air. His plane leaves in less than ninety minutes and he's begging me to "calm down" before word leaks to the front office.

At this point, I'm not too concerned about his career. If truth be told, I'd like to take a baseball bat to it, then to his balls, where I'm betting my launch angle would be better than his.

We're back on camera. I plaster a smile on my face, though I feel like I'm bleeding inside, dying a little at a time. I nearly miss my cue to introduce a live shot until Rodney kicks me under the table. There's a fire in Harlem, a jazz club where Billie Holiday used to perform. We have a reporter at the scene, standing in front of shooting flames as firefighters battle the blaze.

While she reports on the potential cause—likely electrical, according to the fire flack—I catch a glimpse of myself in the back-wall mirror and adjust my blouse. It's limper than week-old lettuce. Don't ever wear silk in 70 percent humidity. Even though they keep the studio at a comfortable sixty-eight degrees, I can't stop sweating.

My phone vibrates with another text. I'm sure it's Kit again but before I can look the reporter tosses back to the desk.

"Thanks, Heather. Please continue to keep us apprised of this important story," Rodney says.

He and I have been coanchoring *Good Morning New York* for four years now. Kit likes to call Rodney my work husband. He's definitely my best friend, especially now that I'm on the East Coast and Avery is in San Francisco, though things aren't great between my sister and me. Even before I moved away, I could feel an undercurrent of resentment from her. Sometimes, I think she's jealous of all my success.

I guess she'll have the last laugh now. By far, Dad will be the most disappointed. He thinks Kit is the second coming of Christ, even if he plays for the Yankees, my father being a lifelong Giants fan.

We go to a commercial break. I wish I could run to the restroom and send Kit a nasty message, like "rumor around the newsroom is your slut has herpes," but we only have a few minutes to set up for the next segment, a cooking demonstration with David Jung.

When I joined WNBC's morning show one of my first interviews was with David. He's a well-known New York restaurateur and we became fast friends. I like to think it's because my father is a chef and owns a popular restaurant in San Francisco, which makes David and I kindred spirits of sorts. But I intuitively know our friendship has more to do with me being on television and my husband being the first baseman for a legendary baseball team.

As shallow as it sounds, I enjoy the fame and all the perks that come with being famous. And I'm about to take it to the next level because if things work out as planned—fingers crossed—I'm about to go network, which means my face will be in front of nearly nine million viewers nightly. Not too shabby, considering I started at the bottom at a small station in Salinas, California, and worked my way up to the local NBC station in the Big Apple. If I can make it here, I'll make it anywhere, right?

David, who is already on set in the studio kitchen, kisses me on both cheeks. "So good to see you, Tess."

"You too, David." I don't know how I'm managing to hold it together but I am.

Even Rodney appears unaware that I'm about to crack any minute. He usually knows my moods before I do.

"So, what are we making today?" I ask David, smiling broadly, like the great pretender.

"We're doing a simple vegetable stir-fry with sesame. This is something anyone can do at home with whatever ingredients are in season. In Korea, we typically use just one vegetable. But I'm zigging a little here, using an assortment. I've got some parsnips, some delicious Jerusalem artichokes..."

I tune out, returning to the morning I've had, to Kit, to my marriage. For the first time in my life, I don't have a plan. Oh, I want to get even all right. I want him to hurt as much he's hurt me. But what do I do after that? Leave Kit, who I still love, despite everything he's done?

And hate. I hate him so much I want to strangle him.

"See what you think?" David says, turning my attention back to the show with a heaping forkful of stir-fry.

I do the thing where I take a bite and pretend to have a food orgasm on screen, when in reality, the vegetables are undercooked and too salty. Barely edible. My father would laugh his ass off.

"Delicious," Rodney says and catches my eye, silently communicating how awful it is. "And so easy even I could make it."

We laugh because all our viewers know Rodney is a lousy cook. Our ratings spike every time he regales them with a story about his failed kitchen escapades.

We break for another commercial. David and I make a few minutes of small talk before I have to return to the main set.

My phone chimes with another text. Kit. He's boarding the team plane and as soon as he gets home, he wants to talk. I don't have time to respond before we go live again, nor do I want to. Let him stew, the bastard. When he gets home, he'll be lucky if I haven't changed the locks.

Next up, Rodney and I talk beach reads with a romance author from the Bronx. I plaster on the face again, going through the motions, when what I want to say is romance is dead and men are whores, every last one of them. Except Rodney, Dad, and Bennett; they're the good guys. Instead, I fake it, letting Rodney do the heavy lifting.

By the time we finish the segment, my stomach feels like there's a sailboat capsizing inside of me. I keep hearing her voice in my head, then Kit's trying to explain away everything, gaslighting me until I don't even recognize him.

We were all out, celebrating...She was drunk and didn't have a room... mine had two beds...Nothing happened...I can't believe you don't trust me.

What does he take me for, an idiot?

We break for another set of commercials, and I have just enough time for Cindy to touch up my face and hair, which if I bothered to look must be frizzy beyond redemption. Cindy brushes out my waves and smooths each lock with her cache of styling products.

"What's up with you?" Rodney whispers. "You're off your game."

"I'll tell you later." If I tell him now, I'm liable to break down and won't be able to pull myself together in time for the rest of the newscast.

He nods and before he can say more, we're back on camera. We go to another live shot of the Harlem fire, which by now has been mopped up. Heather gives us an update and does an interview with the manager of the jazz club, who hasn't been allowed to go in and estimate the extent of the damage, blah, blah, blah. The truth is I'm barely paying attention and am relieved when we go to network for the national news briefing.

I have the sudden urge to call my sister but it's not even dawn yet in California. Besides, I know what she'll say. Leave him! Avery is a take-no-shit woman. She works in a kitchen full of men, including my dad. Macalister "My Way or the Highway" Stone isn't the easiest. But Avery is every bit as stubborn as our father. And she'd kill Kit with her bare hands for hurting me.

The thing is as much as I'd like to kill him myself, I'm not sure I want my family to hate him, even if I do. And right now, I hate him so much I can't see straight.

"Girl, you look like you're about to wilt," Rodney says. "After the show you want to get drinks and tell me what's going on?"

"At eight in the morning?" Who am I kidding? A bracer sounds perfect right now and the place across the street serves a mean Bloody Mary.

"Okay, breakfast."

"Maybe," I say, not sure I want to tell Rodney either. He worships Kit. Everyone does. And I don't think it's just because Kit plays first base for the Yankees or that he's hitting over 300.

He's the kind of guy who walks into a room and everyone stops what they're doing to stare at him. Not because he's the best-looking man in the place—there are always better. Don't get me wrong, he's handsome enough. Six-two, blue eyes, a full head of brown hair. But he's not Hollywood handsome or nearly as attractive as Rodney, who has a classic square jaw, cleft chin, and smooth dark skin. Kit just has a certain kind of bearing that makes him stand out in a crowd, something that says, "I can get us out of any mess there is," and you believe it. You believe in him.

I guess that was my first mistake, believing in him.

It was easy to do. When I first met him four years ago, I'd barely started at WNBC. New job, new city and the stress of succeeding was like a pressure cooker. To say I was overwhelmed is putting it kindly. There's only so much fake-it-until-you-make-it a person can pull off before imposter syndrome sets in. And I was experiencing a bad case of it the night I co-emceed a charity auction with Kit for the Boys and Girls Club of Manhattan.

The station had volunteered me for the event to raise my visibility. Everyone was expecting Sherita King, WNBC's six and eleven o'clock anchor, who pulled out at the last minute. She's an icon in New York and part of the reason guests had paid a thousand bucks a plate to attend was for the chance to rub elbows with her.

While Kit was still a rookie at the time, the buzz was that he was the next Don Mattingly. His profile was definitely higher than mine. I was convinced I'd hate him on sight. I once dated a forward for the Sharks who was a jerk and had covered enough stories about self-entitled athletes to give me a bad taste in my mouth. I figured a rising star in the Yankees had to be a towering tool.

But it turned out he was the opposite. Sensing my bad case of nerves, he took me under his wing. And our auctioneer chemistry was off the charts. We were riffing off each other, cracking jokes, acting like we'd known each other for years. By the end of the night, we'd broken the record for the most money raised, and I was a little bit in love.

For the next two weeks we were inseparable, and I was a lot in love. A year later we were married, a gorgeous ceremony and reception with three hundred guests. And though he's away a lot, we've managed to keep the romance alive. Or so I thought.

We're on again and it's almost time to wrap up the broadcast, thank God. I don't know how much longer I can maintain the charade of the perky blond morning show host when all I want to do is cry into a Bloody Mary with Rodney or go home and start breaking stuff. Kit's stuff.

"Gavin Hunter, the man who invented Quizle, the trivia game that's taken the country by storm, is here with us to talk about how it all started as an anniversary gift for his wife." The camera pans in on Hunter, who's joined us on set.

I turn to Rodney and give him a collegial shove. "You love this game."

"I'm addicted. Seriously, it's not healthy."

"Gavin, did you ever expect that this sweet gesture to your wife, who as I understand it, is a huge *Jeopardy!* fan, would become an American pastime?"

"Never in a million years." He laughs. "It's a little overwhelming."

"Tell us how you planned this surprise for your wife and how it ultimately exploded on the Internet?"

Gavin goes into a dissertation while I disappear in la-la land. Oddly enough, I'm thinking about my father's pot roast. About how just the mere scent of it bubbling on the stove top could warm my insides like the greatest kiss on earth. About how when Avery and I were kids it was the cure-all for everything from a bad grade to a broken heart.

And suddenly I want to go home, to my parents, to San Francisco. To Avery. If it wasn't sweeps, I'd board the next direct flight to SFO and head straight to my father's pot roast. But the station has a strict no-vacation policy during the ratings season, especially for us anchors. The show must go on.

Gavin, game inventor extraordinaire, has exited the set and the floor director is winding his finger in the air to wrap it up.

"Speaking of games," Rodney says in that overly chipper banter we use to close out each show. "That was one heck of a battle last night against the Twins. Twelve innings." Rodney lets out a low whistle. "Kit's game winning hit...he'll never have to buy another drink in this town again."

I doubt that but the suits love it when we talk about Kit and me on air. The all-American couple, beautiful, prosperous, living the dream.

What a joke.

"You know how he celebrated?" I ask, unable to staunch the well of anger and disappointment I'm feeling, unable to let common sense and self-preservation prevail. "He spent the night and the wee hours of the morning fucking none other than our very own Annabel Lane. That's right, Rodney, Annabel isn't just covering the team, she's fucking them."

I feel Rodney's hand pressing hard on my leg, but I can't seem to stop myself from ranting about infidelity, about Annabel, about Kit, about what a swine he is.

It isn't until later that I realize audio cut my sound. But by the time they'd made the split-second decision to drown me out, it was too late.

Avery

It's barely dawn and the streets are empty, only a few delivery trucks and an occasional dog walker. The city won't wake up for another thirty minutes or so. But bakers keep strange hours.

I pull my car into the narrow driveway behind Stones, the restaurant that has been in my family for three generations.

In the beginning, under my grandfather's helm, Stones was near the water, where tourists traversed the piers, dining on the catch of the day. But after the Loma Prieta earthquake, when the Embarcadero Freeway was torn down and that part of the city got seedy before it got good again, my father relocated the restaurant to the Financial District, where it became something of a San Francisco institution.

I go inside, turn off the security alarm, flick on the switch, and stare at my ring finger, admiring the way the diamond sparkles and glows in the illumination of the light. I move my finger from left to right, bedazzled by the prisms of gray and white. The ring feels heavy and foreign. I shouldn't have worn it to work, not when I'll be elbows deep in dough and chocolate all day. But the temptation to show it off is too great to leave it at home.

In about an hour, the staff will start trickling in to prepare for the lunch service. For now, though, I have the place to myself to do my baking.

I hang my bag on a hook, place my phone on the counter and wash my hands in the large sink, careful that my ring doesn't slip off and wind up in the drain. Wearing this rock is going to take some getting used to, I think as I wiggle my finger.

My phone vibrates, piercing the silence of the empty kitchen, and I glance down at the screen. Ten heart emojis from Bennett, which makes a smile blossom in my chest.

Five seconds later, he calls.

I dry my hands and cradle the phone between my ear and shoulder. "Hey, you're up early."

"I've got a presentation at eight and thought I'd get in a workout. What's cooking, good looking?" He always says that and as corny as it is, it always makes me smile. Every single time. "You tell anyone?"

"It's barely six in the morning. No one's here yet." I laugh.

Last night, Bennett Lamb asked me the four words I've longed to hear from the moment I laid eyes on him.

I'm not going to lie, the road to here has been long and bumpy—and even torturous—but we're exactly where I always wanted us to be. And Bennett is trying so hard that it no longer seems important that I wasn't his first choice.

Take his proposal for instance. It was the cutest of all time. After dinner last night, he carried me piggyback from the kitchen to the baby grand piano that takes up our entire living room and played me a jingle. His jingle, the one that unbeknownst to me he'd been working on for two solid weeks.

At first, I thought he was testing out one of his new ad campaigns on me. But when he asked me to marry him to the tune of something that sounded vaguely like the Folgers in your cup commercial, I cried. And after I said yes, we laughed until our sides hurt, and I made him sing the jingle all over again.

"Let's celebrate tonight. I can come to Stones, and we can raise a glass with the family, then come back home and get naked," he says, and my stomach flutters the same way it did that first time.

I'm not exaggerating; from the minute I saw him sitting in the restaurant five years ago, I knew he was the one. The Italians call it the thunderbolt because that first meeting is so powerful, so intense that it reverberates in your chest like a burst of lightening. It sounds crazy but that's exactly how it was. At least for me.

"Naked it is," I say. "I'll call you when I tell everyone." No way will I be able to keep it a secret until tonight. Mom will take one look at the ring and scream and the whole restaurant will know by lunchtime.

I hang up, shrug into my chef's jacket and get to work. Today, it's chocolate layer cake, apple pie à la mode (I made the French vanilla ice cream yesterday, even though we're closed on Mondays), butterscotch pot de crème, which my father insists we label as pudding on the menu, and cheesecake with a caramel sauce.

On Wednesdays, I take things up a notch with carrot cake and go fancy on Fridays with a bananas Foster that'll blow your mind. Occasionally on

Saturdays I'll do a baked Alaska as a throwback, my homage to midcentury modern. And the kids get a kick out of seeing me light it on fire.

I've been making these desserts so long I could do it in my sleep.

Like our savory dishes, the desserts here are classic, nothing too out of the ordinary or too challenging. I went to one of the most respected culinary schools in the nation and my pastry repertoire consists of desserts a fifties housewife would've made.

But my father's philosophy is less is more. He likes to say, "Why push it? Stick with a good thing and they'll come."

And they do.

Even before farm to table or sea to fork was a thing, Stones used fresh and local ingredients. My grandfather believed that all food should taste like the food his grandmother used to make, using produce she grew in her garden or canned in her kitchen.

How we differ from the scores of four-star restaurants in this town—and believe me, there are a lot of them—is that we're not especially cutting edge or even striving for interesting. Our menu doesn't change daily. No trendy small plates, because Dad believes that even an appetizer should feed a family of five. Sous vide and foams would be laughed out of the kitchen. People come here because they want to eat their nonna's dishes, not haute cuisine.

That isn't to say we aren't best in class. No one does a seafood stew, meatloaf, or pot roast like my father.

The truth is, you can't operate a restaurant in San Francisco unless the food is topflight, even if it's simple fare. You'd be run out of the city. And at Stones, people line up for our stick-to-your-ribs menu. Even Northern California's Michelin-starred chefs hang out here in their off-hours, gobbling up Dad's cioppino.

Stick with a good thing, right?

And not to toot my own horn or anything, but part of the reason Stones is so popular is because of me. Sometime in the last decade, San Francisco's culinary kings decided the layer cake and its ilk were dead. I brought them back to life with a vengeance.

My cake is so popular that people call first thing in the morning to reserve a slice for fear there won't be any left by the time they get here. The *New York Times* called it one of the best chocolate layer cakes in the country and "maybe the world" (their words not mine) and year after year it ranks in the top ten recipes chosen by the *Times*'s readers.

So clearly my father has a point. Elevating a classic to best in show is a winning formula, even if it isn't all that exciting.

I let the sheer pleasure of mixing and rolling take me through my morning routine. Only this time, I'm humming Bennett's jingle.

I'm about to get the pies in the oven when I hear a key turn in the lock. It's not even eight yet.

"Avery?" my father calls and before I can answer he's in the kitchen beside me.

"Morning." I slide as many pans as I can hold into our ancient but trusty Vulcan and set the timer. "You're here early."

Dad ties on his apron and takes out two slabs of shoulder meat from the walk-in cooler. Beef stew is the special today. For as long as I can remember, it's always been on Tuesdays.

I glance over at him and he's already slicing and cubing the meat at the *rôtisseur* station. His movements are so fluid it's like an interpretive dance.

When I was little, I used to watch him for hours. He'd sit me up on the counter while he prepared the day's mise en place, gliding through the kitchen with an economy of movement that he bragged saved his feet. He would always give me small jobs to do. Stirring a pot of soup, rubbing salt on the chickens, lining up containers of garnish in perfectly straight rows. I was his tiny kitchen helper.

Tess, on the other hand, couldn't be pried away from the front of the house. She liked standing at the hostess stand with my mother in one of her frilly party dresses, greeting diners, basking in their oohs and aahs.

What a beautiful little girl. Aren't you precious? Look how clever you are. Here stands the future of Stones.

Nope, not Stones. Not any restaurant for that matter. Tess's true calling is broadcast journalism. She anchors the top-rated morning show in New York City. I was the one who followed in my father's footsteps. This wonderful old kitchen has always been my home. My heart.

"Dad, how come you're here so early?" I ask again. My father sometimes gets so caught up in his work, in his love for the ingredients, for the food, he forgets anyone else is here. Javier, our chef de cuisine, will have running conversations with him where Dad never speaks a word.

"Thought I'd get a jump on things." He doesn't look up and there's a tightness in his voice that makes me suspect he's lying.

"You and Mom fighting?"

He stops and lays his knife down. "When have you ever known your mother and I to fight?" He pauses, then throws his head back and laughs.

I've always loved my father's laugh. It's like his stew, deep and hearty with so much richness it fills you up.

"What's it this time? Is she still on you to hire a manager?"

My parents have been managing the restaurant themselves all these years, which is kind of crazy. The job requires endless amounts of paperwork, dealing with vendors, and constantly putting out unforeseeable fires. A leaky toilet, an impromptu visit from the health inspector, an avocado shortage. And it's not as if my mother and father don't already have enough to do. Between Mom operating the front of the house and the waitstaff and my father's executive chef duties, they're running themselves ragged.

"Nah." He gives a half shrug. "We're not fighting. I have a meeting today and I wanted to get things squared away in the kitchen. Javier's got enough on his plate."

"A meeting?" My father rarely if ever takes meetings. He can't sit long enough, and people generally annoy him. He has no greater pleasure than feeding them but having to actually interact with them on any level other than food drives him nuts. Mom is always the one to take the meetings, not Dad. "What kind of meeting?"

When he doesn't answer, I prod. "Dad?"

"Mind your own business." He winks, then goes back to cubing meat.

I know him well enough to know it's hopeless to press. I also know him well enough to know something is up.

As soon as my pies are out of the oven, I disappear into the alleyway behind the restaurant to call my mother.

The street is littered with cigarette butts, more than likely left by Wen and Carlos, who like to take their smoke breaks out here. My mother has been on them for years to quit. They keep telling her "tomorrow."

Mom's phone only rings twice before she picks up. There's noise in the background, music maybe.

"Where are you?"

"Getting my hair done. Is everything okay?" It's always her first question when we call, Tess and I. *Is everything okay?*

I have news, I want to say. But for right now I'm focused on my father. "Why does Dad have a meeting today?"

There's a long pause and then, "Well, I suggest you ask your father."

"I did. He's being his usual cranky self. Is it a medical thing Tess and I should know about?" Because that's the first place I go when Dad is being secretive. Last year, we had a scare with his blood pressure. He was experiencing chest pain and shortness of breath. We forced him to go to the emergency room, where he was diagnosed with hypertension.

The doctor warned that if he didn't make significant changes he was at risk for a stroke or heart attack. Besides meds, Mom and I forced him to reduce his sodium intake. He complains it's like eating at an old-age-home cafeteria but swears he's adhering to the diet, which is a bald-faced lie because I've caught him sneak more than tastes in the restaurant.

"It's nothing medical, Avery."

"You promise?" I don't really have to ask because my mother never lies, not even if her husband explicitly asks her to. Besides having a code of ethics that could rival the late Mother Teresa's, she can't keep a secret to save her life.

Once, Tess threw me a surprise birthday party. I'd just graduated from college and was on my way to the Culinary Institute of America. Tess was working at KNTV. It was before we'd both met Bennett. Anyway, she'd gone to extraordinary measures to keep the party secret from me, even making up some convoluted story about how I needed to go with her on a story assignment because the guy she had to interview, a tech mogul who was having a hospital wing named after him, was a perv. The interview was merely a ruse to keep me away from Stones until the guests arrived.

In hindsight, the story made no sense (Tess always travels to her interviews with a cameraperson) but at the time, I didn't think to question it. If my big sister needed me, I was there. Period.

Except, just as we were leaving the restaurant to go on this alleged assignment of Tess's, my mother blurts, "Make sure you're away for a good hour." I might've missed the slip—I'm kind of clueless that way—if she hadn't immediately covered her mouth and muttered, "Oh shit."

"Avery, honey, Sandra is ready for me. I have to go." Before I can ask again about the meeting she hangs up.

Relieved that it's not a medical issue, I tell myself I'm being ridiculous and go inside to start on my layer cakes.

The kitchen is buzzing with activity. Somehow, Wen and Carlos managed to sneak past me and are prepping vegetables. Javi is at the sink, peeling potatoes. My father is playing the Grateful Dead, his favorite band of all time.

I finish the batter for my layer cakes and get them in the oven, humming along to "Uncle John's Band." While they're baking, I prepare my ganache for the frosting and get to work on the cheesecakes.

Before I know it, it's noon and I can hear the buzz of the dining room. Mom pops her head in the kitchen. Her gray hair is tamed into a smooth bob that falls just below her chin. I like it better curly than when Sandra blows it out with her big round brush until it's straight and sleek and not at all anything like my mother. Tess calls it anchor lady hair, which she's managed to avoid in all her years as a news broadcaster.

"Mac, you better come see this."

A few minutes later, we are in the kitchen, huddled around Mom's phone, watching my sister have a seismic meltdown on the morning show, which has gone viral on YouTube.

We keep hitting replay, trying to absorb exactly what we're seeing. It's a little difficult because halfway through her tirade someone muted her sound, though not before she managed to get in a couple of f-bombs. What is clear is Kit had an affair with someone from Tess's station. And no matter how many times Mom tries, Tess won't answer the phone.

"I can't believe she isn't picking up," my mother says, and my father puts his arm around her.

"She'll be okay," I say. "She's probably with Kit." Or with a good divorce attorney. Knowing my sister, it's the latter. Good! If any of this is true, he deserves to be drawn and quartered, the son of a bitch.

"Who's this Annabel Lane?" my mother asks. "Why have I never heard of her before?"

"She's a WNBC sports reporter," Dad says, not that he keeps up on these things as far as I know. But her picture and bio have been all over the Internet and Dad's been scrolling ever since Mom cued up the YouTube video for us. "Why does it matter?"

My mother shrugs. "I don't know why but it matters. Try to call Tess, Mac. Maybe you'll have better luck."

"Already tried. She's not picking up for me either." My father waves his phone in the air, starting to look more worried than he was a few minutes ago. He gazes up at the clock. "Should we close, Beatriz?"

It would be the first time in memory that Stones didn't have a dinner service during its regular operating hours. Not even during my father's high-blood pressure scare did we close the restaurant. Mom, Javi, Carlos, Wen and I managed to hold down the fort without him.

"No." My mother shakes her head, though I can tell she's torn. "It's already after three in New York. There's nothing we can do for Tess tonight. I'll see about booking a flight tomorrow. Avery will have to help out with the front of the house."

I nod, though I hate working the front of the house. I've always only wanted to be in the kitchen, where the action is. That's one of the drawbacks of a family restaurant; everyone has to pull their weight even if it means doing a job they don't like.

"In the meantime, I'll keep trying her," my mother says. "You too, Avery. If she answers anyone it will be you." She gives me that look, a look that says she knows more than she lets on.

I take a break in the alley again to dial Tess. Her phone rings five times before her voice, a recording of it anyway, comes on and says to leave a message.

"Tess, it's Avery. Mom, Dad and I are worried about you. Please call one of us. And fuck Kit."

The minute I hang up, I consider calling Kit because I'm that concerned. It's not like Tess to go MIA at a time like this; generally we'd be the first people she'd call, milking it for all it is worth. I just hope she isn't doing something stupid.

But I don't call Kit because it would be weird. *Hi, I'm looking for my sister. Is she with you or is this your night with the sports reporter?* I suppose I could call Rodney but I don't have his phone number and I'm assuming TV personalities aren't listed.

I settle for a text: "Call Mom! She's freaking out."

Then I go back to the kitchen, where things seem to have settled down. Everyone is at their station, quietly dicing and chopping.

A part of me feels guilty that I'm not making more of an effort. I could call WNBC, though her workday ended hours ago. But maybe someone knows where she is. It's what a good sister would do. Scratch that. A good sister would be on the first plane to New York City. But things are complicated between Tess and me.

Besides everything else over the past four years—and I'm ashamed to admit this—I'm pissed at her for upstaging my big announcement today with her devasting one. No one even noticed my ring. I know I'm being petty, selfish, and even heartless. But I can't help the way I feel. I can't help it because for as long as I can remember, Tess has been outshining me.

She's always been the star of the Stone show and I've always been sloppy seconds. Maybe that's unfair; it's not Tess's fault she was born more beautiful, more charming, and more outgoing than me. It was just the luck of the gene draw.

And for a long time, I didn't mind living in her shadow. There were times when I even preferred it. I could bake and work in the restaurant and no one, least of all me, expected more. All eyes were on Tess and her meteoric rise in the world, a world she seems to own just by smiling.

By sixth grade, she'd gotten herself a modeling gig with Old Navy. She'd somehow learned that the company was doing a casting call for a commercial at the flagship store on Market, showed up without my parents' permission and got one of the coveted ad spots when my mother agreed to sign the paperwork. That led to an agent, who got Tess more work. The Gap, Levi Strauss & Co, Williams-Sonoma—any San Francisco company that needed "young talent" (that's what they called it) used Tess. She had the face and attitude to sell whatever they were hawking.

We all thought she'd grow up to be a professional model, but the truth was she was too short. Five-seven barefoot if she stood up real straight. And frankly I don't think she would've been content staring into a camera all day long. Tess is brilliant, not to say there aren't fashion models with Princeton educations. But she would've been bored stiff parading around in swimsuits or posing in evening gowns for a living.

I was only a little jealous of her short-lived modeling career and everything that came after. In a way, I rode her coattails. When the kids at school weren't idolizing her, they were looking at me, the younger sister of a minor celebrity. I was more than willing to settle for her crumbs.

That is, until Bennett. It wasn't until Bennett loved Tess first that I loved her less.

Tess

It's funny how life can change in an instant. Before yesterday, before I found out about Kit, before I went ballistic on *Good Morning New York*, my world was perfect. Or as near perfect as it can get. I had a husband I adored—and trusted—and a career that was about to reach the pinnacle of any broadcast journalist's dreams.

My future was certain.

Then it all went to shit in the blink of an eye.

After my "unprecedented" outburst I was put on unpaid administrative leave and escorted to the door by two security guards as if I were a common criminal. Cheryl, the station's news director and my boss, called later to see if I was okay, which was nice, then told me she hoped I got the help I needed (not so nice).

So, here I am at my agent's office, trying to do damage control. I've only been here once before. Usually, Elsa and I talk on the phone or meet at a restaurant.

The space, the thirty-third floor of a Madison Avenue high-rise, is pretty much what I would expect for an agent of her caliber. Tasteful and extremely expensive.

The walls are painted in earth tones and the two sofas that face off next to a floor-to-ceiling window are creamy white with too many throw pillows. The rug is Persian and quite possibly an antique, though I'm no expert in these things, having grown up in a home where tasteful meant we got it at Macy's. The light fixtures alone, a tiered wicker basket situation that looks African, probably cost as much as a year's salary at KSBW in Salinas. Ah, who am I kidding? Probably more like two years' salary before taxes.

There's a gallery of framed photographs of Elsa with various news talent. Katie Couric, Lester Holt, Anderson Cooper, Savannah Guthrie, Gayle King, and some people I don't recognize but instinctively know are important.

Her desk, a lacquer table, is a high-gloss beige. With the natural light coming in, the color almost appears a pale pink, which seems highly impractical (I would be worried about ink stains). And it's got to be an ergonomic nightmare. But it's gorgeous, what my mother would call "a *piece*."

I turn my attention back to Elsa. "If they fire me they have to at least pay me through my contract, right?" I have sixteen months left on a three-year deal, not a small chunk of change. But my hope is they won't can me. So far, the fans on social media are on my side. It is Kit and Annabel in the wrong here, not me.

"That's unclear. You used profanities on air in your newscast. That could easily be seen as a violation of your morals clause, not to mention a violation of a host of other provisions in your contract. It certainly doesn't help that you publicly maligned Annabel Lane. NBC doesn't like backbiting between employees." Elsa lets out a breath.

"Backbiting? The woman is sleeping with my husband, Elsa. Jesus, whose side are you on?"

"Here, let me read from the employee handbook." Elsa picks up a booklet from her desk. It seems she's been studying regulations and protocol at WNBC. "There's a long list of what is considered misconduct, including, and I quote, 'maligning coworkers online and violating standards on workplace collegiality and inclusivity.'" She puts down the book and glares at me.

"I didn't malign anyone on social media."

"No, you did it on live television."

Elsa James is one of the most respected TV news talent agents in the business, so she damned well better have my back. At five-eleven without her signature three-inch stilettos, steel-gray bob and piercing blue eyes, she's a force to reckon with. Case in point: she got me a $40,000 signing bonus and a $50,000 clothing allowance—unheard of in today's media market—when she negotiated my contract with WNBC.

"Don't kill the messenger here." Elsa holds up her hands in the classic surrender position. "We'll work through this, I promise." Then why along with her Chanel suit is she wearing the face of doom?

"Should I put out a statement or something?" I don't have a PR team like Kit, who has an entire machine working for him. Before all this, WNBC handled all my publicity.

"Yes, but we need to consult with Senali first." Senali Kumar is the crisis manager my agency sometimes hires to clean up its high-profile clients' messes.

And according to Elsa, this is a mess of epic proportions, though I'm still having a problem seeing what all the fuss is about. I deliver news and current events for a living and yesterday morning I did just that. It was a public service, really. Now the world can see what a lying, cheating bastard the almighty Kit Reid is.

He didn't even bother to come home last night, just sent a text that said, "Are you out of your fucking mind?"

That seems to be the sentiment of everyone I know, including Rodney, who, God bless him, has been standing by me ever since I was thrown out of Thirty Rock. Even my parents seem befuddled by what happened.

My father: "Tess, honey, you don't always have to say everything you're thinking."

My mother offered to come but I told her to stay. The last thing I need right now is a babysitter. I'm sure by next week this whole thing will blow over and New Yorkers will have a new scandal to embrace.

While Elsa rings Senali, I stare at my phone, scrolling through my Twitter feed.

@RealTessStone Annabel Lane is a skank. #KitReidsucksballs

@RealTessStone Way to stand up. #BoycottWNBC #Metoo

@RealTessStone If you want someone to talk to, I'm available for long walks on the beach and whatever you need, darling. #JasonGiambiisstillking #TessStoneissmokinghot

I grimace at that last one and keep reading, skimming the good ones for the bad just to measure my audience.

@RealTessStone You're an idiot. Everyone knows what happens on the road with professional athletes. What makes you special? #Golddigger #Bimbo

@RealTessStone If getting a little on the side helps the Yankees then it's fine by me. #Dealwithit #Takeonefortheteam

@RealTessStone I used to start my day every morning with you but not anymore. What kind of example do you think you're setting for young people when you use vulgarities on television? My kids were watching. #Dobetter

I can see #DobetterTessStone is trending. Do better, my ass. I want to tell the trolls that spending your day on social media hashtagging about someone you don't even know isn't doing better, it's pathetic.

"I don't think that'll work," Elsa says to the person on the other end of the phone, presumably Senali. She looks at me. "Are you willing to go into rehab?"

"For what?" I raise my arms in the air. "Last I looked, I didn't have a drinking problem."

"I told you," Elsa says into the phone. "Yeah, let's go with a simple apology but heavy on the remorse. 'I feel ashamed...I shouldn't have used my platform to air details about my marriage...My language was unconscionable...If I could take it all back, blah, blah, blah.'"

"An apology? For what?" I yell. "What in God's name do I have to apologize for?"

"For saying 'fuck' like three times on air," Elsa shouts back, cradling the phone between her ear and neck while shaking her head at me. "On live TV, Tess."

Okay, granted, throwing out the f-word wasn't a good choice. But people should understand that I'd just found out my husband was with another woman, a colleague for God's sake, and I was out of my mind with anger, panic, and hurt. In that moment, I wasn't myself. Or maybe I was exactly myself. Shouldn't I at least get points for being genuine? For being human.

They tell you in broadcast journalism school to be real, to be conversational, to be one with your audience. And the first time I do it, really do it, I get bitch-slapped to kingdom come.

"Tess, if you want to go to network, you'll have to trust us. I don't think you understand the gravity of what's happening here."

"What's happening here, Elsa?" I roll my eyes because does she actually believe I've been asleep for the last twenty-four hours?

"What's happening here is you're this close to getting canned." She makes the inch sign with her thumb and forefinger.

I doubt it. The more I think about it the more it seems unlikely they would actually sack me. My Q ratings are through the roof and last year I won an Emmy for a package on counterfeit designer china. Who knew it was a billion-dollar industry? Besides, there are anchors who have done a lot worse than talk about their cheating husband on air. Take Matt Lauer for instance. Need I say more?

Anyway, everyone knows I'm on my way up. You don't let your golden goose go. Nope, to appease the viewing public, Ralph Doran, the general manager of WNBC, who makes all the big decisions at the station and who by the way loves me, will more than likely take me off the air for a month, send me to some kind of broadcast anger management school, and say I'm rehabilitated. In other words, a slap on the wrist. Losing a month's worth of pay won't be great but it's not like I can't afford it. Kit's salary alone is enough to finance a small country.

Kit. That's a whole other story.

The one good thing about everything that went down yesterday is that I haven't had time to focus on my marriage. Other than the one text, Kit and I haven't spoken to each other. It's probably good. We could both use a cooling-off period, time to gather our thoughts so as not to do anything we'll later regret. Like yesterday.

Though I'm not so sure I would've done anything differently, except for the bad language. If I'd taken time to consider my choice of words, I probably would've used better ones or at least less offensive ones. Still, I'm banking that the whole messy episode will soon be history.

Elsa and Senali are still on the phone crafting a statement. There's a built-in console on the other side of the room with a mini fridge, coffee maker, and snacks. I didn't eat breakfast this morning and deliberate on whether to wander over for a look-see at the selection. On second thought, though, I'm not sure I can keep anything down.

I keep visualizing Kit writhing in bed with Annabel, and Annabel's breasts, which is admittedly an odd place to go, considering the trouble I'm in. But they're spectacular breasts, bigger than mine, perkier than mine, the kind of breasts that stop people on the street. Clearly, I'm in a bad place because I'm actually wondering if maybe I should get a boob job.

I flash on Avery, who would be disgusted with me for even considering such a thing. This in turn reminds me that I really need to call my sister. I've been putting it off, putting off having to tell her about Kit, about my job, about sinking so low that I'm sitting here mentally imagining myself with larger breasts. It's stupid because she already knows about Kit and my job. The whole damn world does.

But like I said before, there's a sharp undercurrent between Avery and me. Really just Avery. And for that reason, I don't want her to see me at a low point. Not because it'll be a schadenfreude moment for her, Avery's not like that. And not because I have something to prove to her, or anyone else for that matter. Because I don't. But there's a part of me that suspects she'd like to see me taken down a notch. It's sad because I only want the best for her. She's my baby sister after all. And when this is all over, which I hope is soon, I'm going to do something about patching up my sister and me, getting us back to the way we used to be before I left for New York.

"This looks good," Elsa says to Senali over the din of her printer, then hands me a hard copy of the statement.

I read it and roll my eyes. "A bit over the top, no?" You would think I was apologizing for slaughtering kittens in front of a group of toddlers.

"No, not even a little over the top." From her tone, Elsa may as well add, "You stupid bitch."

I give her points for restraint, though I do pay her salary after all. "Okay, fine. When and how should we disseminate it?" You would think I'd know, being in the news business.

"We'll post it on your Twitter, Facebook and Instagram accounts and I'll make sure to send it to the *Post*, the *Daily News*, and the *Times*."

"Did they even cover it?" The *Times*. The *Post* and *Daily News* had screaming fifty-point headlines on their front pages. Page Six in the *Post* did a whole item on the incident, including citing anonymous sources saying Annabel and I have always been competitive. I barely know Annabel and she covers sports. What could we possibly be competitive over? Except for of course my husband.

Elsa lets her glasses slip down her nose and pins me with a look. "Everyone covered it."

Jeez, what passes for news these days?

"Maybe we can hire a plane to skywrite it over the Hudson."

Elsa leans forward over her lacquer desk, its whimsical lines at odds with her dour expression. "Once again, I'm going to remind you what's at stake here. A little humility might be in order."

I shrug. "My marriage is a dumpster fire, Elsa. You'll have to excuse me if I don't feel particularly sorry about a few bad words uttered in the heat of the moment. Having said that, I do appreciate everything you and Senali are doing to make this go away." The sooner the better, so I can focus on Kit and me.

I quickly scan my phone for the hundredth time to see if he's texted or called but there's nothing. The fallout for him has to be even worse than it is for me. To say the MLB frowns on its players screwing their local sportscasters is an understatement. My guess is he's facing a firing squad right about now.

"Are we good, Elsa? Can I go home?" Between the phone ringing off the hook and me tossing and turning most of the night, I didn't get much sleep and am exhausted.

"Yes, go home." Elsa pushes her glasses back up her nose. "And, Tess, lay low for a while, okay? That means no talking to reporters."

"Got it," I say, then call for my driver to pick me up in the front of the building, where I wait in a corner of the lobby until he parks at the curb.

Having a driver is a perk of the station and apparently no one thought to take away this perk when they suspended me, which I see as a good sign.

In the back of the Escalade, I scroll through my phone while Dimitri makes his way onto the FDR. What should only be a six-minute trip from Elsa's office to my apartment could take more than thirty minutes in traffic. Today is definitely one of those days.

I have twelve missed calls, mostly 212 area codes. Rodney called twice without leaving messages. My mother wants me to call her and my father is "Just checking in, kiddo." There's a couple of voice mails from, wait for it, reporters, including ESPN, which I quickly delete. The last one is from Avery. "Call me." There doesn't appear to be any judgment in her voice but then again it's hard to detect attitude in two words.

I check my watch. It's a little past ten in the morning in California. My dad and Avery are already at the restaurant and my mom is probably on her way there. I deliberate on whether to call, the thought of killing three birds with one stone at once appealing and daunting. Instead, I slip my phone back into my purse and stare out the window at the East River, losing myself in the water, in the blueness of it. Maybe it's my own blues that draws me.

If I was smart I'd call a lawyer. A good lawyer because Kit has the resources to get the best. But a part of me is hoping lawyers won't be necessary, that we somehow can get past this, though I don't know how. Right now, I don't know anything.

Dimitri pulls up to my address, a prewar co-op on Park Avenue designed by Rosario Candela. As legend goes, Gary Cooper held his wedding here. And at one time, Vera Wang could've been my neighbor. Unfortunately, she's long moved on.

We spent way too much money on our twelfth-floor apartment, a price tag that even made me flinch and I'm from San Francisco. But Kit had gotten endorsements from Toyota and Nike, and well, we just did it. We told ourselves it was a good investment.

The apartment was originally a three-bedroom but I converted one of the rooms into a walk-in closet. Kit and I use the second bedroom as an office and guest room for when our folks visit. Or his brother, who would move in full-time if he had his way. I like Jonas but Kit's younger brother has a bad case of failure to launch and would become a permanent appendage if I didn't put my foot down.

The kitchen is the stuff of dreams. My dreams, because nothing looks like it's ever been used. My father laughs at the pristine Viking stove and the impractical Sub-Zero, which has less cubic storage space than a counter-depth fridge and cost roughly three times as much.

Don't get him started about the built-in Miele coffee maker (which I actually use). "What's wrong with a good old coffee press?" he asked the first time he saw it, running his hands over the digital menu while shaking his head. He's the only professional chef I know whose home kitchen appliances come from Sears.

My earliest memories are of him standing over our old thirty-inch white Kenmore stove, making Avery and me grilled cheese sandwiches. The best grilled cheese I've ever had in my life. His trick was the cheese, a French-style gruyere from a creamery in the Napa Valley and a young, mild cheddar from a farm on Northern California's coast. The bread, thick slabs of Tartine's country loaf. When the heirloom tomatoes were in season and if they were especially good, he'd add thin salted slices under the hood. In the winter, he'd replace the tomatoes with spicy chorizo and a warm cup of homemade soup.

Later, Avery tried to replicate his sandwich. Hers was always delicious but never quite as good as Dad's. Her pastries, however, are another story. No one can beat them and I often think she's capable of so much more than the desserts she makes for Stones.

But that's a family business for you.

It's probably why I don't cook when everyone else in my family does, even Mom, who also grew up in a restaurant family. Her folks owned a roadside cafe in Modesto that served mostly Portuguese dishes to the other Portuguese families in the area. We lived for her caldo verde, potato soup with cabbage and chorizo, which she made every Sunday to hold us through the week.

My father still jokes that she should be the one in the kitchen and he at the front of the house. If you know my father you'll get the joke. He's not exactly a people person. But he's our person, our favorite person, even if he is an obstinate curmudgeon.

"Thanks, Dimitri," I say as I step out of the car, wondering if I'll find Kit sprawled out on our sofa. He doesn't have a game until tomorrow and it's at Yankee Stadium.

I'm not sure if he has practice today. What I am sure of is that I don't want to talk to him until I've had a few hours of sleep and a decent meal. I want to be rational but I'm still so angry that it's burning me up inside.

I get as far as the door to my building, expecting Howard our doorman to open it, when I'm blindsided by a man who practically knocks me over. My heart stops and despite all the self-defense classes I took in college I freeze, fearing I'm about to be mugged, and pray Howard is calling for backup.

At seventy-two, he's nowhere near a linebacker and spends a good amount of time sleeping behind the front counter. A few members of the co-op board have hinted that they'd like to replace him. But he's been the doorman here for more than forty years. Kit circulated a petition to save his job and most of the residents signed, buying poor Howard a few more years.

Before I can scream for help or hit the man, he shoves an envelope in my hand. It's too aggressive to be construed as a request for an autograph, though I get those a lot, often from weirdos who are a little bit scary. But this guy is a lot scary. Tall, broad and dressed all in black, his hood drawn over his head. That alone should set off alarm bells because it's at least eighty degrees out.

I stiffen my back, preparing myself for...I don't know what. A punch, a grab, him fleeing with my purse. But all he does is leave me off-balance as he says, "Those are legal documents," hops on a bicycle that I just now notice, and takes off.

I look down at the manila legal-size envelope in my hand. My name is scrawled across the front and my breath catches in my throat.

"Are you okay, Ms. Stone?" Howard has opened the door and is standing on the sidewalk.

"Did you see that guy? The one in all black with the bike?"

"Yes, ma'am. He came in asking about you and I sent him on his way. I got the sense he was one of those process servers. They've been here before. He must've been hiding in the alley, waiting for you to come through the door. You've got a well-known face, Ms. Stone."

"Well, he got me." I hold up the envelope and let out a breath.

"Sorry, ma'am."

"Nothing to be sorry about, Howard. He was going to find me one way or another." I head to the elevator and for a second consider asking him whether Kit's home.

I don't of course, instinctually knowing that the answer to that question is in the envelope I'm holding. The door slides open, and I rush inside before Howard can see the tears in my eyes.

Avery

I know I love Bennett more than he loves me.

Five years ago, Bennett Lamb walked into Stones, sat at the bar, ordered my dad's famous chicken potpie and an after-work cocktail. A martini if I recall correctly. Or perhaps I'm remembering a martini because I know it's his drink of choice. He always sets aside the tiny skewer of olives and saves it for last.

In any event, he was at the restaurant that night, capping off his dinner with dessert. I was in the kitchen, helping my father on the line because Javi was on vacation, a trip to Disneyland with his grandkids.

Our two lives, Bennett's and mine, might never have collided if not for two things.

First: my killer chocolate pot de crème (pudding, according to Dad). Second: the fight that broke out in the dining room.

Hesper Johnson came in like he does every evening. Hesper is homeless, or partially homeless. Six months out of the year he lives with his sister in Antelope Valley in Southern California. By February, the two of them are so sick of each other that his sister inevitably kicks him out and gives him enough bus fare for a Greyhound back to San Francisco, where he sleeps under the Bay Bridge or in one of the single room occupancy hotels in the Tenderloin, depending on his cash flow situation.

In September, when Hesper has had enough of living on the streets, the cycle starts all over again. He calls the annual pilgrimage to Antelope Valley his fall and winter sabbatical.

But while he's here, we feed him most every night. Occasionally, he'll take out the trash for us or do some other menial job in a show of appreciation. Mom always loads him up with leftovers at the end of the night, which he shares with the rest of his bridge posse.

Anyway, one of our diners took exception to him sitting up at the bar. To be honest, he doesn't smell too great. The diner told him to take a bath. In return, Hesper told the diner to do something anatomically impossible. One thing led to another and before too long the men were brawling, like actually throwing punches in the middle of our family-friendly restaurant.

Dad and I ran out from the kitchen as my mom and our bartender, Cybil, tried to pull them apart. Carlos called the cops. But by then, the two men were on the floor, hitting and kicking each other. It was absolute mayhem.

Then, out of nowhere came a loud whistle, the kind that comes from sticking two fingers in your mouth, the kind the hero in a movie uses to catch a cab, the kind I've never quite been able to pull off.

Startled by the ear-piercing sound, everyone stopped to see where it was coming from. And there was Bennett.

He hopped off his barstool, dashed over to the melee, pulled the diner up by his J.Crew collar and walked him to the door. "Do you mind? We're all trying to eat."

There was a round of applause from the room. Carlos sent the cops packing with cake, so their quick response wasn't in vain. And Hesper went back to his soup while I stood at the corner of the bar transfixed on Bennett. On his kind, open face and his green eyes that I would later learn were hazel.

And then I did something I rarely if ever do at Stones. I walked up to him and said, "Your meal is on the house."

His lips slid up in a smile that made my breath catch in my throat. "Nah, you don't have to do that."

"You sure? Because I'd...we'd really like to thank you for what you did," I said, trying not to stumble on the words.

"Yep, totally sure. Nothing to thank me for. But if there are any more of these left, I'll take another one." He tapped his spoon against a ramekin that had been scraped clean except for a small trace of chocolate around the edge. "Best thing I've ever had."

More than even his smile, the words went straight to my heart. Especially because he had no way of knowing it was my pot de crème. I'd never seen him in the restaurant before.

I flagged down Mandy, Mom's favorite server, and asked her to get Bennett another one.

"I take it you've got clout in this place." He motioned for me to take the stool next to him, which I did even though they needed me in the kitchen.

"I'm the pastry chef here and my last name is Stone, so yeah, a little bit of clout."

"Pastry chef, huh? Does that mean you made the pot de crème?"

"With my own two hands."

"Wow, you've got some talented hands."

Ordinarily, the "talented hands" remark would've skeeved me out but from his tone there was no double entendre in his meaning. He was being complimentary in all the right ways.

"Thank you."

"So what's the difference between pot de crème and pudding?" Mandy brought a second ramekin to the bar and Bennett pushed it in the middle, between us. "I'm willing to share but only a little of it, so don't be getting any ideas." He got up and filched a spoon from a nearby table and handed it to me.

I'd never shared a dessert with one of our diners, it's a tad too intimate. Even creepy. But I didn't hesitate to dip my spoon in and take a bite. I taste everything in the kitchen as I go, yet I wasn't prepared for just how good it was. Rich, smooth, and so chocolaty it melted in my mouth.

"My father, who's the executive chef here, would tell you there is no difference," I said, addressing the pot de crème versus pudding question, which by the way I get a lot. "But there is a distinct difference if you're a baker. Both are custards. But pudding is thickened with cornstarch and chilled for at least three hours. Pot de crème is looser than pudding and is thickened with eggs and baked in the oven in a water bath. Probably more information than you wanted to know." I laughed because I tend to geek out when I'm talking about food.

"Wow, who knew? I just thought pot de crème was the French word for pudding. You learn something new every day." He grinned again and I felt his smile all the way down to my toes.

"So what brings you into Stones, I mean besides dinner?" My face turned red because it was a silly question and sounded like a cheesy pickup line.

"Word on the street is it's good and I'd never been before. Thought it was high time I gave it a try. Glad I did. Besides the food being really good and the dessert outstanding, who doesn't love a good barroom fight?"

"Yeah, sorry about that. Would you believe me if I told you that's never happened before? Or at least not as long as I've worked here."

He laughed. "And how long is that?"

"My whole life."

"You came here straight from the womb, huh?"

"Pretty much." Which felt like the truth. I can't remember a day when Stones wasn't part of my life.

"You're a local, then," I said. Because the way he'd made it sound was that he lived here and wasn't just passing through.

"Born and raised if you count San Jose."

I chuckled because San Franciscans have a thing about San Jose. A friend of my late grandfather used to say the last time they had a crowd in downtown San Jose was for a hanging. Given that San Jose is the epicenter of the tech world, San Joseans are having the last laugh.

"What brings you to our fine city?" I asked.

"I live here. Work a few blocks away."

"And this is your first time at Stones?" I made a face.

"But it won't be my last." He shoved a heaping spoonful of my pot de crème in his mouth and when he finished, said, "How's this?" and to the tune of the Rice-A-Roni jingle sang, "Stones ain't phony, it's the San Francisco treat. Stones is homey, the flavor can't be beat," then threw his hands up in the air. "Okay, best I could do on short notice."

I laughed again because the rewritten ditty had a ring to it. "How'd you come up with that?" I didn't think anyone, at least our age, knew the commercial anymore. I only did because some of the DeDomenicos, the family who invented Rice-A-Roni, ate in the restaurant from time to time.

"It's what I do," he said.

"Make up jingles on the spur of the moment?"

"Make up jingles, yes. But not on the spur of the moment. Like your pot de crème, it's a fine art. And fine art takes time." He winked as if he was letting me in on a joke.

"Seriously, you make up jingles for a living?"

"Seriously, I do, though we call it advertising."

"Wow, name a couple." I'd never met a person who wrote jingles.

He ticked off a few that I recognized but nothing like the "Nationwide is on your side" or "Every kiss begins with K" (thank God) commercials. Still, it was impressive. He was impressive. But the best part was he wasn't impressed with himself. It's a rare quality in this city. Most single men here think they're the second coming, which made me check his left hand for a ring. There wasn't one, which didn't mean he was single.

But it felt like he was. More importantly, it felt like he liked me.

I glanced at my watch, knowing it was only a matter of time before Dad sent out one of the line cooks to find me. But I hadn't wanted it to end with Bennett. I could've asked him for his number, but it seemed highly presumptuous. For all I knew, there really was a significant other hiding in the wings.

He must've sensed my dilemma because he followed my gaze to the swinging doors that led to the kitchen and said, "Do you have to get back to work?"

"Yeah, I'm filling in for our chef de cuisine this week," I said, then casually threw in, "Most of the time I'm off by five."

"Well, I'll be back tomorrow for one of these." He held up the now empty ramekin. "If you're not too busy, come out and say hello."

And true to his word, I found him on that same barstool the next evening. I even made and put aside a couple of pots de crème just for him in case he showed because it was Friday, bananas Foster day.

He came on Saturday and Sunday, too. I finally had to break it to him that if he wanted to continue eating my desserts, he'd have to branch out a little, that the chocolate pot de crème was a specialty item. Tuesday, he tried the butterscotch pot de crème and lost his mind. Wednesday, he deemed my carrot cake the best in the world.

By Thursday, I'd prepared him a small table in the corner of the kitchen, so he could eat lunch (he had started coming for lunch too) while I baked and we could still carry on a conversation. We talked about everything. My job, his job, his love of opera and how I hated it, my love of shoes and how he only owned three pairs. How we both wanted to buy a house someday near the water. How neither of us had ever been to Hawaii but desperately wanted to vacation there.

To my amazement, Dad never said a word, going about his business, pretending Bennett wasn't there.

For four glorious weeks, we spent lunch in the kitchen and dinner at the bar. I was sure he was working up to asking me on a real date, somewhere away from Stones. Somewhere where we could kiss for the first time away from the prying eyes of my parents, Javi and the rest of the staff.

But that day never came. What happened next is hard to explain. Probably because I should've seen it coming but was too caught up in Bennett to think it could.

Tess.

She walked into the restaurant one evening after work, her hair sleek and shiny, her dress not too fitted but just fitted enough, flashed those baby blues and Bennett was a goner. I could see the moment it happened, the way he instantly turned his head toward her entrance and glanced at her a little too long. His hazel-green eyes a puddle of wonder.

She waved at me and in a voice that could only be described as awestruck, Bennett asked, "Do you know her?"

"Mm-hmm, she's my sister," I croaked, telling myself that everyone was like that when they first met Tess. That in a second, he would come to his senses and remember I was the one.

"Are you going to introduce us?"

No. Go away, Tess. "Of course," I said, trying to sound like it would be my greatest pleasure.

Tess sashayed over, looking beautiful and poised, and from that minute on, I was forgotten. A piece of day-old bread that had once been fragrant and fresh...and so, so stupid.

I slipped away, unable to watch him slip away from me. It was easy, no one even noticed as I left. It was just Tess and Bennett. I got as far as the kitchen before breaking into tears.

"Avery, honey, what's wrong?" Dad, sweaty and smelling like freshly chopped onions, pulled me into his arms.

"I hate her." I sobbed into his stained chef whites.

"Who, honey? Who do you hate?"

I stopped, unable to say my sister's name, trying hard to pull myself together. And for the next eight months, trying for the sake of my pride to pretend I didn't care as Tess and Bennett got closer and closer.

He still came to the restaurant, devoured my desserts, raved about how delicious they were, oblivious to my suffering. I no longer invited him back to the kitchen to the private little table I'd set up especially for him. And I kept our conversations cordial but short. If he noticed he never said anything, which I suppose was best for both of us.

I hated him and loved him but it was Tess I resented most. An argument could be made that she knew nothing about my feelings for Bennett and if I'd told her the truth, she would have backed away. But I wasn't angry with her for taking him. I was angry with her for being more desirable than me.

I told myself that I would get over Bennett, that we'd only known each other for a mere thirty days. But my infatuation with him never subsided. The only thing that lessened was the closeness I shared with my sister. The fissure between us grew as deep as the Grand Canyon. By the time she left for New York, we barely talked anymore.

By the time she left Bennett behind I was all too ready to pick up the pieces.

It happened right before Christmastime. Tess got an offer to anchor *Good Morning New York*. She'd already been anchoring the weekend news here at KNTV. But WNBC would give her a higher profile and pave the way for her to make it to the network. She jumped at the chance. What she didn't jump at was taking Bennett with her. In fact, she made it clear she was leaving Bennett...and his heart...in San Francisco.

Soon after, photographs of her and Kit Reid began to appear under headlines that the two were romantically involved. Of course, I already knew. We may not have been talking but she still spoke to my parents regularly. Sometimes twice a day. We've always been close and a little too dependent on them in that way.

At first, Bennett was too devastated to come around. The restaurant reminded him too much of Tess, which was ridiculous because she hardly ever came in. But little by little he began to emerge again, ten pounds lighter than he used to be.

He took his old place at the bar, often telling Cybil or whoever was making drinks that night that he wanted to say hello. Initially, I made up excuses. I was too busy in the kitchen to come out. I had to leave early for a date (I wasn't dating). Or that I had called in sick that day, then I snuck out through the alley so he wouldn't see me.

He was persistent, though, coming to eat almost every evening. Mom felt sorry for him while all Dad felt was disgusted. "The boy really needs to get a life."

It appeared his life was Tess, who had moved on, trading up from a jingle writer to a major league baseball player. That was Tess for you, always climbing the ladder.

On a cold, foggy evening in May I finally broke down and joined Bennett at the bar. It was baked Alaska day and I wondered why he had nothing better to do on a Saturday night.

"How you holding up?" I didn't really want to hear how he was still pining for my sister but was afraid it would be insensitive not to ask.

"Moving on, I suppose."

Judging by the loose fit of his clothes and his slumped shoulders, it didn't seem like he was moving on to me. But I nodded and ordered us both martinis.

"How 'bout you? Everything good?" he asked, but not in a way that implied he was asking about whether things were good between us.

The truth was, in his eyes there never was an us. Whatever flicker of interest he might have had for me was quickly extinguished the day Tess walked in the door and across the restaurant floor. He considered me a friend and that was all.

"Pretty good," I said. "I'm thinking of adding a mille-feuille to the menu." Dad had already nixed the idea but I was still fighting him on it.

"What's that?"

"Thin layers of puff pastry with custard filling, whipped cream, or even fruit. Basically, a Napoleon."

"Sounds fantastic."

"It's better than fantastic. I learned how to make it in culinary school."

The next night, I had him test my revised recipe and by summer we were back to our old routine in the kitchen. Dad rolled his eyes but left us alone to our conversations.

In late June, we had our first real date, a bike ride on the Silverado Trail in the Napa Valley. It was a gloriously sunny day as we cycled from vineyard to vineyard, admiring miles of rolling hills and grapevines. We ate dinner at Bouchon Bistro in Yountville and shared our first kiss in a dusty parking lot in the center of town. It was still faintly light outside but the sky had turned a multitude of colors. Oranges, reds, blues and yellows.

I remember clinging to Bennett, feeling his heartbeat as he cupped the back of my head, taking the kiss deeper. Later, I told myself it was the best kiss I'd ever had, slow and thorough and oh so romantic with the countryside as our backdrop.

As Tess's relationship with Kit moved forward, mine and Bennett's kept pace. Every day I fell more deeply in love with him. So much so that I ignored simple warning signs, like when he asked too much about Tess or moped when there was a new headline about the incredible first baseman for the Yankees.

In what seemed like a whirlwind to the rest of us, Tess and Kit got engaged the following year and were married just a few months later. The wedding, a big to-do, was held at the Carlyle hotel. I was Tess's maid of honor. And though Bennett was invited as my date, we both thought it best if he skipped the event.

It was a beautiful ceremony and an elegant reception. My sister was breathtaking in her backless sheath wedding gown and I could tell she was really in love. And the happiest I'd ever seen her.

Here's the really sad part: Instead of being happy for her I was happy for myself because she was no longer a threat to me being with Bennett. I know it's pitiful but that's how much I love him.

After the wedding, my relationship with Tess got better, or at least not so strained. For her part, she was so wrapped up in her own life I don't think she ever realized that I'd pulled away. As far as me dating Bennett, she never gave it a second thought. For her, it was water under the bridge.

Where once I used to avoid her phone calls, we now talked at least once a week. She would entertain me with stories about the morning show and being a professional baseball player's wife. We talked about the restaurant and how Mom and Dad worked too hard. About Javi and Wen and Carlos and Cybil and even Hesper. About my latest recipe. But I refrained from discussing Bennett and me, irrationally afraid she could still take him from me.

And while things were better between us they weren't the same as they used be. I suppose I still secretly resented her.

When my father got sick, she and Kit came home. The two of us closed ranks and it almost felt like the old days, when Tess was my favorite person on earth. But then I caught Bennett looking at her. Longingly. It could've been my imagination or paranoia. And Tess didn't even look back. Still, it brought out my hostility all over again.

And now she's coming home. This time, alone.

Tess

I spend most of my flight dreaming up ways for bad things to happen to Annabel Lane.

I keep coming back to the one where a dog eats her face and she has to go on air wrapped up like a mummy. It's a toss-up between that one and the one where she gets fired and has to support herself working as a waitress at Denny's and is forced to serve me twenty Grand Slam breakfasts at the same time. I send all of them back, complaining they're not hot enough.

As I down another cocktail (they're free in first class, bought with all my miles because why the hell not?), I get more creative. I slip that awful medication they give you the day before a colonoscopy into her drink and she gets explosive diarrhea during her sportscast.

Yes, I think I like that one the best.

It's a five-hour-and-thirty-minute flight from JFK to SFO, so I have plenty of time to come up with ways to torture her.

Payback for serving me with a slander lawsuit in front of my apartment building for the whole world to see. Or at least Howard.

And it's not like I have anything else to think about. I'm jobless.

Yes, my bosses waited ten days to permanently let me go. In other words, I was fired. And for the time being, I'm also homeless while Kit and I take some space. My idea, while I figure out what to do, though I hardly need space when he's on the road a good part of eight months out of the year. The real reason, I suppose, is that I need my family.

And I need to be far away from Kit before I smother him in his sleep.

I'm not sure if it's the turbulence or the plane's "beef Wellington" but I've got a bad case of nausea. I put down my drink and flag down the flight attendant for a glass of ginger ale. She instantly recognizes me (I can see it in her eyes) but before she can gush, she remembers I'm the spawn of Satan who said the f-word on TV and abruptly pretends not to know who I am.

Fine. What do I care as long as she gets me my ginger ale?

Ten minutes later, I'm feeling mildly better and scroll through my phone for lack of anything else to do. May as well take advantage of the free Wi-Fi, another perk of flying first class. Like an idiot, I forgot a book and was running too late to stop in the airport gift shop to get one.

I just want this day to be over and for me to be sleeping in my old bed after a bowl of my father's pot roast or my mother's soup and Avery's tiramisu. The upside of being fired is I can get as big as a house if I want without having to suffer the slings and arrows of mean viewers e-mailing me the South Beach Diet and pictures of Porky Pig.

Once, I got fifty e-mails in a row, lambasting me for wearing the same sweater twice in one week. For the record, it was a different sweater, same color. Sue me, like bitch-face Annabel Lane.

I take the time to dwell once again on the sheer gall of it all. Can you imagine *schtupping* another woman's husband and then suing said woman for calling you out on it? Shameful, right? Wait, I'll one-up that. Then the aggrieved woman, the one who's been cheated on and sued, is summarily fired for slandering her husband's whore.

"How can that be?" you ask.

Beats the hell out of me.

I scroll some more while the man next to me has a running conversation with himself. I actually think he's dictating something into a tape recorder. My first inclination is that it's rude. But after further consideration, I conclude that it's no different than if he were talking to the person sitting next to him.

I go back to my phone. There's a long e-mail from Rodney, who's still convinced that Ralph will come to his senses, realize what a big mistake he's made, and beg me to come back. In the meantime, Rodney hates Camila Resnik, my temporary replacement, and thinks she looks like a reptile. I actually like Camila, who anchors the weekend news and welcomed me to the station with a big gift basket when I first started. Unfortunately, she does slightly resemble a reptile. I think it's her eyes.

He also thinks Annabel has something cooking at ESPN and is suing me to save face with the brass over at the sports network and to show the world that she's innocent. Both she and Kit swear nothing happened that night. And I'm just stupid enough to want to believe them.

If it's true nothing happened, I made a huge mistake. A mistake that hurt Kit in the eyes of his fans. Could hurt Annabel professionally. And killed my career at WNBC, though Elsa says the network is still interested.

These are the things that keep me up at night. It's why I needed to leave New York and clear my head.

But I'd be lying if I said I didn't miss my job. Losing it is a lot like losing myself. I fully admit that much of my self-image, even some of my self-worth, is wrapped up in being on TV. Perhaps it's not healthy but it's who I am and I won't apologize for it.

I check my watch, noting I have four more hours on this insufferable plane. The nausea is back again. I measure the distance to the bathroom while my hand searches the storage compartment in front of me for a barf bag just in case. It's a bumpier than usual flight and it doesn't help that my stomach is in knots from everything that has happened.

I finish my ginger ale and to distract myself, peruse my phone again. There's nothing from Kit but he's got a game tonight in Tampa. And I'm not talking to him anyway.

The guy who was talking to himself has drifted off to sleep. There's a drool stain on his pillow. I turn on my side and rest my head against the cool window, hoping that if I close my eyes I'll drift off as well.

I wake up to a voice over the loudspeaker saying we've begun our descent. The same flight attendant who recognized me is walking around the cabin to make sure we're all buckled in. She has to nudge drool guy to put up his tray.

I lift the shade over my window and peer down at the Pacific Ocean. Otherwise, there's only a sliver of land to see in the distance. No fog or air traffic today, or else we'd still be circling. Sometimes it takes thirty minutes or more to get a runway because of poor visibility.

I toe my purse to make sure it's under the seat and try to keep my stomach from pitching when we land and speed down the runway.

Hallelujah! I can't wait to get off this plane. I've had to pee for at least an hour now and hate using the plane's loo. It's silly, but I have this deep-rooted fear of crashing and the NTSB finding my body sprawled across the tiny toilet with my undies around my ankles.

At the same time, I'm in no rush for my family to see my shame. It's not that they're judgy—well, Avery sort of is—but they've always seen me as this supernova and now...not so much. I suck in a breath and wait for the first-class passengers in front of me to gather up their luggage before opening the overhead compartment for mine.

I tried to travel light but at the last minute packed a second suitcase, which I had to check. That's okay. Other than desperately needing the ladies' room, I'm in no rush. It's the lunch hour and despite my mother's protestations that it wouldn't be a hassle to leave the restaurant to pick me up at the airport, I know better.

By the time I pee and wrangle my excessive luggage to the Uber stand, I've worked up a sweat. Unlike New York in summer, it's dry here and not all that hot. If it wasn't for the fact that I'm only thirty-six I'd think I was having a hot flash. The exhaust from all the cars lining up to pick up passengers assails me and I try to gulp in fresh air.

My Uber driver is only four minutes away, according to my phone. I spend the time reciting the speech I've written in my head about where I go from here. Because let's face it, everyone is going to ask.

A Honda Accord pulls up and I check the license plate to make sure it's my Uber. Covering the news, I've learned you can never be too careful. The driver helps with my suitcases and we head off to my childhood home, a combination of dread and happiness coalescing in the pit of my stomach.

I haven't been back in a year, not since my dad was rushed to the hospital with chest pain. We thought he was having a heart attack but it turned out his blood pressure was through the roof.

Thankfully, traffic is light and it only takes twenty minutes on the freeway to get to Octavia, the exit to my parents' house. I stare out the window at the city, at the pretty houses and the not-so-pretty houses as my driver hangs a left on Fell and then a right on Baker Street to the Victorian I grew up in.

For as long as I can remember we lived in the Haight, otherwise known as Haight-Ashbury. My folks moved here in the early nineties, long after the hippie movement. Though there are remnants of it everywhere, in the last couple of decades the area has become more $500 hair extensions than flowers in your hair. When I was a kid it was fairly working class but like everything else in the city, the neighborhood was gentrified and real estate prices skyrocketed.

My parents are probably one of the few here who haven't added up or on. In fact, not much about my childhood home has changed. Same thrift-store furniture that my mother reupholstered with her own two hands. Same gallery of family pictures lining the hallway walls. Same cozy hook rugs handed down from my grandparents.

The second I walk in, the familiar scent of old wooden floors, furniture polish and freshly baked bread hits me. There is no other way to describe it other than it smells like home. If I could replicate and bottle the familiar fragrance I would.

I drag my two suitcases upstairs to my old bedroom where, like everything else in the house, nothing has changed. A faded pink Shabby Chic comforter still covers my full-size bed and the dresser Mom and I bought at the Alameda flea market and painted white still sits next to the window. On top of it is a chipped pitcher filled with pink lilies, which I'm sure Mom bought at the Flower Mart on Brannan Street.

I deliberate on whether to hang my things in the closet before they become a wrinkled mess and decide to screw it. If they're not wrinkled beyond recognition by now a few more hours won't hurt them. I'm starved and decide to go downstairs to hunt up something to eat.

There's a note pinned to the refrigerator with the Frida Kahlo magnet I got during my fifth-grade field trip to the San Francisco Museum of Modern Art that says "Fresh muffins are on the sideboard and Dad's pot roast is in the fridge, help yourself. Love, Mom."

I wander into the dining room, grab a muffin off the plate and stuff half of it in my mouth (oh if the viewers of WNBC could see me now). It's boysenberry and so delicious I remember what homemade tastes like. My mom is no Avery but she can bake.

I finish the other half and debate whether to eat another one or nuke myself a bowl of pot roast. The phone rings—my parents still have a landline—and I wonder whether I should pick up. Before I can get to it, my mother's voice floats through the answering machine. "Tess, honey, are you there?"

I stub my toe on the hallway console as I rush to scoop the cordless off its holder. "I'm here."

"You made good time. How was your flight?"

"Good. No delays, just smooth sailing."

"I'm glad. Did you find the pot roast?"

"I haven't looked yet. I was too busy eating a muffin."

"How do you feel about coming to the restaurant for dinner? We're not going to get out of here until late and I can't wait that long to see you."

I squeeze my eyes shut and silently curse. "Mom, I'm not ready to see a bunch of people yet." Javi, Carlos, Wen, Mandy...they all know. Do I have to face them my first night back?

"Oh come on. What are you going to do, hide in the house the entire time you're here?"

Sounds good to me.

"Your dad, Avery, Bennett and I are dying to see you, Tess."

I start to argue that I'm tired from the flight, the time change, yada, yada, yada but instead fold like a cheap suit. "Fine, I'll come over about six."

"Want to take the car? Your father and I drove in together this morning."

"Nah, I'll Uber over. That way I can get good and drunk."

"Ah, Tessy."

"I'll see you later, Mom." I hang up and let out a long breath. There goes my quiet night of feeling sorry for myself.

I climb the stairs, open my bedroom window to let in some air, lay on my old bed, and stare up at the ceiling. A nice breeze ruffles the lace panels, bringing with it the smell of jasmine from the backyard. It seems late for jasmine but Mom's the gardener not me.

I can't remember ever being this tired. All I seem to want to do is sleep. I roll over, scoop my purse off the floor where I left it and search for my phone. One missed call. Not Kit, though. Rodney.

I punch in his number and cradle the phone with my pillow against my head.

"You make it okay?" This is how he answers.

"I did. How was the show?"

"It sucked. Camila laughs too much, tries too hard. She ain't you, baby."

"No one's me. Fuckers. I still can't believe it, Rod. And yet Annabel still has a job. There's no justice in the world."

"Something's up with her. When I left today, she was in Ralph's office. I saw her go in and shut the door. I tried to hang around, see what I could see but she was in there too long and it was starting to look suspicious, me hanging around like that."

"You think she's doing Ralph, too?" I'm only half joking.

"What I think is she got an offer from ESPN and is seeing what she can squeeze Ralph for. If it had something to do with the eleven o'clock she'd be talking to Cheryl."

"Do you think Kit's telling the truth about her...about them?"

There's a long silence, then, "I don't know, Tess. It's possible he is."

"But you don't think so?"

"That's not what I said. Don't go twisting my words, girl."

My phone beeps with an incoming call. It's Kit, so I let it go to voice mail.

"Just be honest," I say. "It's me for God's sake. You know I can take it." But what I really want is for Rodney to say I should believe Kit, that my husband is telling the truth.

There's another long silence and I have my answer. That's what I get for asking for honesty.

"I've got to go," I say. "Drinks when I get back."

"You know it."

I click off and roll over on my side so I can stare at the vase of flowers instead of the ceiling. Kit calls a second time and I once again let it go to voice mail. If he wants to know if I made it alive to San Francisco he can check the obit page in the *New York Times*.

But he's relentless, calling every ten minutes.

Finally, I answer. "Stop calling me," I say and quickly switch off.

But he's at it again a mere five seconds later. This is when I should probably ask myself why I don't simply turn off my phone. The answer, I suppose, lies somewhere between getting a perverse pleasure out of listening to him grovel and really wanting an excuse to talk to him, even if it's just to yell at him.

Apparently, it's the latter because I pick up after his tenth attempt.

"Don't hang up," he says.

"Can you please leave me alone."

"No, we need to talk, Tess."

"We actually don't. The people who need to talk are our lawyers. Mine will be calling yours very soon." It's a bluff because I don't have a lawyer, just like I don't have a job or a faithful husband. I've got a whole lot of nothing.

"We're not getting lawyers, Tess. Look, the game starts in sixty minutes, so I have to go soon. I just wanted to make sure you made it safely to San Francisco."

"I'm here. I'm safe. And I'm still not talking to you. So, no need to call again."

"Come on, Tess, don't do this to me before a game."

"I can say the same to you. Don't have your girlfriend serve me with a lawsuit in front of the place where I live, where my neighbors can see my humiliation. So don't ask me to give a shit about your game. Because I don't."

He lets out a long, exasperated sigh like he's the most put-upon man in the universe. "We've been over this over and over again, Tess. I love you. I'm at the Vinoy if you need me. I'll try to call you tonight. We've got an early game tomorrow, so I've got batting practice in the morning."

I wonder if he's telling me all this so I won't try to call him in the morning, which of course I have no intention of doing. Typically, batting practice is about an hour before game time and I know for a fact they don't play until one o'clock tomorrow. I checked the schedule. Then again eleven is morning to Kit, who would sleep until noon every day if he could.

"You going to the restaurant tonight?"

I answer with a terse "Yes."

"Yeah, I figured. Say hi to everyone for me."

I don't respond. I don't think I've ever met a person so unaware, so damn clueless.

"I've got to go, Tess." Thirty minutes before game time they're supposed to turn off. No phone, no music, no video games, no arguments with their wives. "I love you."

He waits for me to say it back but I don't. Instead, I hang up, then dissect the conversation, such as it was. Did I detect a hitch in his voice when he told me he loved me? My favorite is that he'll "try" to call me tonight. How damn hard is it to pick up a phone? The game will likely be over in three hours, leaving him plenty of time to say a quick good night. Unless he's planning to go out afterward and do a little carousing. See, that's where my mind automatically goes.

At least I know Annabel won't be there because Rodney saw her at the station. But who knows, maybe she'll fly out after the eleven and stay with him at the Vinoy.

I blow out a breath and tell myself this is no way to live. I'm filled with rage, rage that Kit has put me in the position of questioning his every move, of doubting his love for me, of doubting my love for him. And for making me lose my job. Okay, I have to own that last one but it's fair to say he helped drive me to it.

What kind of married man lets a woman, not his wife, sleep in his room? I'd have to be pretty gullible to believe nothing happened between them, yet I want to. I want to so badly that I'm willing to rationalize and make excuses for him. What does that say about me? When did I go from being a confident, take-no-prisoners kind of woman to a whimpering dupe?

I lie here, thinking about it, once again staring up at the ceiling, looking for answers and coming to the obvious conclusion that it's because I love him.

I wonder if this is how other women do it. Do they tell themselves this is just a curve in the road of marriage? That twenty-five, thirty years from now they'll be sitting with their husbands on the front porch of their dream home, grandchildren playing on the lawn, deliriously happy and secure, that one small indiscretion forgotten as if it never happened?

Can I be one of those women? Can I love Kit more than I love myself?

Avery

We're at Mission Rock Resort, sitting on the deck, the San Francisco Bay stretched out before us, endless. Mom insisted we celebrate Bennett's and my engagement here instead of Stones.

"It'll be fun to venture away from the restaurant," she'd said. "And you two love their fish tacos."

It's true, we do. But it's a little off-kilter to be celebrating in someone else's restaurant. Every milestone I can remember we've commemorated at Stones, including all our birthdays, Tess and my graduations and Mom and Dad's anniversaries. Even our dog Jasper's memorial service was held after hours at the restaurant.

"I can't believe you didn't tell me," Tess says to me.

It's only been twenty-four hours since she's gotten here and already my stress level has ratcheted up to a 6 on the Richter scale. For reference, the 1906 earthquake was a 7.9, so nearly two-thirds of the way there.

"We were too busy focusing on you," I say through gritted teeth.

Bennett drills me with a look. "What Avery means is with everything... going on...we wanted to wait to tell you."

One of the things I love best about Bennett is he always says the right thing at the right moment. The problem is I'm feeling uncharitably mean today, even though I should be feeling the opposite toward my sister.

"Well, I'm thrilled for you guys." She reaches across the table and takes both our hands and just like that, a rush of guilt floods me.

"Thank you," I say.

"Have you picked a date?" she asks and three pairs of eyes land on Bennett and me.

I blurt "Fall," which is only two months away. Bennett and I haven't even discussed a venue, let alone a date.

"Wow, we have a lot of planning to do in a short amount of time." My mother exchanges a glance with my father, who gives an imperceptible nod.

There's something going on. I've witnessed enough of the silent way my parents sometimes speak to each other to know they are keeping a secret. Dad has had two more "meetings" since the first one and won't say what they're about.

I tell myself not to get worked up over it. Dad's a private guy to begin with and if it was something serious, like his health, Mom would tell us.

The server comes to take our order and goes around the table. As soon as she leaves, the conversation immediately turns to plans for the wedding. Do we want the reception at Stones?

I look again at Bennett who looks back at me.

"Whatever you want, Avery. I'm great with Stones but if you want it somewhere else I'm great with that too."

Tess leans forward and rubs Bennett's arm. "This one's a keeper, Avery Bear."

I bristle and try to tell myself it's because of the nickname, born out of the fact that when I was a toddler I didn't go anywhere without Tess's hand-me-down Care Bear, a pink stuffed bear with a rainbow belly badge.

I bristle even more when Bennett turns to Tess and says, "If this is weird for you...I mean because of...Kit...say the word and we'll—"

"What? We'll what?" I give him a hard look.

Before it turns into a minor scene my mother comes to the rescue. "If you do want it at Stones, I'd like to get it on the books as soon as possible, so we can let our customers know we'll be closed that day," Mom says. "We can rent a dance floor, put a band or a DJ in the back where the communal table is, fill the place with flowers. Remember when Sylvia had her wedding at the restaurant? It was gorgeous."

Sylvia is my first cousin. Two years ago, she married a guy she met in law school. They threw a big reception at Stones with two hundred guests. It was a little tight but my aunt and uncle haven't stopped talking about it.

My cousin and her husband moved to Los Angeles last spring because he landed a job in a big firm that specializes in entertainment law. Last I heard, he represented all kinds of movie stars. I'd thought about him for Tess. Maybe he could threaten her old station with a lawsuit and get her job back, or at least a payout on her contract.

"I think Bennett and I have to talk about it," I say, hoping he'll agree to having the ceremony at City Hall, which is probably one of the most beautiful civic centers in the country.

The original city hall was destroyed in the 1906 earthquake by fire and replaced with a beaux arts building with a gilded dome that is positively breathtaking. The entire hall takes up two city blocks and is nineteen feet taller than even the US capitol. It's where Marilyn Monroe and Joe DiMaggio got married.

The first time I stepped foot in the grand rotunda, I knew it was the place where I wanted to be married. The sweeping staircase, the way the light reflects off the pink marble floor...well, I can't imagine a better backdrop for our wedding portrait.

Secretly, though, I have mixed feelings about having the party at the restaurant. I want something that is mine and Bennett's alone. A place where there's no history of Tess. Maybe a winery in Yountville, where we had our first date.

"Take your time, but not too much time," my mother says. "Fall will be here before you know it."

It is short notice for a wedding, which may leave us no other choice but the restaurant. Or a longer engagement. But instead of saying anything I change the subject.

"How long are you staying, Tess?" The minute I ask, I know it's the wrong question because the whole table goes silent. My mother is glaring at me as if I'd belched in public. And Bennett gives my arm a gentle squeeze, a silent warning. Could he be any more solicitous of Tess?

Jeez, all I asked is how long she's staying. What's the big deal?

"I don't know yet," Tess says and stares out over the water.

Bennett pushes his chair away from the table, making a horrific screeching noise, and excuses himself to go to the men's room.

The server comes with our food and Bennett returns from the "bathroom." My guess is he bypassed the john for the bar and got himself a shot of Patrón. Because you know...poor Tess. She always has a way of sucking all the oxygen out of the room.

We're halfway through our fish tacos when I'm gnawed by guilt and, yes, shame. It's her first time back since Dad got sick and her life is falling apart. Maybe it's selfish but I just wanted time to savor my engagement while it's still shiny and new. But I'm better than that and Tess deserves the good me.

I get up, walk around the table, and give her a big hug. "I'm glad you're here and I love you."

On the way home Bennett says, "That was good what you did back there. I'm proud of you."

I don't say anything because it feels a little like he's patronizing me. We drive the twenty minutes home in silence. Bennett pulls into our narrow driveway and kills the engine. But instead of getting out of the car we just sit there, staring at our small stucco house, a Tudor revival with a neatly trimmed yard.

"Avery, are you angry with me?"

"No, why would you think that?"

"Oh, I don't know. Maybe because you've been staring daggers at me the whole ride home."

I turn in my seat to face him. "What was that crap about poor Tess? 'If this is too hard for you...'" I mimic him from earlier. "This is about us, not about her."

"Excuse me for trying to be a decent person. How would you like someone talking about their wedding plans as your marriage is falling apart?"

"So I'm not supposed to celebrate or even discuss the happiest time of my life because Tess's husband cheated on her? Is that what you're saying?"

"What I'm saying is we don't have to throw it in her face. That's all."

"No one was throwing anything in Tess's face. The whole purpose of the dinner was to celebrate our engagement."

I can't help but wonder whether Bennett is just being sensitive, like he would be to anyone in either one of our families, or if it's more. I should be past Bennett and Tess, more evolved than I was five years ago, but her being home is like déjà vu all over again.

"Is it difficult being with her?" I ask, my voice quiet.

"Who, Tess? No, why would it be difficult?"

I want to say because you loved her, but I can't seem to get the words out of my mouth. And now I'm sorry I ever brought it up. We never talk about Tess in that way. We've made an art form of pretending there was never a Bennett and Tess, that there's only us.

"I'm with you, Avery. You!" he says. "Everything else...I'm just trying to be a good guy here."

"I know." Sometimes, though, that's the problem. It makes me wonder how far being a good guy extends. Is he marrying me because he's a good guy or because he loves me as much as I love him? If he wasn't such a good guy, would we just be friends?

I start to ask, then stop myself, afraid of the answer, afraid I'm being insecure and trying to sabotage what I have with Bennett. And the longer

I sit here, the more I blame Tess for ruining what should've been a perfect day. A perfect celebration.

"Let's go inside." I start to undo my seat belt when he reaches over me and catches my lips with his mouth, kissing me sweetly, making me forget I'm perturbed with him.

"How about we go away next weekend, book a room in a swanky hotel, and stay in bed all day?" he says.

"Really? You don't know how much I'd like that. Maybe we could start making plans for the wedding."

"Fall? Seriously?" His brows wing up but he's beaming, and everything seems right again.

I kick myself for second-guessing him, for second-guessing me. How many times am I going to do this?

"I like fall." I smile against his lips. "Best time of the year to get married, in my book. Maybe we should push it up to early September."

"You think?" His lips have worked their way to my neck, to the soft spot behind my ear, and I lose my train of thought.

When his warm hands slide up my sides and press my skin under my shirt, my need for him is overwhelming. "Bennett?"

"Hmm?"

"We really need to get inside."

* * *

When I leave the next morning, Bennett is fast asleep. I stand in the doorway of our bedroom looking at him, his dark hair curled against the pillow, his broad bare shoulders tan against our white sheets.

Just seeing him like that makes something in my chest move, and I whisper, "I love you."

In the kitchen, I make myself a cup of coffee. I finally broke down two months ago and got one of those single-serve pod coffee makers. It seems silly to go through the rigmarole of brewing a pot just for me. Bennett won't be up for hours and he's not much of a coffee drinker anyway.

I look around the room. It's an old-fashioned kitchen but cheery with its buttery walls, white glass cabinets and white tile countertops. At some point, the landlord shoehorned in a dishwasher and the only change I made was adding a professional stove, which I'll take with me when we leave. We stowed the old one, an inexpensive General Electric, in the tiny garage. It was fine for regular cooking but the oven's temperature was just uneven enough to throw off my baking.

Bennett and I have been saving to buy a house and I've made a file of pictures of the kind of kitchen I want. It's a long way off but in the meantime, I like this house. It may be small—Bennett's baby grand barely fits in the living room—but the neighborhood is peaceful and we're only a few blocks from the beach.

Sometimes, on a particularly quiet night when the window is open in our bedroom, I can hear the water at Ocean Beach lap against the shore and the seagulls squawking.

For a Tudor, the house is sunny with a dozen quirks that I find charming (Bennett, a lover of all things modern, not so much). Like the little mail niche in the foyer, the weirdly textured walls and the iron light fixtures that look more appropriate for a medieval castle than they do for a cozy cottage. I love the parquet floors and the cove ceilings and the extra bedroom Bennett and I use for an office. And even though the garage is really too small to park a car, it's great storage.

I finish my coffee, grab my keys off the hook in the hallway, and tiptoe to the front door.

By the time I get to the restaurant, the sun is coming up. In other words, I'm late. Still, I find myself alone and if I'm lucky I'll have at least an hour to myself before the cavalry shows up.

I start on my pie crusts. While my dough is chilling, our produce supplier delivers crates of fruit and vegetables. Dad has been doing business with the same San Joaquin farmers for twenty years. July's bounty is always my favorite, plenty of berries and stone fruit to work with. Today's delivery is so gorgeous, I snap a picture and post it to Instagram with the hashtags #Seewhat'scookingatStones #local #farmtotable.

After Bruce unloads, I reorganize the pantry and cull the olallieberries and apricots for my pie fillings. The music goes on in the kitchen—The Band—and I know I'm no longer alone. I come out of the pantry to find Dad already in his chef whites.

"Morning," he says, eyeing my armful of berry baskets. "I see Bruce was here."

"Yep. Lots of goodies. The fava and lima beans look out of this world."

He nods and heads to the *rôtisseur* station, where he already has a slab of marbled beef laid out.

"Yesterday was fun," I say.

To this, he raises his head from his dicing and arches his brows. "You could cut the tension with this." He holds up a meat cleaver.

Okay, he's got a point. But in my own way I made nice.

"Come here." He crooks his finger and opens his arms. I'm there in an instant. "Your sister isn't always easy but she loves you and now, more than ever, she needs your love back."

"I know," I say softly, ashamed.

"We all get that it's supposed to be your day in the sun and that Tess and her current situation has overshadowed that. But kiddo, you're not twelve anymore. This is life."

I know this too. "You think she and Kit will work things out?"

He gives a half shrug. "Time will tell. The Yanks are here this weekend, playing the A's. Hopefully they'll talk, get things out in the open."

I can't read his voice as far as his attitude toward Kit. Dad tends to keep his opinions to himself. Mom, on the other hand, has made no secret about her feelings. She loves Kit but wants to strangle him.

I make my berry mixture and let the fruit macerate while I start on the apricots, pitting and slicing, letting the rhythm of the work take me away. Then I roll out my pie crusts and line up the pans in neat rows, ready to get them in the ovens.

Dad, lost in the music and the sound of his own chopping, doesn't look to make any more conversation. We both like it quiet in the morning. There will be enough noise when the rest of the team gets here.

By nine thirty, I'm surprised to find I'm ahead of schedule. I even have time for a quick coffee break at Top Me Off, two short blocks away. Besides the café having terrific coffee, it's nice to get outside for a little while.

I'm about to slip out the alleyway door when Dad says, "Don't make any plans this evening. We're having a family meeting."

"A family meeting?" We haven't had one since Dad got sick, and it was called by us, Mom, Tess and me, not him. Did I mention my father hates meetings? "What's it about?"

"That's the whole point of a meeting, Avery. Your mother wants to do it at seven." He goes back to preparing his beef stew, signaling that's all I'm going to get for now.

I'm on my way to Top Me Off when my cell buzzes with an incoming call. I fish it out of the pocket of my apron, which I forgot to take off before leaving the restaurant. It's my sister, who ordinarily never calls this time of morning. She's always at work and I'm busy at the restaurant.

"Hey, Tess."

"What's this meeting about?" She cuts right to the chase.

"Your guess is as good as mine."

"Seriously, Dad hasn't told you anything? He always tells you stuff."

The only person our father tells stuff to is Mom. The rest of us are on a need-to-know basis, so Tess is wrong on that front.

"You think it's about the restaurant?"

"Tess, I don't have a clue." But if it is about the restaurant I'm surprised Tess has been asked to attend. She's never really shown an interest in Stones. I suppose there's a chance my parents figured she's here with nothing to do, why not make her feel part of it?

"I heard Kit's in town this weekend," I say, changing the subject.

"Yeah," she says with all the enthusiasm of a corpse.

"That'll be good, right? You two can talk."

"I have nothing more to say to him." She pauses, and then in a complete turnaround says, "He swears he wasn't unfaithful."

I want to tread lightly here but can't help asking, "Do you believe him?"

"I don't know what I believe. Do you?"

The question catches me off guard. Probably not. But I don't know Kit the way she does. I only know ballplayer stereotypes, which isn't fair to either of them. "Tess, I'm not in a good position to say."

"Why? Where are you?"

I laugh. "That's not what I mean and you know it. I've met Kit what, five times?"

"Six, I think, but who's counting?" There's another long pause and I wait for it. I wait for another Kit excuse because when it comes to love, people only want to believe the best of their partners. They tell themselves whatever lies it takes. No one knows that better than me, not even Tess.

Tess

I woke up at eight, which is really five, which is one hour later than I normally wake up. My body is so screwed up from being three hours behind—but mostly from not having to get up at four in the morning any longer—that it doesn't recognize what time it really is. It's like suffering from constant jet lag.

I probably wouldn't have woken up at all if Kit hadn't called. My phone buzzed on the nightstand, ringing through the house.

"Don't hang up," were the first words out of his mouth. It's become his standard greeting these days.

"Go away." But I stayed on the phone, lying there, waiting for him to beg some more. It's what I do now.

"Not going to happen," he said. "And you don't want me to or else you wouldn't have answered the phone."

It hurts to know how true that is, to know how weak I am when it comes to him.

"I want to see you this weekend."

"Because it's all about you. Not this weekend, Kit. I have plans." I hung up before he could talk me into it.

After Kit, I called Avery about tonight's family meeting—the only real plans I have. She seemed as surprised by this sudden meeting as I am. My parents aren't really meeting types. It's way too formal for them. If something needs to be said, they just say it. The only family meeting I can remember is when Dad got sick and even that was just Mom, Avery and I sitting around the dining room table, coming up with a game plan on how to keep Dad in line eating- and rest-wise.

Needless to say, I'm worried. And I know Avery is too; I could hear it in her voice. I don't think it's Dad. He looks hale and healthy, a lot better than the last time I saw him. Yet I'm girding myself for the worst.

I head out to the backyard with my coffee, the fourth cup today. It's unseasonably warm for July in San Francisco and the sun feels good. In New York I'm sure it's sweltering.

The yard is large by city standards but a bit grown over. My parents never had a gardener. Mom manages to fit in the yard work with everything else she does. As a result, it's always a little like a jungle back here. Roses climbing the wall, overtaking the roof of the small shed where we've always kept our bikes, and out-of-control camellia trees pushing against the windows.

Despite its unkempt appearance there's always been something charming about it, like something you'd see in an old Italian villa in a Tuscan hill town.

The only new addition appears to be a gas barbecue. Growing up, we always had a Weber. Dad made burgers every Sunday night in summer and we'd eat outside. Avery made ice cream in the KitchenAid and we'd have sundaes for dessert, or my parents would take us to Swensen's or Joe's.

It strikes me that I have nothing to do all day. Under better circumstances, I might've called Lori, an old high school friend I'm still in touch with. She owns her own PR firm and has an office on Market Street. We could've gone shopping. By now, though, I'm sure she's heard about my situation. The whole world has. As Kit likes to remind me I have only myself to blame.

I decide to try Elsa again. She hasn't returned any of my messages, which isn't like her. This time, I dial her cell and bypass her office altogether. I'm not in the mood for her assistant, who brushes me the wrong way. She's not bitchy per se, just officious, which comes off as condescending.

"Ah, you're alive," I say.

"How's San Francisco, Tess?"

"Good...boring. Have you heard anything?"

"No. But when I do you'll be the first person I call."

"Maybe you should tell NBC I have other offers." Light a little fire under those network bosses' asses.

"But you don't," Elsa says curtly.

"Why again haven't we contacted CBS or ABC? It's not like I'm married to NBC, especially after the way WNBC treated me."

"Because we've already started a dialogue with Chandra. This isn't going to happen in a day, Tess. You're not exactly a hot property right now. Be patient."

Patience has never been a virtue for me. "I'll be a nobody if we wait too long."

There's a long pause, then, "Don't take this the wrong way, Tess, but that might be preferable. Let's just hope the folks at the network have short memories."

I sigh. It all seems so ridiculous. One bad day and suddenly I'm a pariah. "Why does Annabel go unscathed in all this?"

"I don't know that she is, I'm not her agent. What's going on with the lawsuit?"

"My lawyer is dealing with it."

"It would help if it went away, otherwise it's liable to draw more attention to the whole situation, which isn't helping your situation."

"What are you saying, I should pay her off with a settlement? I wouldn't give her the satisfaction."

"Do you want to fight, Tess, or do you want to win? Because unemployment doesn't feel like winning. Think about it. I have to go now."

Before I can even say goodbye, she hangs up.

I go inside and make myself scrambled eggs and toast. When Avery and I were kids she used to make us cinnamon toast for breakfast. And it wasn't your run-of-the-mill cinnamon toast either. She melted the butter on top of the stove and added sugar and cinnamon until she had a thick slurry, which she drizzled over fat slices of fresh bread from the bakery. It was heaven.

Despite her crappy disposition lately, I wish she was here. I wish we could spend the day together, doing all the things we used to like to do. I don't know what her problem is. You would think she'd be glowing with engagement happiness instead of looking like a sourpuss.

I eat my rubbery eggs and nibble on my toast. None of it tastes particularly good but it's something to do while I scroll through my phone. These days I try to stay off social media and stick solely to my e-mail account.

Today, though, I'm feeling adventurous and skip over to *Mad as Hell*, a broadcast news gossip blog. It's mostly filled with acquisition news and newsroom shake-ups. Occasionally, though, it'll be the first to report on anchors and reporters leaving their posts for new jobs.

I scroll, looking for news of Annabel. I don't know why I'm obsessed with her. Who cares if she goes to ESPN or anywhere else for that matter? But I suppose it's easier—and less damaging—to snoop around in her life than it is in Kit's. Because with him who knows what I'll find?

There's nothing remotely interesting in *Mad as Hell* unless you count the fact that the ABC affiliate in Billings, Montana, is becoming an O&O, meaning it'll be owned and operated by the network.

I switch over to my e-mail account. I have a fraction of the mail I used to get when I was still working at *Good Morning New York*. PR people begging me to do stories on their clients' events, books, wine or e-mailing just to kiss my ass. Now, it's mostly spam and the occasional Nigerian prince who has chosen me of all people to share a huge fortune with him.

I close out of my e-mail and toss my leftover toast in the trash. Maybe I'll be a nice sister today and buy Avery and Bennett an engagement gift, an expensive trip to somewhere exotic on Kit's credit card. The Arashiyama Bamboo Forest in Japan or Lake Atitlán in Guatemala or Machu Picchu in Peru.

Or maybe just Mendocino.

I decide to do a little travel research on the Internet, which calls for a real computer, not my phone. Twenty years ago, my parents turned our old butler's pantry into a small office with a desktop computer and a printer. I bring my coffee and make myself at home, firing up the computer and plugging in the password they use for everything, the address of the restaurant. I know, original. But handy.

Soon, I'm exploring weekend trip possibilities, wishing I could take a few of them. Nope, not until I land a new job and I'm back in the game.

All these places look great but I can't book a date without knowing Avery and Bennett's schedule. I remember from when Bennett and I used to date that he had weekends off. But weekends at the restaurant are busy and I know Avery likes to be there to help out Mom and Dad. It's probably better to buy gift certificates and let them make their own plans.

I settle on the Mendocino Inn, a refurbished Victorian with gorgeous views of the ocean, beautiful gardens, and from the pictures, a charming restaurant that Avery would love. The whole setup looks incredibly romantic with wisteria growing over a white lattice arbor, rattan rocking chairs on the porch and wrought iron tables and chairs spread out across the lawn. There's even a croquet court, which Bennett will like.

I search for a few restaurants in the area that I can also buy gift cards for. The most famous one, of course, is St. Ornish, known for its wild game and foraged food. The place was originally a loggers' boardinghouse until a few Bay Area folks bought it and turned it into a hotel and restaurant.

My parents' best friends got married there at least two decades ago. Avery and I were flower girls at their wedding. I still remember the white eyelet peasant dresses we wore, which in hindsight were probably hideous.

I loved walking down the aisle, spreading rose petals, striking a pose for all the guests. Avery cried and my mother had to hold her hand part of the way.

While the place is spectacular and holds nice memories, I don't think Avery is into wild boar or venison, so I skip it. There's plenty of other restaurants to choose from, including a few that get great Yelp reviews. I pick a seafood place right on the water and a café in an antique farmhouse that looks perfect for breakfast or brunch.

I'm just about to add a gift card to my basket when I elbow my mug, knock it off the desk, and spill coffee everywhere. In a panic, I quickly move papers out of the way before they get drenched as the pool of coffee begins to spread. Then I make a mad dash for the kitchen to find a towel or napkins to sop up my mess.

I get it all cleaned up, take the papers that got wet to the sink and try to blot them dry. That's when I notice what they are. I have to look twice, three times, but there's no mistaking that they're part of a contract.

It takes some sifting through the mess I've made. Everything on the desk is now in disarray. But I finally find the missing pages. I stare down at them, reading each paragraph over and over again, trying to cut through the legalese. It's confusing but not so confusing that I don't get the basic gist.

I do some sleuthing on the World Wide Web, find my phone in the mess, and hit automatic dial for Avery.

"Can't talk now, Tess. I'm slammed."

"I know what the meeting is about and you're going to want to hear this. Is Dad there?"

"Of course he's here."

"Go to the alley."

She lets out a long sigh, but I can hear the squeak of the door and street traffic.

"Okay tell me. But for the love of God make it fast, I've got cheesecakes in the oven. Is it bad?"

"Not bad, just seriously bizarre. Mom and Dad put a deposit down on a house. And get this, it's in Tahoe."

"What? Whoa, slow down. What you're saying makes zero sense. How did you come up with this?"

"I found the paperwork on their desk. I was using the computer and spilled coffee on the contract. It's there, plain as day. I looked up the place and it's one of those golf-course communities. I think it's Mom's way of getting Dad to take more time off. You know, a vacation home. It's not far from Dave and Carol's cabin." Dave and Carol are good friends of my parents. On rare occasions, Mom and Dad borrow their cabin for a quick weekend getaway.

"Why wouldn't they have told us?" Avery says.

"They are telling us. That's what tonight's about."

"Mom and Dad are not vacation house kind of people. They barely spend time at Baker Street."

"That's probably the point. If they're three hours away it won't be so easy to run to the restaurant for every little thing. They'll actually relax."

"Can they even afford a second home? The restaurant does well but Mom and Dad are thrifty. I've never known them to do anything remotely extravagant. And a vacation home in Tahoe..."

"It's about time they're finally rewarding themselves for all their hard work. I mean Mom's still driving the same car she brought us home from the delivery room in. Dad's idea of living large is a new gas barbecue."

"Shit, my cakes will burn if I don't get back in there. This whole vacation house thing is crazy but at least it's not Dad. At least he's not telling us he has three months to live."

"Nope, not Dad. See you tonight."

Avery is just about to disconnect when I remember to say, "Oh, and Avery, act surprised."

Avery

We're in the back corner, near the bathrooms, a few feet away from the bus tubs. It's the same round table where we always sit when we have family dinners in the restaurant. While it's not what you would call prime real estate, it's private and somewhat quiet.

Nothing is worse than trying to have a relaxing meal—or in this case a meeting—in the middle of your own restaurant. First, you want to tell one of the servers that table five has been waiting for water for more than twenty minutes. And second, everyone can eavesdrop on your conversation.

At least it's a spacious dining room, especially by San Francisco standards. The restaurant used to be a bank in the 1920s and my parents have kept the original dark mahogany wainscoting, encased windows, wall sconces and Douglas fir floors. The only major change they made was adding an antique mahogany bar they got in a salvage store in Berkeley that supposedly is as old as the Gold Rush. It took six men to carry it from the truck to the restaurant.

But even back here in our private corner, diners are gawking. Not at the Stone family, but at Tess. Wherever she goes she gets appreciative stares. She may not be a television celebrity anymore, but she still draws attention as if she is. It's been this way my whole life.

A server brings us a big platter of Dad's juicy pork tenderloin, a steaming bowl of mashed potatoes, a fresh salad, and a basket of bread and butter. We help ourselves, eating family style, no different than if we were home. That's the thing about this place; it is every bit home, as much as the house on Baker.

"Bennett couldn't come?" Mom asks.

"He had to work." The truth is I didn't ask him. Not that he isn't family because he is. My family. But it just didn't feel right. When we're married... well, then it'll be different.

"Did you talk to Kit, honey?" Mom asks Tess.

"Earlier. He sends his love." Tess rolls her eyes.

Dad passes the bread, and we all take a piece, Tess and I pretending we don't know what the big announcement is.

I want to say just spit out the news so we can get back to our regular programming.

Tess sniffs the air. "What smells so funny?"

Mom glances over at the bus tubs and shakes her head. "I don't know. What does it smell like?"

"Fish or something. It smells foul."

Okay, either it smells like fish or it smells like fowl. Why does Tess always have to be so dramatic?

Dad gets up and carries the bus tubs into the kitchen and returns a few minutes later. "Better?"

"I think so," she says, scrunching up her nose.

I hold my patience because there was nothing foul smelling. Maybe she got a whiff of the salmon we're serving, which is fresh caught and smothered in a dill lemon-butter sauce. It smells and tastes delicious. But that's Tess for you.

We eat in companionable silence, my parents taking their sweet time about telling us. There is no sense pushing. I learned a long time ago that Dad says what he has to say in his own good time.

Dad flags Daphne, our server, and asks her to bring a bottle of sparkling wine for the table. Daphne runs off to do Dad's bidding and returns a short time later with a bottle of Roederer Estate L'Ermitage, the good stuff.

Tess and I exchange a glance and she mouths, "Told you."

I suppose she thinks she's freaking Woodward and Bernstein now.

Dad takes the bottle from Daphne and uncorks it himself without losing a drop. I remember in culinary school, watching some of the wine students whack open a bottle of champagne by slicing off the top with a saber. It's a technique called *sabrage* and is mostly reserved for douchebags who don't mind losing half the bottle of bubbly for a spectacle. The same kind of people who buy cult wines for thousands of dollars, then let it gather dust on a shelf to show off to all of their friends.

Dad pours each of us a glass and holds up his flute. "Your mom and I have an announcement to make."

Tess's mouth curves up as we lock eyes. She really does think she's Walter Cronkite's protégé.

"We got an offer on the restaurant," Dad says.

My jaw falls open. An offer on the restaurant? Did I hear wrong? I cut to Tess, and she gives me an imperceptible shrug.

We got an offer on the restaurant.

What does that have do with a house in Tahoe? My mind isn't working fast enough to compute it all.

"I didn't realize the restaurant is for sale," I say, still dazed by the news, but working up toward anger. Why didn't anyone discuss this with me?

"It wasn't...it isn't." My mother presses her hand against my father's arm, a signal that he should stop talking, and tries to smooth over his abrupt delivery. "Jeremy Gains came to us. It was out of the blue. At first, we didn't even take it seriously. Your father met with him, intending to brush it off. He didn't want to sell. But...well...the offer is significant. It's not something we can say no to without real consideration." She looks at Dad and then back at Tess and me. "But we wanted to talk to you girls first. This is a big decision, and it includes all of us, not just your father and me."

JEREMY. GAINS. Those are the only words I hear.

Jeremy. Goddamn. Gains.

It's what we all call him around here. He's only a few years older than me, and he owns ten restaurants. Two in New York, two in Vegas, two in LA, one in Napa and three in San Francisco, one of which is his flagship restaurant and home base. Four of them, including the one here, have Michelin stars.

It's not that I have anything against the guy. Objectively, he's beyond impressive. The thing is his cooking philosophy—the more is more approach—is the exact opposite of Dad's. In fact, the reason we call him Jeremy Goddamn Gains is because his food is overly fussy, overly complicated, and overly pretentious. Don't even get Dad started on Jeremy's portion sizes. As my father likes to say, "A child's plate." Or "Is this food or a sculpture?"

So whenever we're somewhere where the food is particularly obnoxious, one of us will say, "Jeremy Goddamn Gains."

"Dad?" I turn to him because the notion that he would give up our family's legacy to Jeremy Goddamn Gains, or anyone for that matter, is unfathomable to me. I don't care how *significant* the offer is. "You don't really want this, do you?"

"Avery!" Tess stares me down. "This is a lot for Mom and Dad." "This" being the day in, day out drudgery of running a restaurant. "This" being

Dad's health. She doesn't have to say it for me to know exactly what she's saying. In other words, her words, I'm being selfish.

Except I'm not.

Without this restaurant Dad would wither away. This is his lifeblood, his everything. She should know that but as always Tess has to be the "good" daughter, the one who knows what's best for our parents.

"Nothing is settled yet." My mother looks directly at me as she says this. "It's a big decision and we have time to think about it."

I note that my father isn't saying a word. He's just sitting here, pretending that selling the restaurant is a viable option. But there's a deep well of sadness in his eyes. And it's taking everything I have to keep from screaming, "Am I the only one who sees that selling will destroy him?"

"We don't want to do anything without both your blessings," my mother says.

I don't even know how to respond. Both our blessings? A flash of burning anger shoots through me like a bullet. Tess, who could never be bothered with the restaurant, is suddenly an equal in all this.

"He's very impressed with you, Tess," Dad says. "Loves everything you do. Doesn't he, Beatriz?" My mother is all smiles.

I laugh. As if suddenly Jeremy Goddamn Gains's opinion is something Macalister Stone gives a shit about.

Tess reaches into her purse and pulls out the papers she found. "What about this?"

Mom and Dad exchange a glance.

"Where'd you find that?" Dad asks, none too pleased.

"In your office at home. I wasn't snooping, I was using the computer. It was in plain sight."

I want to say what does it matter where Tess found the papers, since when does our family keep secrets from each other? Since when do they hold clandestine meetings with Jeremy Gains? Since when do they consider selling the restaurant without telling anyone?

But I don't because Tess the reporter isn't cowed by Dad and launches right into "When were you going to tell us that you bought a house in Nevada?"

"We didn't buy a house," Mom says. "We put a fully refundable deposit down to save our place in the queue." She emphasizes the "fully refundable" part.

I'm lost and from Tess's expression she is too.

"Can you please explain what's going on?" Tess says, and for once I'm thankful she's being her usual demanding self, though for me the revelation that Mom and Dad are considering selling the restaurant far outweighs this mystery house in Nevada.

"Remember when we stayed at Dave and Carol's cabin up in Tahoe last year?" Mom says, and Tess gives me a see-I-told-you-so look, the only thing she's gotten right so far.

It was last year, right after Dad's health scare. They went up for a weekend because Mom thought Dad could use the fresh air, fresh air being a euphemism for getting him away from the restaurant so he could convalesce.

"We were tooling around Incline Village when we saw a billboard for a new development," Mom continues. "On a lark we took the tour and fell in love with the place. The salesperson told us the lots wouldn't last and for a few thousand dollars we could reserve one of the yet-to-be-built homes, and if we changed our minds there were no strings attached."

"So, like as a vacation home?" Tess asks, trying to prove her hypothesis, which has been upstaged by the bigger news. The devasting news that I'm still reeling from.

"Originally, that's what we were thinking," Mom says. "A place the whole family can use. It's really something. Swimming pools, tennis courts, a golf course. A little slice of heaven. And truthfully, we got a little caught up in the fantasy of it, especially after the scare with your father, and acted impulsively."

"But you're not thinking in terms of a vacation home anymore?" Because I see where this is going.

"We don't know yet," Dad says.

"If you sell the restaurant to Jeremy, you'd move there full time," I say, not letting him off the hook. Besides losing the restaurant, they'd sell the house on Baker Street, the house Tess and I grew up in. It was where I lost my first tooth, had my first kiss, and is the first place I go when I need the warmth and familiarity of home. They'd trade all that for some wannabe ski chalet in a retirement community in Nevada, of all places.

I don't get it. They put everything they had into our house. Every nook and cranny has their personal stamp. Mom planted every flower and tree and stayed up nights, sitting at the dining room table with her Singer sewing machine, making the silk douppioni drapes that still hang over the bay windows in the front room. Dad painted every square inch of the house with whatever colors matched their moods, including my and Tess's bedrooms at least three times as we grew out of bubblegum pink into a more sophisticated palette in our teens.

And this city. Dad was born and raised here. Mom may as well be the ambassador to San Francisco. Besides being the face of the restaurant, she sits on at least three nonprofit boards that I know of.

I can't grasp my parents retiring. They may be in their midsixties but they're young and robust. They're the same people they were when I was fifteen and twenty and thirty, just with a few more wrinkles and gray hair. I can't imagine my father leaving his kitchen and whiling away his days playing golf or pickleball. Or my mother spending her afternoons with a group of blue-haired ladies, playing canasta.

"Let's not get ahead of our skis." Dad breaks off a piece of bread and pops it in his mouth. "Why don't the two of you take a little time to mull over everything. It's a lot but we want to do this as a family."

We eat in complete silence. I have a million things I want to say to plead the case for keeping the restaurant, top among them being why not me?

Later, I buttonhole my father in the kitchen. He goes back to remind Javi about something or maybe just to escape Mom, Tess and me for a few minutes—proof to me that he's not as on board with all these changes as he's pretending to be. I pull him into his office, away from the others.

"Is this what you really want, Dad? Because this plan of selling the restaurant and moving to a retirement community seems sudden to me."

"It's a good offer, Avery. Maybe even a once-in-a-lifetime offer. The retirement community...well, that was your mother's idea."

"That's what I thought." There is an edge to my voice, not because I'm angry with Mom but because I know this couldn't possibly be my father's decision.

"Watch it," he says and holds up his finger in warning. "Your mother is worried about me."

"Is there a reason for that?" I cross my arms across my chest, concerned—and to be honest a little bit pissed—that he and Mom haven't told us the whole truth about his health. Maybe it's worse than we know.

"Avery, I don't need to tell you how much work this place is. Your mom and I, we're not kids anymore."

"Dad, are you really sick?"

"I'm healthy as a horse. But I can't do this forever, nor can your mom. The restaurant was always my dream. It's Mom's turn now to have hers. Think about that." He slings his arm around my neck. "Nothing has happened yet. We're still tossing this offer of Jeremy's around. And as much as I wish I could give you the restaurant, kiddo, I can't. Even if I could, I don't think I'd be doing you any favors." My father pauses, then says, "Change is sometimes a good thing, Avery."

Later, as I'm driving home, I think about what my father said. I think about how he bought the restaurant from my grandfather, then invested everything he and my mom had to move it from the water to the Financial District. How they purchased the run-down old bank building on California Street and spent hundreds of thousands of dollars retrofitting and converting it into a restaurant. Everything they have is tied up in Stones.

My phone rings and Tess's number comes up on my dashboard screen. I hesitate, then answer hands-free. "What's up?"

"Nothing, really. Just wanted to check in."

"Tess, I just saw you ten minutes ago. Go ahead and say what you've called to say." Because she eventually will anyway.

"Okay. You were kind of unfair to Mom and Dad back there. They've worked hard their whole lives, Avery. They deserve to be able to retire with financial peace of mind."

"I'm not saying they don't, Tess. I just want to make sure this is what Dad wants."

"Dad can take care of himself. I think this is more about what you want." She doesn't say it cuttingly and if I was in a better frame of mind, I'd say she hit the nail on the head.

"It's our family's restaurant, Tess. It might not mean much to you but it's everything to me."

"Of course it means something to me. Why would you even say that? I may not work there but it's a piece of my history just like it is yours. All I'm saying is, be fair about this. Mom and Dad spend every waking hour running that place. Why do you think Dad has a health condition? And you shouldn't do it, you shouldn't take over Stones. Because I know that's what you're thinking. Look, I speak from experience when I say all work and no play is bad for a marriage. Is this how you want to start your life with Bennett? Just think about it, Avery. I'll call you tomorrow."

I head west on California Street toward Battery. It's only seven miles from the restaurant to our little house on Forty-fourth Avenue. Early mornings I can make it in sixteen minutes flat, even with stoplights. Tonight, about the same.

Too little time to contemplate all the things Tess said. All the things she didn't say but was thinking. Frankly, I'm still trying to digest it all. The restaurant. Mom and Dad selling their house and moving away. It's a lot of change and despite what Dad said change isn't always good, or at least I'm not always good at adapting to it.

I suppose I should've seen it coming. It wasn't as if my parents were going to work forever. I just didn't expect it now and all at once. And I never anticipated they would let Stones go and leave it in the hands of a stranger.

Tess was right about me not taking over the restaurant. I can't afford a down payment on a house, let alone a business that includes real estate in one of the city's most expensive commercial districts. It's not like I run with the kinds of people who invest in such ventures. Most of my friends are struggling chefs and bartenders.

She was wrong about everything else, though. Taking over Stones wouldn't hurt my marriage. The only thing that can hurt my marriage is Tess.

Tess

Not to dwell on it or anything but it's stunning how fast I went from being a peacock to a feather duster.

I used to get inundated with phone calls, everything from pleas from charity leaders to host their events to "friends" wanting to grab a drink in the evening. But today the only call I've gotten is a robot telling me I need to extend my car warranty. Funny, because I don't own a car.

I console myself that in no time I'll be back on top, that this is only a momentary setback.

To make myself feel better I've dressed up in a black sleeveless sheath dress I bought downtown yesterday at the Armani store with Kit's credit card. It's too dressy for a casual dinner at Stones but it shows off my curves and gives me a bump in the boobs department, though there's no one in particular at the restaurant I want to impress. I guess it's more accurate to say I want to impress everyone. But tonight, it's just Avery.

My sister gets off at five and we're planning to have drinks at the bar. Mom's idea not Avery's. I think my mother wants us to discuss and come to terms with the sale of the restaurant. The truth is, selling the restaurant may give Avery the nudge she needs to leave the nest, so to speak. I would never tell anyone this but she's wasting her skills at Stones under my father's thumb.

She's capable of more, like her own baking show on the Food Network. I've seen her reinvent the simplest chocolate chip cookie or the most basic fruit crumble in a way that makes it hers and hers alone.

Not only are her pastries out of this world, they're also gorgeous. Two years ago, she made a four-tier wedding cake that looked like a Monet painting for one of her old high school friends—an art historian—that was so breathtaking that the photo wound up on the cover of *Brides*. Her croquembouche, made with a pate a choux so delicate and flaky it beats all others, is almost too beautiful to eat.

I wish Avery would see this as an opportunity because it could be if she doesn't stand in her own way.

I take one last look in the mirror, like what I see, and head out. Halfway to the street where my Uber is waiting, my phone rings. It's Kit. His game against the Oakland A's must be over. How nice for him. I slide my phone back in my purse and get in the car.

Traffic is light for a Friday evening, and I get to Stones in record time.

And wouldn't you know it, Kit is waiting at the door. I motion for him to move aside but he continues to stand there, all two hundred pounds of him.

"I told you not to show up."

"I told you I'd call so we could get together to talk but you don't answer your goddamn phone."

"Because we've said all we need to say. Now move aside before someone sees you harassing me and calls the cops."

"Come on, Tess, let's go to dinner."

"I am going to dinner. At my family's restaurant, where you are no longer welcome. So move out of the way."

"A drink," he says. "Just one drink. There's a nice bar down the street."

"I was born and raised here, Kit. I know where all the nice bars are." I try to step around him but the man has outstanding reflexes and blocks me from getting inside.

"Please, Tess." He holds up his finger. "Just one drink, then I'll jump off the Golden Gate Bridge if you want me to."

"That's not funny."

"Please."

I roll my eyes and tell myself it's just one drink and that it's better than making a scene in front of Stones, in front of a hundred diners. All we need is to show up in the tabloids again. "One drink. That's it."

He moves aside and I lead the way to the House of Whiskey, which is two blocks down from Stones. My feet are cursing me. That's what I get for wearing new four-inch Stuart Weitzman heels. Kit, of course, doesn't so much as slow his stride in his loafers. Though he could probably climb Mount Shasta in my shoes without taking so much as a single break. Bastard.

"Tess, honey, you want me to carry you?" He smirks as I stop to adjust my strap.

"Shut up or I might say yes."

The bar is dark with a hipster vibe. Lots of exposed pipes, tattoo sleeves and flights of locally made whiskey. Last time I was here, it was a chicken potpie shop. The good news is no one recognizes Kit, which would never happen in New York.

We take one of the small booths, a whole Chesterfield leather situation. A waitress, dressed in a black see-through crinoline and lace up boots, takes our order. I get a glass of Pinot Gris, an odd choice for a whiskey bar but I don't like whiskey. Kit orders a Jameson. I'm sure the waitress thinks we're two rubes from Fresno but whatever.

Kit gets a call and says, "Sorry, I have to take this," answers and holds up the two-minute sign with his fingers. The person on the other end of the phone is doing all the talking, with a few sporadic grunts from Kit, so I can't tell if it's his agent, his masseuse, his strength and conditioning coach, or a reporter from *Sports Illustrated.* For all I know it's Annabel.

"Your concubine?" I ask when he hangs up.

"Seriously?" He shakes his head, leans over and kisses me before I can stop him. "You look fantastic, by the way." He takes a long, visual stroll down my body.

"You like it?" I run my hands down my sides, watching his eyes heat, and I say, "Good. Because you paid for it and it cost as much as a small airplane. The shoes too." I stretch my leg out from under the table and point my toe like a ballerina.

"You look beautiful, Tess."

I want to say fuck you, Kit. Save the compliments for someone who cares. But what's the point? Instead, I find myself focusing on his hair and how it's still damp from his after-game shower. I've always loved the way it curls at the nape of his neck.

He reaches across the table to touch me and I pull away. I may have dressed for seduction but not by him. Every time he gets affectionate with me, I see Annabel's face and her perfect boobs.

Our drinks come and I remind myself that I told him just one. It would be so easy to let myself believe that I overreacted, that nothing happened that morning with him and Annabel. It would be so easy to believe he's telling the truth about him being a gentleman and letting her use his room to crash.

Admittedly, the story is plausible, especially because it's Kit. He really is the kind of guy who would lend his room to a damsel in distress. And I've always been way too distrustful, it's the reporter in me. And until Kit, I hadn't had the best luck with men. My high school boyfriend cheated on me with a girl who went to Lowell, across the city. The two of them later married, got divorced, and married again.

During my sophomore year in college, I caught the guy I was dating with my roommate in the shower. His response was to ask me to join them. See, I've had some real winners, except of course Bennett, who was always a gentleman. A keeper, though I threw him away.

At the time, I thought we were on the same wavelength of keeping things light and in the fun zone while I pursued my dreams. He was cute, sweet and had an interesting job, though I never understood why he was willing to settle for writing jingles. Some of his tourism ditties, like the ones promoting San Diego and Alaska, were catchy and poppy enough to be hit songs. I guess that was the sticking point between us. He was satisfied with his life just the way it was, and I'm always reaching for the stars.

I don't want to say he was a placeholder because that sounds callous. But in effect, that's sort of how it was. At least for me.

And now he's marrying my sister.

"My parents got an offer to buy Stones," I say, because the restaurant has always been the center of our family's universe. And even though I hate Kit now, besides Avery, he's my best friend. Or was my best friend.

"A good offer? Are they going to sell?" He's as surprised as Avery and I were.

"Yeah, it looks like they're serious. I think after last year, after Dad's diagnosis, he and my mom took stock of his health, of how Stones wasn't helping it and decided working this hard wasn't the way they wanted to spend the rest of their lives. Especially if they didn't have to."

"Wow, good for them. What'll Avery do?"

I shrug. "We haven't talked about it much but she's so wildly talented she can work anywhere."

He's barely touched his whiskey and I have only nursed my Pinot Gris. At this rate we'll be here all night and that isn't my plan.

I make a show of looking at my watch as if I have somewhere important to be. "What did you want to talk about, Kit? I have limited time and not a lot of patience."

"I want you to come home. We can't work this out with you on the other side of the country."

"That's rich coming from a guy who's on the road most of the year. What am I going back to? Last I looked, I still don't have a job. Or a loyal husband."

"So, you're sitting back, hanging out at your parents', waiting to hear from NBC?"

From the tone of Kit's voice and his facial expression I can tell he thinks it's a bad strategy—because he is an expert after all on all things broadcast journalism.

"I'm doing what my agent told me to do, Kit. Because believe it or not, she didn't get where she is by giving stupid advice. But maybe we should call Annabel Lane. I hear she's got lots of tricks up her sleeve for clawing—or is that blowing—her way to the top."

"Keep your voice down." Kit looks around the dining room. "You really want to do this here? Jesus, Tess, I thought we were past this."

"Well, we're not. Especially when you're being a sanctimonious asshole. You—and she—are the reason I'm in this position in the first place."

"How many times do I have to tell you nothing happened?"

"What would you do if you were in my place, Kit? What would you do if one of my sources spent the night in a hotel room with me? Would you believe nothing happened?" We've had this conversation so many times that I sound like a broken record.

"For all I know Rodney has slept in your hotel room a dozen times. Do you hear me accusing you of infidelity?" he whispers.

In the same hushed tone, I say, "Good one, Kit. As if you don't know Rodney's gay."

"How do you know Annabel isn't a lesbian?"

"Is she?" I pin him with a look.

"How the hell would I know?"

"Even if she is, do you know how unethical it is for a reporter to sleep in the same room as her source?"

"I'm not her source, Tess."

"You are by nature. She covers the Yankees. Last I looked you're a Yankee. But that's not the point."

"What is the point?" He sounds exasperated. "Fucking enlighten me." He's acting like the aggrieved partner here. And maybe he is.

"The point! The point is, the reason I now have to look for a job is because the two of you decided it would be a good idea to share a hotel room. And God knows what else."

"No. The reason you got canned is because you jumped to conclusions and lost your shit on the air, Tess. That's on you, babe, not me."

He's partly right, though I don't want to admit it. Not to him, anyway.

"Look, can we just give it a rest tonight? I want us to have a good time and try to put this behind us." He leans across the table. "I'm sorry I let you down and I love you."

Does he? I never had to wonder before.

* * *

It's Saturday and Kit's back again. I give him credit for perseverance. The man is nothing if not persistent.

He walks into Stones like nothing has happened, like my whole family couldn't possibly hate him, and like everything is normal between us and I'm expecting him. The last part is true, though I expected him to show up at the house on Baker after the game. That's why I'm at the restaurant.

I'm sitting at the bar, folding napkins like I used to when I worked here as a teenager. It's a monotonous chore but at the same time there's a sort of zen to it. Repetitive and mindless, perfect for daydreaming.

His eyes light on me from across the dining room and he saunters over like he owns the place and trails a kiss across my neck.

Before I can push him away, Avery comes toward us. I instantly can tell she's surprised to see Kit here. But she quickly covers it up by plastering on what she likes to call my "anchorwoman" smile. It's too bright to be real. And in this case, the smile is a little maniacal, like she'll stab him if I say the word.

She may have some imagined beef with me but she's loyal to her core. I love her so much for that. No matter what, she'll always have my back in a storm. Like the time Jenny Tuberville carved "whore" into my eighth-grade desk with a penknife and Avery got even by putting gum in Jenny's hair. Or like all the times she drove to Santa Barbara to bring me homemade cupcakes or brownies to salve my latest college breakup or help me through a particularly trying roommate situation.

Before things went sour between us, we were inseparable. Maybe because Mom and Dad were always at the restaurant, and it was just the two of us fending for ourselves and each other. Latchkey kids with just enough freedom to get into trouble.

I don't know why she has a hair up her ass where I'm concerned, whether it's some ridiculous notion that I somehow left her behind. But every time I try to talk to her about it, she blows me off and pretends like I'm crazy and that everything is fine.

No matter what, though, I know she's on my side. Still, I really don't want her to hate Kit.

Avery hugs Kit, pretending like she's happy to see him. "I didn't know you were coming in." She turns to me, silently asking whether she's missing something.

I didn't tell anyone about our rendezvous at the House of Whiskey last night. It was a momentary weakness that no one needs to know about.

"Yep, Tess and I have dinner plans tonight," Kit says.

Dinner plans? This is news to me—and infuriating that he's putting me on the spot like this.

"I wanted to see you all before I leave tomorrow," he continues without missing a beat.

He has one more game with Oakland Sunday before the team continues its West Coast swing. And in case you are wondering, the Yankees beat the A's four to two today. Kit got a home run and hit a double. Winning!

"You have time to join us for a drink?" Kit asks, and I seriously want to kill him. Is he really this tone-deaf or is it a ploy to get my family to rally behind him?

"Uh...sure," Avery says, and looks to me for confirmation.

Mom sees us in the corner and comes over. "Kit, now this is a surprise." Her voice is cold. But for the sake of not making this any more awkward than it already is, she gives him a superficial hug.

Mom is making it crystal clear she's not on Team Kit. Either he's too clueless to notice or he plans to win her back by wooing me in front of my family. He does genuinely love the Stones, as I do his parents and Jonas, even if his brother is a mooch of the highest order.

"We're having a drink," Avery says, wearing a tight smile. "Should I get Dad?" She looks from me to Mom and grimaces.

Thank goodness Kit is too oblivious to notice. He's never suffered in the confidence department and probably can't comprehend the idea that a female, even my sister, would want to sock him in the face.

"I'll get Mac." Mom returns from the kitchen a few minutes later with Dad by her side.

"I've got a couple of minutes." Dad slaps Kit on the back. "Good game today. I listened to it on the radio."

Under normal circumstances, my father would've broken away from the restaurant for a few hours to go to the game. Kit always arranges for my parents to sit with the other players' families when the team has games in the Bay Area. But these are not normal circumstances, even if Kit is pretending they are.

We take our usual corner table, freshly bussed from the last party that left only minutes ago. In an hour, the place will be packed to the rafters. Saturday night.

Mom flags down one of the servers and we order cocktails. Dad wanders back to the kitchen and returns with a few appetizers, including fried calamari, which he knows I love.

Everyone is trying so hard to make things normal that it feels anything but.

Kit reaches for Avery across the table. "Where's Bennett?"

"As coincidence has it, he's on his way," she says.

Not really a coincidence. Bennett is coming in to talk about the wedding. The possible sale of Stones puts a wrinkle in the restaurant being a viable option for the reception, though I'm sure things can be worked out.

"When's the wedding date?" Kit smiles his big toothy grin and my treacherous heart does somersaults.

"September third."

As if on cue, Bennett comes through the door, glances around the restaurant, and lights up when he sees us in our usual corner. I've always thought he looked like a big teddy bear, not pudgy but stocky with an open face and a wide, perpetually happy grin.

Is it weird that I dated him first? A little bit. Possibly more so for Avery than me.

I felt bad about the way things ended between us. I think of all the men I've been with, Bennett loved me the most, even more than Kit if I'm being completely honest. It was a little too much, if you know what I mean. The responsibility of holding that kind of emotional power over another human being is more than I can take. Perhaps that's why I've never wanted children. All that unconditional love frightens me.

Knowing that Avery and Bennett found each other after I left has helped take away some of the guilt for breaking it off with him. And the fact that he and I have remained friends—and soon in-laws—is a nice piece of fate. For some reason it makes me feel optimistic about the future.

"Hey, everyone." Bennett tries for a group hug but can only fit Mom and Dad in his outstretched arms. Avery and I lean forward toward him in a symbolic gesture that he's got us too.

"Sorry I'm late. Traffic." He reaches across the table and shakes Kit's hand as if it's not awkward that he's sitting here. Another one of Bennett's sterling qualities is tactfulness. "Hey there, Kit, it's been a while. Good to see you."

Mom pats the chair next to her for Bennett to sit.

The men talk baseball, which bores me to tears. I get enough of it with Kit.

Someone passes me the fried calamari and I quickly push it to the other side of the table. I love it but tonight it makes my stomach queasy.

Kit is deep into a story about his walk-off home run from four years ago when the Yankees made it into the playoffs. I've heard him retell this story so many times I could recite it while comatose.

He waxes on about his heroic hit and how he single-handedly saved the day.

I'm tempted to say, "Yeah, but you didn't make it to the World Series." It's mean and petty and I'd like to say beneath me but apparently it's not. Since Annabel, and me losing my job at WNBC, I'm angry a lot, especially at Kit, the winner of life's lottery.

Bennett glances my way and flashes a commiserating smile as I check my watch again. He's not as enthralled with Kit's story as my father appears to be.

Avery clears her throat. "Aren't you guys going to be late to the restaurant?"

I glare at her.

Kit glances at his watch and gets to his feet. "Shoot. We've got to go. Our reservation is for seven. It was great seeing everyone."

And there I am, caught between letting Kit call the shots or making a commotion about it in front of everyone. I opt for dinner, mostly because I didn't eat Dad's appetizers and am starved.

"There's no chance in hell we'll make it on time," I say once Kit has hailed a cab.

"Relax. So we're a little late."

"There's a fifteen-minute rule. Then they give the reservation to someone else," I say because it's really a thing in San Francisco, even for Kit Reid. Because no one here cares that he's first baseman for the Yankees.

The cabdriver takes evasive measures to avoid traffic, wending through the city in a circuitous route that by some miracle gets us there only seven minutes late.

"See," Kit says.

He is pulling out all the stops. The restaurant is French and incredibly romantic, lit almost exclusively by candles. I feel my stress level drop the moment we're shown to our table, a round two-top in a curtained-off alcove next to a window that looks out onto Polk Street.

The sommelier brings us a bottle of expensive champagne. "Compliments of the chef," he says as he pours us each a glass.

I was wrong. Even in the City by the Bay, three thousand miles away from Yankee Stadium, Kit Reid is a freaking icon. And he definitely did his homework. If he wanted to impress me, he couldn't have picked a better restaurant.

"Please send the chef our thanks," I say.

"Shall I close the drapes or leave them open?"

Kit turns to me and I say, "You can leave them open. Less claustrophobic, right?"

A flash of disappointment wreaths his face, which is ridiculous. It's not like we're going to make out in the middle of a restaurant. And even with the drapes open, it's cozy in the alcove. Private.

He nods. "Open is good."

The sommelier leaves us to enjoy our champagne and peruse the menu. A server quickly appears to tell us the specials of the day and without a lot of fanfare we order, anxious for privacy. At least Kit is. I don't know what he's expecting, but if he thinks all it takes is an expensive restaurant to win me back he's got another thing coming.

"Hey." He lifts my chin with his finger. "This is supposed to be fun. Romantic."

Before our lives became consumed by work and public appearances and stardom, we made plenty of time for romance. Plenty of time for fun. Long, chilly weekends on the Cape. Cozy dinners at our favorite Manhattan restaurants. Even a winter trip to Barbados.

"We'll never be able to make this work if you don't let it go, Tess. I shouldn't have had her stay in my room. It was stupid. It was thoughtless. And it was disrespectful to you. But she was drunk and it was late and she's practically part of the team. I guess I looked at her like she was one of the guys. It was a mistake."

"Tell me one good reason I should believe you, Kit. No one else does."

"I don't care about anyone else. I only care about you. Jeez, when have I ever lied to you?"

"There's a first for everything." Or a second or a third, or even a fourth. Because for all I know Kit has been lying to me for years. That's the cynic in me speaking.

But the wife in me yearns to believe him.

Our food comes and I seem to have lost my appetite, though everything smells delicious. Kit probably burned a thousand calories at the game today. He can eat whatever he wants and never gain a pound. I think it's his genes, not that he's a professional athlete. I've seen some pretty tubby baseball players in my time.

In any event, he attacks his beef bourguignon like he didn't just eat enough fried calamari to feed a small nation.

"Taste this." Kit feeds me a forkful of stew, which hits the spot. "Good, right?"

"Delicious." I dip into my own coq au vin, which is every bit as good as the beef.

And as we tuck into our food it starts to feel normal between us, though I know it's a temporary state of mind helped by the food, the atmosphere, but most of all the champagne, which is starting to go to my head. That, and I'm exhausted from being angry all the time. I think it's all the pent-up bitterness that's constantly souring my stomach these days.

We both get dessert, Kit an apple tarte tatin and me chocolate mousse, which isn't half as good as Avery's. She uses three different kinds of chocolate and the mousse is so airy it melts in your mouth.

"Come home, Tess," Kit says to me, his blue eyes twinkling in the candlelight. "Or at least come back to me."

Maybe I'm a fool but I feel myself wavering.

Avery

The whole way home all I can think about is the way Bennett kept sneaking glances at Tess. Okay, to be fair they weren't so much longing glances as they were commiserating glances. At least that's how I'd describe them if it was anyone other than Bennett. Anyone who didn't have a history of being crazy in love with my sister.

Because let's face it, you'd have to be a cold-blooded snake not to sympathize with Tess, whose husband talked incessantly about himself and his amazing feats on the field while my poor sister went from rock star to nobody in a New York minute because he couldn't keep his dick in his jockstrap. Even if Kit's innocent of sleeping with that sports reporter, he gets an F- for showing poor judgment. Judgment that ruined my sister's career, a career she worked so hard for.

Although everything seems to come easy for Tess, my sister is one of the most driven people I know. I've always admired that about her, her willingness to take risks. The word "No"—and man did she hear that word a lot when she first started out as a broadcast journalist—just makes Tess push harder. I remember the dozens of rejection letters she got from the big-market stations she applied to right out of college. It was probably unrealistic for her to start at the top, but that's Tess for you. Still, she wasn't deterred and surprised us all when she took a job in Salinas at a tiny station that paid an even tinier salary, covering the lettuce industry. She didn't know a soul there, and Tess isn't what I would call a tractor-loving kind of girl. Even worse, as the new reporter she was required to work the weekend shift.

The only plus was that Salinas is only a two-hour drive from San Francisco. We all expected her to spend more time at home than in the salad bowl of America. But Tess threw herself into the job like there was fire in her belly, breaking story after story until she caught the notice of KNTV here. She made the jump from small-town USA to the sixth largest television market in the country in only a few years.

We were all so proud of her, no one more than me. And the best part was my sister was coming home. Then, she met Bennett...

Is it always going to be like this? Me wondering if Tess will forever be his one who got away?

Don't think I haven't considered what would happen if Tess left Kit, not that I believe for one second my sister would ever intentionally do anything to hurt me. But would Bennett hope for a second chance? Would he secretly wish he wasn't attached to me?

I round the corner to our small Tudor and see that Bennet has beaten me home. He's parked on the street, leaving me the driveway. He does it all the time, so when I leave early in the morning for the restaurant I won't have to stumble around in the dark. I bet Kit isn't that considerate.

It's awful but for some reason that cheers me. Not because I'm happy that Tess's husband is inconsiderate but because my fiancé is. Bennett Lamb is a good person. It's one of the reasons I love him so much.

He meets me at the door. "What took you so long?" It's a long-standing joke. Bennett will drive through parking lots and take detours on out-of-the-way side streets just to avoid traffic signals. We all make fun of him for it but more times than not he reaches his destination before anyone else does.

"How long have you really been here?"

"Five minutes." Bennett chuckles. "You want to watch TV?"

"Sure. First, I've got to take these shoes off."

I typically wear clogs because I'm on my feet all day. Today, though, I wore a pair of strappy platform sandals and a skirt, of all things. Tess always looks so put together, so glamorous. I didn't want to look like a hausfrau in my apron and black-and-white-check chef pants. I even took a little time with my hair between the lunch and dinner service, instead of wearing it tied back all day.

I head to the bedroom, hear Bennett turn on the TV, and switch out my torturous shoes for a pair of fuzzy slippers. My feet want to cry with appreciation. While I'm at it, I trade my skirt and blouse for a pair of yoga pants and a sweatshirt. It's not like Bennett noticed my outfit anyway. How could he when Tess was wearing Prada or Dolce & Gabbana or whatever that dress was?

"You coming?" he calls to me from the living room.

I put my hair up in a twist and meet him on the sofa. He's poured us both a glass of wine and put out an elaborate charcuterie platter with cheese and crackers, mustards and jams, and fruit. It's beautiful.

"Whoa, what have you done with the real Bennett?" We just ate, after all. But I don't want to rain on his parade, especially because he's gone to so much trouble.

"The real Bennett didn't think Doritos went with grenache," he says.

"Au contraire, they're actually a match made in heaven. Shall I get them, you know, as a vehicle for the cheese?"

"Uh-oh. I may have finished them off. Sorry."

"No worries." I cut myself a slice of the Manchego, spread it with a little of the quince jam. "This is perfect. What's the occasion?"

Typically, Bennett will have a beer in the evening, and I'll have a cup of herbal tea before bed. When we're really shaking things up, one of us will microwave a bag of popcorn.

"I thought a little celebration was in order."

"A celebration for what?" Certainly not because the Yankees trounced the A's. Bennett couldn't care less about baseball, or any sport for that matter.

"Us and our decision to have our reception at Stones."

After Tess and Kit left for dinner, we told my parents we want to throw our wedding at the restaurant, despite my initial hesitation about it. Knowing Stones may not be Stones much longer changed my mind. It seems appropriate that my wedding be the grand finale at the restaurant.

"It's getting real now," Bennett says. "The wedding, I mean. That's a big deal, right?"

It is a big deal. A momentous deal. Yet the question in his voice feels like a forewarning. And just like that I'm transported back to the restaurant, to Bennett and the way he was looking at Tess.

I force myself to ask the question, to confront the elephant in the room. "Was it sad for you tonight, seeing Tess that way?"

"What way is that?"

"Sad about her marriage."

"I thought they were trying to work it out." He takes a sip of his wine and I swear I see his hand tremble.

"They are. Does that make you sad?" I ask softly, holding my breath. I'm not trying to be vindictive or even snarky. But it seems like something we should talk about before we take vows that bind us together forever.

"I'm not a huge fan of Kit but if he makes Tess happy, yeah, I hope they work things out. Don't you?" He puts his wine down and busies himself with building a cracker with a piece of cheese, avoiding eye contact.

"I don't know if I do. My sister deserves better." I take a deep breath and force myself to ask the one thing I've never had the guts to ask, "Bennett, are you still in love with her?"

He jerks his head up. "What? Jesus, why are you doing this again? It's almost as if you're looking for reasons to pick a fight. I'm in love with you, Avery. For God's sake, we're getting married soon."

I don't say anything for a long time, letting his words settle around me. *I'm in love with you, Avery.*

I don't doubt him. I've always believed Bennett loves me—he's proven it in a thousand different ways—but does he love me best? Or perhaps the more pertinent question is, does it matter as long as I love him best?

"I know you love me, but do you still love her?" I don't know why I can't leave it alone, why I have to press. But I can't seem to stop myself.

"Where is all this coming from?" He doesn't sound annoyed as much as impatient.

I shrug. "I don't know. Today...I just felt something between you two."

"You're looking for problems that don't exist. Stop, okay?"

"Because I won't like the answer?"

"Because it's hurtful." He gets up, walks to our bedroom and slams the door, the sound of it reverberating through our tiny house.

I flick off the TV and there is only silence, which in this case, to me, speaks louder than words.

    * * *

By the time Tuesday rolls around, Bennett and I have worked our way back to some semblance of normality. This is to say, we pretended Saturday's heated conversation never occurred and spent Sunday and Monday, my days off, making wedding plans.

July is almost over, leaving us a little more than a month to orchestrate this soiree. If the restaurant wasn't a lock for our reception we'd be in trouble as far as securing a venue on such short notice. And since Stones is our official caterer, we're good in the food department as well. It's all the other things: the DJ, the photographer, the videographer, the florist and countless other details that have to be nailed down.

I'm hoping to make calls during breaks at the restaurant today.

While my pies bake, I start whipping up my frosting for the chocolate layer cakes.

There's a tap on the alleyway door and without thinking I swing it open, assuming it's one of the guys. They're forever forgetting their keys and Dad won't budge on putting in a smart lock. Always old school with him.

I realize my mistake as soon as I'm greeted by a man in a black hoodie. At first, I think he's a vagrant asking for food or money, then quickly realize it's Jeremy Goddamn Gains, dressed like a homeless dude or a millionaire tech programmer. In San Francisco it's hard to tell the two apart.

He's tall and lean with sandy-blond hair, brown eyes and a pair of dimples that are at odds with what is otherwise a chiseled jawline. Objectively speaking, he's nice looking but not nearly as hot as he thinks he is. He's wearing a wide smile, clearly amused by my startled reaction. Either that or he thinks I'm overcome by being in the presence of greatness.

Before I can ask him what he wants, he steps inside like he already owns the place.

"Can I help you?"

"If you don't mind, I came to take a few measurements. Mac said it was okay."

News to me. I wonder if Mac also told him we haven't made any definitive decision about selling yet.

"Nope," I say, though I do mind. I mind very much. "Have at it."

"Great. Thanks."

I go back to my frosting as he uses some kind of laser beam thing to record the dimensions of the kitchen. I would've thought he had people for such a menial job.

I've only eaten once at one of his restaurants. Les Corniches on the Embarcadero. Bennett took me last year for my thirty-fourth birthday. It was a surprise, otherwise it wouldn't have been my choice. For the price of dinner, we could've bought a used car or a nice weekend away.

Let's start with the name. Les Corniches, derived from the trio of cliff roads in the Côte d'Azur of France that go from Nice to Monaco with breathtaking views of the Mediterranean. If I had a dime for every restaurant named after a road or highway in Europe I could finally afford to buy a house in San Francisco.

The restaurant features mostly seafood and Monégasque dishes, like stuffed zucchini flowers, dried cod stewed in tomato sauce, and savory pies made with Swiss chard or olive tapenade.

The lobby has a fish tank the size of something you'd find at the Monterey Bay Aquarium, I kid you not. And the private patio, which overlooks the bay, has crisp white cabanas like the ones you'd see on a beach in the South of France.

And...wait for it...the cabanas all circle around a heated, built-in swimming pool with a swim-up bar. All this for a restaurant in foggy, chilly San Francisco.

It is so over the top that all I could do was laugh.

But here's my dirty little secret. It was the best meal I've ever had.

The *barbajuan*, puff pastry filled with chard, leeks and ricotta cheese, made my heart sing. And I still dream about the bouillabaisse. It came in three parts: first, raw shellfish with fish fritters, then a medley of seafood in a saffron broth, and ended with three gorgeous fish filets served with rockfish-and-crab soup. The dessert was a newfangled *Fougassette Monégasque*, a sweet shortcrust called sablée made with almond meal and topped with anise and almonds. It put every pastry we ever made in culinary school to shame.

Supposedly Jeremy's restaurant in Napa, which pays homage to the Calabria region of Southern Italy, is equally good, according to my culinary school friends who have eaten at both.

"What are the measurements for?" I'm wildly curious. Clearly, he's planning some kind of remodel, perhaps a swimming pool where the ovens are or maybe a jungle gym. Any reason to burn money and be ostentatious.

"The kitchen's tight. I have plans to blow it out, organize it better." He hops up on one of the stainless steel worktables and I make a mental note to sanitize it after he's gone.

The kitchen may be small but there's nothing wrong with its organization. It's twenty times better than most of the commercial kitchens I've been in. Everything is accessible and Dad's a stickler for safety and cleanliness. Every year, we score near perfect on meeting the city's health regulations. But I keep my thoughts to myself. He can spin his wheels all day long, planning how he's going to rip this place apart.

"What do you got there?" He gets off the table, finds a clean spoon, dips it into my frosting and takes a taste. "Needs salt."

I stare daggers at him and he has the gall to smirk. Okay, it's more like a boyish grin. He clearly thinks he's the most charming man in the world.

A friend of a friend used to date him and the rap on him is that his favorite person is himself. The other thing she said is that he's a habitual name-dropper. You know the type.

Thomas (as in Keller) *and I were hanging out with Francis* (as in Coppola) *over at the winery the other day when we ran into Gwyneth* (as in Paltrow) *and she's dying to get me onto the cover of* Goop.

But today he isn't dropping names. No, he is back to sitting on the stainless steel work area, watching me make my frosting. I'll admit it's a bit unnerving. He might be an asshole but Jeremy Gains is an incredible chef. No one says otherwise.

"So, you planning to put in a pool here too?"

One corner of his mouth curves up. "You think I should? It's not really the FiDi vibe but I'm open."

"Maybe you could do a whole stock exchange theme. You know, a bell, an electronic ticker tape that goes around the whole dining room, all the servers can dress in pinstripe suits."

"Not a bad idea." He pretends to consider it. "I'll take it under advisement."

The timer goes off and I take out my pies and slide in my cakes.

"I hear you're getting married in September," he says.

"Oh yeah, where'd you hear that?"

"Your mom. She says you're doing the reception here and wanted to make sure we carve out the date. Mazel tov, by the way."

The "we" sticks in my craw. Jeremy Gains is not only too high on himself, but he's also presumptuous.

"Did you get all your measurements?" It's a not-so-subtle hint that I've got things to do and don't have time to make small talk with Jeremy Goddamn Gains.

"Yep." He strolls over with his hands in his pants pockets, stands over me and inspects my pies. "How 'bout a slice? I left home without eating breakfast."

I cut him a slice. I don't want to but in the hospitality industry we feed each other, it's the way it's done. It was rude of me not to offer in the first place.

"Sorry, I didn't make coffee." I set him up in the same spot where he parked his ass earlier and pull up a high folding chair from the office. "You want it à la mode?" It's a little early for ice cream but that's the way I normally serve my pie. I make my French vanilla using vanilla beans, not extract. It definitely makes a difference.

He considers it for a second, then says, "Why the hell not?"

I go to the freezer and take out the big tub of ice cream I made on Saturday and top his olallieberry pie with a big scoop.

To be honest, I'm nervous. I'm a good baker, really good, but Jeremy Gains has eaten from the best. Even before he interned at the French Laundry, he staged for the late Jöel Robuchon in Paris. My prosaic little pie has nothing on the rich and complicated pastries he no doubt has sampled. Or served. His pastry chef at Les Corniches came from The Dorchester in London, Alain Ducasse's Michelin three-star restaurant.

The pastry chef at his Napa place was featured in the *San Francisco Chronicle* as one of the region's "rising stars." In his Vegas restaurant he has two pastry chefs, a husband-and-wife team, both featured judges on the Food Network's *Extreme Cakes*.

My only claim to fame is that the *New York Times* likes my chocolate layer cake. Irony of ironies is that Jeremy asked for pie.

I can't even look while he's eating and instead turn my attention to taking my cakes out of the oven and putting my bowl of chocolate ganache in the fridge to chill. The last thing I want him to see is me sweating over something as insecure as whether he likes my pie. Give me a break.

The kitchen is quiet, other than the occasional clink of his fork against the plate. He says nothing, not even a content murmur escapes his mouth. I pretend to search through a drawer. The location holds a good vantage of his back. I try to catch a glimpse of his plate to see how big of a dent he's made in the pie but his ridiculous black hoodie is in the way.

At Stones we always know the successes from the failures by what comes back on the plate. If diners leave more than a third of something, the dish gets eighty-sixed.

"An all-butter crust, huh?" he asks blandly. So blandly that I can't tell whether it's a rebuke, a compliment, or just a statement of fact.

"With a little cream cheese." I find it gives the crust an extra flakiness you can't get from animal or vegetable fat.

"Hmm," is all he says. The man doesn't give anything away.

Or there's a chance he's just being polite, trying to make conversation about a dessert that doesn't wow him.

He swivels around so he's facing me and the row of cakes that just came out of the oven.

"Is that the famous cake the *Times* wrote about?"

I'm surprised he knows about that. Jeremy doesn't strike me as the kind of guy who keeps track of the *little people*. My mother or father must've bragged to him about it.

"Yep," I say, feeling foolish.

He nods and pushes his pie plate to the side. I can finally see it and it's... empty. Licked clean, as my dad likes to say. I wait for him to comment about it. *Good pie. That was delicious. Your French vanilla is beyond compare.* Anything. But nothing. I tell myself to take pleasure in the little things. Clean plate.

He takes his dish to the sink, rinses it and loads it into the rack. Color me shocked. I haven't met a chef yet who does his own dishes. Not even Dad, who's salt of the earth and eschews the typical arrogant-chef crap, would stoop to washing plates. I suppose attending the Culinary Arts Academy in Lucerne buys him the privilege.

Jeremy takes his spot at the high table again. For a guy with ten restaurants, he seems in no rush to leave.

I decide to take the opportunity to do a little fishing. "What're your plans for Stones, or are you going to change the name?"

"No, that's what I'm buying, right?"

I laugh to myself because he's full of shit. Outside of Northern California, no one knows the Stone name, whereas Jeremy Gains is as household as Gordon Ramsey or Emeril Lagasse.

"I'm going to keep it pretty much the same with a few tweaks here and there."

"Like expanding the kitchen," I say, not even bothering to keep the sarcasm out of my voice.

"For a start. The dining room could also use a face-lift, though I like its old-timey feel. I like that it was a bank, seems appropriate for the location."

"You have a chef in mind?" That'll give me more of a clue of the direction he'd take the restaurant if he got it. And that's a big if.

"A few. You have any recommendations?"

I get my chocolate ganache out of the fridge and plate my cakes, letting the frosting come to room temperature.

"No, but you should make a place for Javier Garcia, he's our chef de cuisine and is amazing." Javi has given his blood, sweat and tears to this place and while he won't have any trouble being picked up by the city's thriving restaurant community, he should be able to stay if he so chooses. "One of the best I've ever worked with." I've only worked with Javi but Jeremy doesn't need to know that. It's not like my CV is on our Web site.

"Yep, Mac is making that part of the agreement," Jeremy says.

Shame on me for not giving Dad the benefit of the doubt. Javi is my dad's brother from another mother, of course Mac would look out for him.

I nod, then start to frost my cakes. "So you're keeping the Americana concept, huh?" It's sort of like asking Jeremy Goddamn Gains if he's planning to open a burger joint.

"Nouveau American," he corrects.

There's nothing new about Stones. We're as old-school as it comes. It's Jeremy's way of saying he's changing everything.

I don't know how to feel about that. On the one hand, I resent it. My father has built a solid reputation on doing things the old way, not to mention a profit. On the other hand, I would do exactly the same thing if I were him. He's made his bones pushing the limits, why would he stop now?

He nudges his head at the cake I just finished frosting and gets to his feet. "You going to give me a piece of that for the road?"

I blow out a breath. Of course I am but I feel like this is all a big test. Jeremy has no interest in my chocolate layer cake. He has no interest in my chef recommendations or anything else I have to offer. He's playing me. He firmly believes that if he wins me over it'll go a long way to winning over my dad, which in his mind will make the deal for the restaurant go smoother.

Well, I'm onto you, Chef Gains.

I wrap up a big slab of cake in a to-go container. The ones at Les Corniches are blue foil boxes, the color of the sea, with an embossed logo on the top and a white satin ribbon for a closure. Ours are the brown cardboard kind you buy at the restaurant supply store with a regular tab-lock top. Hey, they're compostable and that's not nothing.

"You get everything you need?" I hand him the box.

"For now." Instead of leaving, he just stands there, holding the box, watching me frost another cake.

If I hadn't done this a million times I would find it nerve-racking, like I'm back in culinary school and the instructor is standing over my shoulder, scrutinizing my technique.

"See you around," he finally says and heads to the door.

"See you around, Chef."

"Oh, and Stone, your dad is making you a part of the deal, too. So, no need to worry about a job," he says on his way out.

What a condescending asshole.

Tess

"Why the hell not?" I look Avery in the eye and shake my head.

"Because I don't want to take money from you and Kit."

"First of all, it's Kit's money not mine. And secondly, don't make me keep repeating myself. Why the hell not?"

"Because it's a bad idea to take money from family."

"It's not taking money; it's giving us a piece of the action. We'd be like any other investor."

We've decided—or rather I've decided—that Avery should open her own business, then she won't be at the mercy of Jeremy Gains if the sale goes through. I personally believe she overreacted to Dad making her "part of the deal." He was only looking out for her best interests. But I can see why she would find it insulting. My sister doesn't need our father to secure her a job. Any chef would be lucky to have her.

Avery starts to talk and stops when the whir of the coffee grinder drowns her out. That's why I didn't want to come here. But Avery insisted she needed an espresso and preferred talking away from the restaurant.

For that reason, she made me schlep two blocks in my Jimmy Choos (Yes, I have an extensive shoe collection. Get over it.) to a coffeeshop called Top Me Off and won't even take my husband's goddamn money.

When the grinder finally stops, she says, "Tess, you've gone above and beyond. Seriously, you don't know how touched I am by what you and Kit are offering. But I don't know the first thing about running a bakery. I'm a pastry chef not a businesswoman. It's a lot of money. The last thing I want to do is take you down with me."

"With all due respect we can afford it. Do you know how much Kit's contract is for?" I'm not trying to brag, I just want Avery to see that we have the money. "And you're not going to take anyone down. You've been baking your whole life. Not for one minute do any of us doubt you can do this."

"Apparently Dad does or else he would have offered me first dibs on buying Stones. Not Jeremy Gains."

"Have you ever thought he might've been sparing you? That he didn't want to saddle you with the burden of carrying on his baby if it wasn't what you wanted."

"Why would he think I wouldn't want it?"

I don't say the real reason because my sister's so touchy lately that I don't want her to misconstrue my feelings on this. But the bottom line is Avery hasn't been reaching her full potential at Stones. That's on my dad not her. He's so rigid that she's never been allowed to spread her wings. Maybe for once, he realizes that.

"Have you ever shown interest in running the restaurant before?" I say. "I mean, even as a boy, Dad knew he was going to take over the operation of Stones from Grandpa. He went to the Culinary Arts Academy in Switzerland as much to learn restaurant management as he did to learn how to cook. But you...Your passion has always been baking. We all know that, especially Dad. So if he'd come to you and asked you to take over the restaurant, you would've felt duty bound to do it, even if your dream was doing something different. I'm sure he didn't want to put you in that position."

Our coffees are ready. It only took four months. You'd think they were in the back, harvesting the beans.

"I'll get them." Avery goes to the counter and my feet say a silent thanks. She comes back, carrying two cups and a plate of biscotti.

"To you from the barista." She lets out a snort.

I gaze over at the cash register and a young guy with a man bun smiles at me and gives me a head bob.

"I've been coming here since they opened," Avery says. "Not once have they given me anything complimentary. And I'm a freaking chef."

"Not bad," I say after a few sips. It is really good coffee and may even rival my Miele's. "Look, don't say no. Just think about it, okay?"

"I'll think about it. Promise. Drink up. I've got to get back soon. We've got a party of twenty-four coming in. Someone is retiring from Charles Schwab."

I'm in no rush to walk the two blocks back, even if they are short blocks.

"What's going on with the wedding plans?"

Avery lets out a sigh. "I think I found a photographer. Bennett says he'll lock down a DJ. I still have to find a florist. Mom has some ideas. She knows the florist who does the flowers for Aqua Nova."

Aqua Nova is a seafood restaurant near the Chase Center. The owners have been friends with my parents for decades.

"Feel free to put me to work," I say. "It's not like I have anything else to do."

"What's going on with that?" Avery drains her espresso like it's a shot of tequila. "Any news from your agent?"

"Not a word. You'd think saying fuck on television was up there with murder."

I don't say it to Avery but I'm starting to worry. I've never been out of work before. Even in the lean days when I first started in broadcast, there was always something for me. They might not have been my dream jobs in my dream cities but the phone kept ringing.

These days the only ones calling are telemarketers.

"What are you going to do?"

"Hope it blows over and wait it out until it does."

I can see what she's thinking and not saying. *What if it doesn't blow over?*

It will. I did something stupid not illegal. And I happen to be supremely good at my job. It'll all work out.

"And you're planning to stay in San Francisco until it does?" Avery asks.

If I was a paranoid person, I might think she's hoping I won't. Lately, no matter how hard I try, she pushes me away. Case in point, the money for the restaurant. Who in their right mind would turn that down? Family, my ass. Like I said before, it's Kit's money and I couldn't have made it clearer that we would be silent investors. Neither of us is interested in running a bakery, so no strings attached.

"I've decided to go back to New York."

She tilts her head to one side. "Yeah...and?"

"Kit and I are planning to see a marriage counselor."

"Does that mean you're reconciling?"

I let out a long breath. "You think I'm an idiot, don't you?"

"No, of course not."

For the first time in my life, I can't tell whether my sister is being genuine. "Be straight with me, Avery." I pause because I've never been one to show vulnerability, but this is my sister, the one person in the world I trust beyond all others. "Am I being one of those codependent, weak women who takes her husband back because I don't want to lose the security of marriage, or the life I've built with Kit?"

"That depends," she says. "Do you love Kit or the idea of Kit and the life he's given you?"

"What if the answer is both?" I love Kit with all my heart but would I love him the same if he wasn't who he is and all that comes with it? I don't know.

"Well, at least you're honest. Then, yes, you should fight to save your marriage." She glances at her watch. "But this is a conversation for another time. Unfortunately, I have to table it because I really need to get back to the restaurant."

We walk together as far as Stones. "I'm going to call an Uber back to Mom and Dad's. Think about what I said, about the money. Investors don't grow on trees."

Her face softens and for a few seconds I glimpse the old Avery, the sister who used to think the sun rose and set on me, the sister who isn't cold and distant.

I don't know what sparked her resentment for me and the truth is between my meteoric rise and my spectacular fall, I've been too wrapped up in myself to really explore the reasons. All I know is that it started when I moved to New York. Maybe she felt deserted by me or maybe, just maybe a piece of her envied that I was going for it, grabbing what I wanted by the throat instead of staying behind to work in the family business.

She certainly doesn't have anything to be jealous of now. My career is a dumpster fire, and my marriage is on life support, while she's marrying a man she can trust, who loves her more than life itself. And this thing with the restaurant...well, we'll figure it out. Avery may not have my ambition, but her talent is beyond compare. And I'm not just saying that because she's my sister. I wish she knew her own worth.

"I'll think about the money," Avery says. "And Tess, things will work out for you, they always do." She gives me a quick hug and rushes inside.

I ride home, telling myself that Avery's right. Things will work out. The network will call. Kit and I will get over this awful hump in our marriage. The good people of New York will move on and forget.

I check my phone for a text from Kit. He's supposed to let me know when he lands safely in Seattle.

We had a good time Saturday night, even though it was short and we spent a good portion of it rehashing all the reasons I can't trust him. Nonetheless it felt good to talk it out and to have dinner together again, even if it's only baby steps. By the end of the night we were falling into our old groove where we could finish each other's sentences.

Kit couldn't keep his hands off me and I finally relented. We went back to his hotel room after dinner and I slept with him. To deny him was only punishing myself. And the sex was good, really good, like it used to be before work consumed us.

As far as Annabel, it is exactly as Rodney predicted. She got hired at ESPN. Good riddance, though I suppose the same could be said for me. The difference, though, is she's getting a farewell cake at WNBC as opposed to getting escorted to the door. Whatever. I'm so over her.

When I get to my parents' house, I go upstairs to my old bedroom to take a nap. They say depression makes you sleep a lot. I wouldn't call myself clinically depressed, but I definitely am something. It's all this free time with nothing to do.

I try to keep busy reading the news. That way I won't have to catch up on world events when the network comes calling. But there is only so much I can do without gluing myself to a computer. Kit says I should take up a hobby. Yeah, like what? I'm not a crafts type, never learned to knit, and as I've said before, I leave cooking to the rest of my family. For me it's always been about career.

I wish I could take this opportunity (I'm trying to look at it as an opportunity) to enjoy the things I haven't had time to enjoy in the past. Read, watch movies, go for walks, and try new restaurants. But besides feeling exhausted, I'm too wound up to do anything pleasurable. I wish Avery had more time; we could do more together.

I try to nap but now find myself wide awake. I stay still, trying to visualize a new job, a husband I can trust and the life I've always wanted, a life filled with success. I read somewhere in a self-help book that if you spend an hour a day visualizing the future you want, you can make it a self-fulfilling prophesy. That's what I'm doing.

There's a noise downstairs and I try to remember whether I locked the door. I strain to listen but it's quiet now. I convince myself it's just my imagination and return to my visualization exercise.

Then I hear it again. It sounds like someone in the kitchen. Mom or Dad, except they'd never leave the restaurant. And didn't Avery say Stones was hosting a retirement party?

I roll out of bed and pad to the door in my bare feet, wondering if I should call 911. But it's still light outside and whoever is down there doesn't sound like he—or she—is tossing the place, unless you count raiding the refrigerator.

I tiptoe down the stairs, my finger hovering over the emergency call button on my phone. There's a man in the kitchen who is not my dad. Still, I'd know that back anywhere.

"Bennett?"

He jumps and nearly drops a bowl of Dad's lobster bisque. "I didn't know you were here. Avery said you were meeting her at the restaurant."

"That was earlier." I grab a towel and pat his shirt where some of the bisque splashed onto his chest.

"I'll get it, I'll get it." He turns his head toward the living room as if he's afraid someone will catch him doing something he's not supposed to, then puts down his soup and takes my towel, blotting his wet shirt.

"You come for the lobster bisque?" I point to the bowl on the counter.

"No, I came for your mom's Rolodex. She has a florist in there for the wedding. I stayed for the soup."

Yeah, Mom still has a Rolodex where she stuffs business cards and little scraps of paper with phone numbers in no particular order. I think she's the only one left on the planet who still does it that way.

He takes his bowl to the breakfast nook, my favorite spot in the house because it looks out over the garden. I'd join him but the fishy smell of the soup...I grab one of the dining room chairs and drag it into the kitchen so I can sit with him from a distance.

"I told Avery I'd help you guys with the planning. I'm available to run errands, work the phones or whatever you need."

He nods with a spoon in his mouth. "Thank you," he says without meeting my eyes.

Clearly, it's awkward for him. Why? I don't know. We've been broken up for four years and he's about to marry my sister for God's sake.

"Kit was excited to see you the other day."

"Yeah? I don't know why. We hardly know each other."

I don't recall Bennett ever being combative before. I'm just trying to make pleasantries. And for the record, Kit was happy to see Bennett. He likes him, thinks he's low key and amiable, which in Kit-speak means he leaves the spotlight for Kit. But seriously, everyone loves Bennett.

"Well, we're all going to be family now." I smile, trying to smooth out whatever is going on here because I'm detecting some weirdness.

"Yep, I guess so."

"Is there something you're not saying, Bennett? If so just spit it out. We've known each other long enough not to play games."

"Okay." He pushes his soup away. "You want to know the truth. I think what Kit did to you is fucked up."

"He didn't do anything to me. I got it wrong. I'm the one who fucked up."

He gives me a long hard look and laughs. "Is that what you're going with? Wow. Just wow."

"Are you intentionally trying to be hurtful or are you just a dick?"

He takes his bowl to the sink and pours the rest of the soup down the drain. "I'm leaning toward dick. I've got to go. Nice seeing you, Tess."

Bennett is out the door faster than I can say goodbye. Or good riddance. I don't even know what happened there or whether he got the number he came for. And frankly I don't care. I'm still spinning from how rude he was. It was completely out of character for Bennett, who is usually like a big puppy dog, sweet and eager to please. But today something crawled up his ass and poked him with the mean stick.

Moreover, my marriage is none of his business. So where does he get off making accusations about something he knows nothing about?

I debate whether to call my sister but knowing her she'll take Bennett's side. It takes me a while to let it go but I eventually do, chalking it up to wedding jitters. Or Bennett is suffering from jingle block and is taking it out on the world. Not my problem.

I make myself a cup of coffee, using Dad's press (boy, am I missing my Miele) and drink it in the nook, staring out over the garden. My phone dings with a text and I hop up to grab it off the kitchen counter, where I left it when I thought Bennett was an intruder.

Finally, Kit.

"See you tonight. Be safe."

I read it again, confused. Before I have time to shoot him a message to clarify, I get another one from him.

"Sorry, that was a misfire meant for Jonas. I'm in Seattle. Safe. Love you and call you later."

Jonas? Kit hadn't said anything about his brother meeting him in Seattle. When Jonas is in New York, which is almost always now that we have a comfy guest room for him to park his lazy ass in, he goes to all the home games. But the guy doesn't have two nickels to rub together, so unless Kit is paying for his airfare...

What really seems off is the "be safe" part. It's not the way Kit talks to his brother.

I dial Jonas's number and get voice mail. If he's really on an airplane it makes sense but I leave a message anyway. "I just remembered I have tickets to *Harry Potter and the Cursed Child* for tonight at the Lyric. If you're in town and want them, call me." I don't have any such tickets but mark my words, if my freeloader of a brother-in-law is really in Manhattan, he'll call.

That is if Kit doesn't get to him first.

Avery

It's my day off and I'm meeting Richie Zhao, a friend from culinary school. I need career advice and Richie is killing it with his series of pop-up restaurants.

I find parking across from the Ferry Building, a giant food emporium on the water that still operates a terminal with ferries going from San Francisco to the East Bay and Marin County. It's a gorgeous day, sunny and so clear I can see all the way to the mountains.

Richie suggested we meet here, grab something to eat, and talk outside. It's a perfect day for it but unfortunately everyone else has the same idea. The place is swarming with locals and tourists and the food lines are worse than at Shake Shack on a Friday night.

Richie is waiting by El Porteño. I haven't seen him in more than a year, not since our class had a reunion in downtown St. Helena, a block away from our alma mater, the Culinary Institute at Greystone.

"You look great," he says and gives me a big hug.

Richie was one of my first friends at the CIA. Even though I was baking and pastry and he was culinary, we started hanging out together between classes. We were two of only a handful of students who commuted from San Francisco and carpooled whenever our schedules coincided.

"You do too." He was still wearing his hipster attire, a porkpie hat, black jeans and a Foo Fighters T-shirt.

We're both from food dynasties. His parents used to own one of the best dim sum restaurants in the city and his aunt founded the Golden Bakery in Chinatown, legendary for its egg tarts.

"You want to get some empanadas and see if we can find a table near the water?"

Fifteen minutes later, we're stalking a family in matching Alcatraz T-shirts, waiting to claim their seats as soon as they leave.

That's when I spot Jeremy a table away. He's sitting with an attractive blonde but looking straight at me. My hands are full with a plate of empanadas, so I bob my head at him. He toasts me with a cup of Blue Bottle coffee.

Richie follows my line of sight. "You know Jeremy Gains?" he says in that breathless way reserved for celebrities.

"He's trying to buy Stones."

"No shit! When did that happen?"

"A few weeks ago, he approached my parents about selling to him."

"Makes sense," Richie says. "Every major restaurateur in the city would die for your location. And Stones is a freaking institution. Your parents said no, right?"

"Promise this is between us?" Richie nods. "They want to do it; they want to sell. They're just waiting for my blessing."

He holds my gaze. "You giving it?"

"What choice do I have? That's what I want to talk to you about. Where do I go from Stones? As part of the deal, I'm supposed to have a place at the restaurant but that's not an option. At least it's not on my end."

"Why? Is Jeremy a dick? Some of the cooks I know say he is. But I've never met anyone in our industry who isn't a whiny bitch. Who knows what they say about me behind my back?"

I laugh. "Let's just say he isn't short on confidence. Or attitude."

"Jenny Gladstone works at his Napa restaurant, Da Lucrezia. Says he's anal as fuck. He found out that the restaurant had run out of chanterelles and the chef de cuisine sent the commis, some local kid, over to Safeway to buy more and Gains lost his shit. Fired the chef on the spot and took over that day in the kitchen."

I had heard similar stories. "Well, now you can see why I wouldn't want to stay under his helm. Not to mention it'll be creepy having a stranger take over what has always been my family's restaurant."

The T-shirt folks leave and Richie and I quickly slide into their table.

"Yeah, when my folks sold Zhao it was like that. My brother worked there for a while under the new ownership and eventually left because he couldn't deal with taking orders from the new people."

We both bite into our empanadas and I sneak a peek over at Jeremy's table. He peeks back. I suppose he comes here a lot, given that Les Corniches is next door. And I'm sure he's curious about how I know Richie.

Richie isn't as exalted as Jeremy in the food world but he's definitely an up-and-comer. His pop-up dumpling shop has gotten write-ups in every food magazine known to mankind. Before he went off on his own, he was sous chef at the venerable Chez Panisse and the Porch Swing, a Southern comfort-food restaurant in Oakland that was taking reservations a month out, it was that popular.

Memo to Chef Gains: you're not the only game in town.

Richie finishes his first empanada, lets out a breath and says, "Then again, you can learn from a guy like Gains. And working under him sure looks good on a resume."

While Richie's point is well taken, it's an impossible ask. Not only would it be strange but Jeremy Gains agitates me. That first meeting...well, he threw me off guard and made me lose my center of gravity.

"My sister and brother-in-law want to give me seed money to open my own bakery," I say.

"A bakery, huh?" He takes a swig from his water bottle and assesses me. "Is that something you're interested in doing?"

"Maybe. I don't know."

"You want my take? And be careful here because I'm going to be brutally honest."

"Okay."

"You're a rock star, Stone. You blew us all away in school. We all thought you would go on to do great things." Richie leans in. "A bakery wasn't one of them. You're a chef, Av, you should be working in fine dining. I say this with love and from the perspective of a guy whose aunt owned one of the most famous bakeries in the Bay. This is your chance. Whether it's with Jeremy Gains or somewhere else, take it!"

We finish our empanadas in companionable silence, Richie letting all the things he didn't say sink in.

"I'm not doing great things at Stones." I pose it as a question but it comes out as a statement.

"Hey, it's your family's restaurant. You're doing what they do and it works. It works so well that freaking Jeremy Gains wants to buy it. All I'm saying is this is an opportunity to do more, to get out from under your Dad's shadow and spread your wings."

I let out a whoosh of air because although nothing he's said comes as a big surprise, it still hurts.

"What about Brenda Carmine?" Richie says.

"You mean her restaurant in Mill Valley?"

"Yeah. I hear she's looking for a pastry chef. Her last one left to go to Manresa."

I don't know Brenda well and what I do know I don't like. When she ran Lodi, a vegan farm-to-table restaurant in the Mission District, she treated her staff like shit. I know this because some of the servers came to work for us and had plenty of stories. They'd nicknamed her "Wingnut" and stayed past closing at Stones to celebrate when she was fired. Last I heard, she was opening the place in Mill Valley.

I pull a face and Richie laughs.

"It was just a thought," he says around his last empanada. "Personality aside, she is a great fucking chef and her fan club's got big bucks, all those Silicon Valley douchebags who pretend they know what good food is. It's always good to have connections with deep pockets, even if they are poseurs. I'll keep my ear to the ground for you."

"I appreciate it, Richie."

He checks his watch. "Shit, I lost track of the time. I've got to run." He gets to his feet, busses his food wrappers, and pecks me on the cheek. "Good seeing you, Avery."

I'm just about to leave too when Jeremy slides into Richie's now vacant spot. "Richie Zhao, huh?" He toggles his hand from side to side. "I guess you could do worse."

"I'm not even going to dignify that with a comment."

He grins that stupid boyish grin of his. "You two cut a deal?"

"Not that it's any of your business but no. Richie isn't in the market for a pastry chef."

"What about Brenda Carmine? I hear she's looking."

I glare at him. "Would you work for Brenda Carmine?"

"Not in a million years. And at the rate she's going no one else will either. So what's your plan?"

"Why would I tell you that?"

He shrugs. "Why not?"

Because you're the guy who's likely to be my next boss while you turn my family's restaurant into a theme park. Granted, a very tasteful theme park with transcendent food that adds more stars to your name.

"Because we're competition," I say.

He leans back, his smile changing from boyish to smug. And it's then that I'm reminded of all the reasons I don't like him.

He flips his hand between us. "No competition."

Just when I think his response is exactly what I would imagine from him, condescending and full of bravado, he says the last thing I'm expecting.

"Blood is thicker than water, Avery. If you really don't want your folks to sell to me, you win. Every time, hands down. The question is do you want the status quo or unconventionality?"

There is a grain of truth in what he said. In all of it. But it's the last part that resonates. It's the last part that makes me want to pretend Jeremy doesn't know a single thing about me.

"What I don't want is a swimming pool in my family's restaurant. That's what I really don't want."

He breaks off a piece of my uneaten empanada and tosses it to a trio of pigeons circling a garbage can near our table. "Then don't put one in."

With that, he pushes his chair away from the table, gets up and walks away.

* * *

When I get home, Bennett is waiting for me by his car. He doesn't have to look at his watch for me to know I'm late. We're supposed to meet with the florist my mother found us.

"Sorry."

"I hope it means things went well with Richie."

"He's going to keep his eye out for me."

I tell him about my meeting and about how Richie is against the bakery idea and is urging me to stay the fine-dining course. For no quantifiable reason, I leave out the part about seeing Jeremy there. Bennett has never met Jeremy Gains, only knows him by reputation and that we all call him Jeremy Goddamn Gains.

It's silly not telling him. But there's too much to unpack there and I want to spend the rest of the day on wedding plans, not on presumptuous chefs and my family's restaurant.

"What are you planning to do?" Bennett pulls me in for a hug.

"That's the million-dollar question."

Bennett likes the idea of a bakery but he's adamantly against me taking on Tess and Kit as investors.

"Let's not talk about this now." My head is throbbing.

Bennett squeezes my shoulder. "You need to go inside first or are you ready to hit the road?"

"Hit the road," I say, hoping that picking out bridal bouquets and centerpieces will cheer me up.

The florist is on Chestnut in a trendy area of the Marina District, filled with boutiques, cafés and upscale gift shops. I typically avoid the Marina because I find it too glossy, like it's Southern California with its sorority-fraternity party atmosphere. It's probably where Tess would live if she ever moved back to San Francisco.

Gloria greets us at the door of her shop, and I apologize for being late. My mom wasn't kidding when she said Gloria was good. On the counter is a huge centerpiece that appears to still be in progress. But even incomplete, it's dazzling with at least ten different flowers in various shades of purple.

"Where's that going?" I ask.

"The Fairmont."

"Wow, it's gorgeous."

"Thank you." She leads us to a small table where there's a stack of photo albums. On the walls are framed pictures of floral arrangements, including an extravagant floral topiary from the opening night gala of the San Francisco Ballet and a dolphin made completely out of flowers for a fundraiser for the Nature Conservancy.

"Your mother says we're doing a wedding."

"Yes," I say but am starting to think Gloria is out of our league. "It's just a small wedding, only eighty-five guests, at my family's restaurant. We don't need anything as elaborate as this." I wave my hand over the album that's open to pictures of spectacular bridal bouquets and boutonnieres of all shapes and sizes.

"What are your theme colors?" Gloria asks.

I turn to Bennett and we both shrug at the same time, which makes me laugh at how ill prepared we are.

"We haven't gotten that far," I say. "I'm making the cake and it's beige with white if that makes a difference." I've designed the cake in my head so many times I know exactly what it'll look like.

"We can go with an all-white bouquet if you'd like and white centerpieces. Very elegant. Are there bridesmaids or a maid of honor?"

"No bridesmaids." I'd wanted to have three of my best friends but then I would have to include Tess. To avoid the awkwardness of that, I decided to eliminate the whole bridal party thing. I never told Bennett why, but he knows. I know he knows. And frankly he seems relieved.

Gloria turns to Bennett. "A best man or any attendants?"

"Nope. We're doing this streamlined." He winks at me and my chest flutters.

"All white sounds pretty," I say.

Gloria flips through the pages of one of her binders until she finds examples of all-white arrangements. "Will there be flowers on the cake?"

"No flowers. Instead, I'm doing a technique that will make the entire cake look like it's covered in white antique lace." I scroll through my phone until I find the picture of the inspiration, a cake I saw on the cover of a bridal magazine and knew instantly was the one.

"Oh, that's beautiful," Gloria says. "And you can do that?"

"I can." I've never actually tried it before but have pulled off much more intricate designs in a cake decorating course I took while Bennett and Tess were together. Some people drink to soothe their grief; I take baking classes.

Gloria spends the next ten minutes talking about the various flowers we can use and how she sources them from farms all over California. We agree to all her suggestions.

It's funny, in all my wedding fantasies I never once thought about flowers or centerpieces, not even the bridal bouquet. It's always been about the food. About a Viennese table sagging with all the beautiful pastries I dream of making but are too fussy for Stones.

Mom and I have already determined the menu. We start with my father's lobster bisque, then a fresh frisée salad with pine nuts and goat cheese. For the main course, a choice between Dad's Chilean sea bass with a mango chutney or his filet mignon smothered in mushrooms and sherry sauce. The sides: cauliflower gratin, a creamy risotto, and chilled asparagus with a lemon cream, served family style on my parents' colorful Heath bowls and platters.

To Mom's horror, we're doing Evites. It took Bennett and me less than thirty minutes to pick out and customize our invitations. All we have to do now is hit the send button to our eighty-five guests.

Bennett got a DJ, a friend of a friend. And I've already sent a deposit to the photographer, someone I met through a food blogger acquaintance of mine. Even on short notice, the planning has been ridiculously easy. It's of course a huge help that we already have the venue and catering covered, otherwise we'd never be able to pull it off.

Still, everything seems kind of rushed. My wedding, the sale of Stones, my parents' looming retirement.

"I know this is more last minute than you're used to," I say by way of an apology.

Gloria nods. "The timing is tight, but we can make it work."

But can I?

Ever since Tess came home, I'm back to the place I was before she left. The place where Bennett loved her first.

I wish I could feel good about the wedding. But it all seems hurried, like we're in a race to make it to the finish line before one of us backs out.

Tess

I'm in New York. On the spur of the moment, I decided to surprise Kit. He's playing Boston tonight at Yankee Stadium and my plan is to show up unannounced.

It's been a week since he accidentally texted me. And although Jonas corroborated that the message was indeed meant for him and that he'd gone to Seattle to watch Kit's game, I can't help but believe he was coached. Maybe I'm just being paranoid but my spidey reporter sense tells me Kit's lying. Again.

I don't expect Kit to be home when I get to our apartment from JFK. He's got his game day routine and I'm fine with that. Gives me plenty of time to snoop.

What I find is a mess. There are dishes in the sink. Fast food wrappers in the living room (thank you, Jonas) and two unmade beds—one in the guest bedroom, the other in our en suite. While I'm here, I take the opportunity to search both our bedroom and bathroom, looking for any telltale signs that a woman who isn't me has been here. But all I see is the clutter of one very sloppy man. It makes me wonder if Kit has fired our housekeeper.

I strip and change the linens and make up both beds, then load the dishes into the dishwasher and toss the garbage. It's stuffy and smelly in here, so I throw open the windows, letting in the fresh air. Or as fresh as the air can be in Manhattan.

Six hours on a plane and I'm exhausted. I contemplate taking a nap but hop in the shower instead. The hot water gives me a boost and I spend the next hour picking out something to wear to the game. I don't want to look like I'm trying too hard but I want to look good just the same. I settle on a pair of white jeans and a clingy navy halter top that shows off my shoulders.

I fire up my flat iron and give myself a head full of beach waves. Then I apply my makeup with a light hand. There were no stylists at the small TV stations where I worked before WNBC and I learned to do my own makeup and hair.

Satisfied with the reflection staring back at me in the mirror, I grab a Yankees cap on my way out and take a cab to the ballpark.

My reserved seat is with the rest of the wives, who I haven't seen since my downfall, what Rodney and I have now dubbed the "Incident." It'll be uncomfortable for sure but I have a feeling a good many of them have been in similar situations. In other words, they're Team Tess, or at least I hope so.

Besides, haven't I been punished enough? I lost my job for God's sake and I'm being sued. And even though I want to believe Kit that nothing happened with Annabel, here I am, sleuthing around, looking for clues of something untoward. Something slutty.

Before going to my seat, I hit the clubhouse for some liquid courage. There are a few of the wives huddled in a corner and the moment they see me everything goes quiet. Then, just as quickly, one of them comes forward, pulls me in for a hug and clamors over how good it is to see me. And just like that I'm being embraced by the others.

"It's been too long," says one of them. I can't remember her name but I think she's married to one of the outfielders. At the risk of sounding catty, they all kind of look the same.

It seems prudent to go for it, just rip the Band-Aid off, get it over and done. "I've been in hiding and decided it was safe to emerge," I open with, feeling like it's a safe starter.

"So you and Kit are still together?" says outfielder wife, wearing a baffled expression on her face. Or maybe that's just the filler and Botox. I give her props for her directness, though. A woman after my own heart.

"Yep," I say. "I, uh, may have jumped to conclusions I shouldn't have. And well...here I am." I flash my anchorwoman smile, fooling no one, judging by the other women's frowns.

"I heard she's at ESPN," says one of the other wives, at least I assume she's one of the wives. I've never met her before. And by "she" I'm sure she means Annabel.

"That's what I'm told."

"I never liked her," says the same woman. "There's something about her that's off-putting."

I'd like to agree because at the very least I think Annabel's unethical. At worst, a home-wrecking whore. But the thing is, "off-putting" is usually code for I don't like her because she's beautiful and successful and I'm threatened by that. I've been a victim of the "off-putting" label myself more times than I can count. Women should root for each other, not tear each other down.

But I'm no saint and appreciate the words of solidarity.

"Is she still suing you?" one of the others asks.

I nod and quickly say, "My attorney has asked me not to talk about it."

"You would think under the circumstances Kit would avoid her like the plague. Why on earth would he pull all those strings to get her references for the ESPN job?" the blonde says and I'm struck silent.

What strings? What references? What the fuck is Blondie talking about? Kit has never once mentioned helping Annabel, the woman who wants to take me to the cleaners, get a job at ESPN.

I try to rebound, knowing that if I don't I'll be a headline on Page Six by tomorrow. These women may be on my side but they're not above squealing to the press if it'll get them in the good graces of the *Post*'s gossip columnist. "Sorry, ladies, I can't talk about it." Another anchorwoman smile and a wink, wink, nudge, nudge.

"Oh." Blondie's eyes grow wide. "I get it. Smart, really smart."

For a second, I start to believe my own bullshit. At least I want to. Did Kit trade his influence in exchange for getting Annabel to drop her suit against me?

I have no choice but to wait until after the game to confront him about it. And here's the part I don't tell people: I don't love baseball. I actually find it boring. And tonight, the game seems to drag on forever while I'm champing at the bit to take Kit to task.

Don't jump to conclusions, I tell myself. There's a good chance Blondie doesn't know what the hell she's talking about. Isn't rushing to judgment what got me into trouble in the first place?

So I wait, my earlier excitement of surprising Kit gone because all I want to do is cut his balls off. I wonder if Annabel is in the press box. I don't know what her new beat is or if she is even covering the Yankees anymore. But if Blondie is right Kit helped her get the job, leaving me with a big why.

Finally, the game is blessedly over. Boston won. I'm actually happy about that because it means the guys won't spend too much time in the locker room, celebrating. I'm rushing out of the box to greet Kit when I see her. Annabel. She's on the field, interviewing one of the Red Sox, the pitcher, I think.

She sees me, stops what she's doing and our eyes lock. I don't see any animosity there, only pity. And in that second, I know. I know everything.

* * *

"It was one time, I swear," Kit says. "I was drunk, she was drunk, one thing led to another...It didn't mean anything. Jesus, Tess, I love you."

I'm crying. I'm sitting in our living room, sobbing my head off. How could I've been so stupid?

"It means something to me, Kit. God, you're such a piece of shit. You know what the worst part is? The worst part is you acted like I was a horrible person for not trusting you, for accusing you of doing things you didn't do, of telling the world what a cheater you are. That everything that happened to me was my own fault for being unhinged. Hysterical. And the whole time you were lying. What kind of person does that?"

Kit rubs his hands down his face. "The worst kind." He tilts his head back and pinches the bridge of his nose. "I knew you would leave me if I told you the truth. And I couldn't live with that. I can't live without you."

"But you can live with being a scumbag liar?"

"No. Look, I made a mistake. A really shitty mistake."

"Correction. You made multiple shitty mistakes, starting with screwing that woman and ending with helping her get a job. You've broken my heart, Kit. Do you realize that? I've lost everything, including my self-respect. But nothing hurts more than your betrayal."

I grab another wad of tissues and wipe my nose, trying not to lose it, trying to breathe and stop crying.

"It's time to come clean, Kit. Are you still seeing her, sleeping with her? And don't lie to me this time."

"I swear I'm not, Tess. It happened once. Just once. And if you forgive me I swear to you it will never happen again."

"How am I supposed to believe that? After everything, after all the lies, what person with half a brain would believe that?"

I'm crying again, hating him so much that I want to strangle him. Loving him so much that I don't know how I'll let him go. But this time I have to.

"Why would I ever trust you again? My God, you're gone more than you're here. How am I supposed to believe you're not out there, sleeping with someone else, with Annabel for that matter? How am I supposed to live like that?"

I don't know why I'm bothering to lecture him when what I should do is get up and walk out. Forever.

He lets out a breath and drops his head between his legs. "I don't know. But I love you. I understand if I fucked up so bad that your love for me has changed. But I'm begging you to give me another chance. I'll spend the rest of my life making it up to you."

"Give me a break, Kit. What does that even mean? You'll spend the rest of your life making it up to me. You took a vow and you broke it. And now you want to offer up empty platitudes."

"All I'm asking is that we work through this. Do the counselor thing, like you said."

"What exactly am I working through? You're the one who cheated, you're the one who lied, you're the one who needs to work through it, not me."

"So you don't even want to try? You're going to throw away four years of a life together because I made one goddamn mistake."

He gets up and brings me back a glass of water. "I'm sorry, Tess. If you only knew how sorry I am."

I try to hold on to my temper, and my sanity, because I'm on the brink of...I don't know what. But inside, I'm dying a little at a time. And I'm angry at myself. It's not in my nature. But I wanted so hard to believe.

"If you're so sorry why on God's earth would you help that woman get a job? I lose my entire career, everything I've worked for, and you're out gathering up letters of recommendation for your mistress. She sleeps with you and her career blossoms. I complain about her sleeping with you and I get fired. In what world is that fair?"

All he has to say to that is "She's not my mistress."

"I need to know why, Kit. Why the hell are you helping her? It sounds to me like she means more to you than one night."

He just sits there like a lump on our sofa, looking like a wounded bird, saying nothing. I've never been a violent person but the urge to hit him, to slap him, even to stab him is all-consuming right now. It's taking everything I have not to rip out a hunk of his hair. Or better yet, break his fingers so he can't finish out the rest of the season.

"I thought if I helped her she'd go away," he finally says.

"What does that mean, go away? What are you implying? Oh let me guess, you're like crack. Once Annabel had a taste of the almighty Kit Reid she was hooked and now she's stalking you." I could gag.

I'm tempted to tell him that I've had Kit Reid and it was nothing to write home about. In fact, Bennett Lamb was better. But out of respect for my sister I won't drag Bennett into this.

"She's trouble," he mutters and looks away.

"You're telling me she's trouble." I laugh but it comes out as a choking sob. "Perhaps you should've thought of that before you screwed her."

"I'm trying to fix it, Tess. I'm trying to make this whole thing go away."

"This whole thing?" I say. Kit is really something. He actually thinks he's the hero in this tragedy, a tragedy of his own making. "I don't know if I want to laugh or throw up."

It's the latter that has me running to the bathroom and hugging the bowl. It's either the stress of this situation that's gotten to me or the nachos I had at the ballpark. Either one, I vomit until there is nothing left in me but dry heaves.

Kit kneels down behind me and holds my hair out of my face. "You okay?"

"Do I look okay?"

He lifts me up and washes my face with a wet cloth, then carries me back to the sofa. "I know I don't have the right to ask this but will you stay in New York, give us a chance to work things out?"

In other words, he's asking me to hang around in an empty house with no job and no life while he travels around the country doing God knows what with whom. And the sad part is I'm still making up a million excuses for him, for why it's important for me to stick around and try to save our marriage.

Has there ever been a bigger fool?

"Why did you help her get a job at ESPN, Kit?" This time I want an answer. A real answer.

According to Rodney, because of the brouhaha of Annabel sleeping in Kit's room, Cheryl was going to take her off the Yankees beat. Annabel could remain as the lead sportscaster but Don would take over the station's baseball coverage.

For all I know Kit used his influence to keep her close, so they could continue their affair.

"So she'd drop the goddamn suit against you and leave me alone." He waits for me to respond and when I don't he continues, "She wants more and she can make a lot of trouble for me, Tess. For us."

"Why does she want more?" Kit's making her out to sound like a deranged groupie but I don't think so. Of all the horrible things I can say about Annabel, of which there are legion, she's a smart cookie. If she wants more it's because Kit gave her the impression there is more to be had.

"How the hell should I know? The woman is off her fucking rocker."

"Ah, so it's all her fault."

"That's not what I'm saying. The one-night stand was as much my fault as it was hers. But I've told her more than a dozen times that there's nothing between us, that us sleeping together was a mistake, that I love my wife. She didn't take it well and started making threats. I hoped if I helped her get the spot at ESPN, she'd leave us alone."

"Last I looked there was still a lawsuit filed against me. Guess it didn't work out as well as you thought." The man must take me for a moron. "What did you tell her, Kit? That you loved her? That you were going to leave me for her?"

"Jesus, Tess, where do you come up with this shit?"

"You tell me, Kit." It comes out as a hiss.

I smell of dried puke and should probably shower but I'm so livid all I want to do is fight. "What did you do to make her believe there could be more? Speak now, Kit, or forever hold your peace because if you lie to me one more time there's no hope for us."

I doubt there is any hope for us anyway but for now I'm letting him think otherwise. I want the truth, every last drop of it, even if it kills me. It's got to be better than my imagination, which let me tell you is pretty vivid. Oh, the things I've seen in my fourteen years as a news reporter. None of them pretty.

Kit leans his head against the back of the sofa. It's nearly two in the morning and he's facing off against the Red Sox again tomorrow, which is really today. Oh well.

"This is going to sound bad, worse than you think. But we'd been flirting for a while. She mostly with me. After games and in the locker room. A few times, we went out for drinks. Nothing happened, I swear." He takes a deep breath, and I can see he's trying to choose his words carefully. "You're not easy, Tess. Love with you is always transactional, instead of unconditional. And you were so caught up at WNBC and getting to the network that—and I'm not proud of this—I welcomed the attention."

Apparently, this is all my fault. I realize I'm not easy. I'm demanding, self-entitled, vain, and ambitious to the point of neglecting the people I love. But give me a break. How dare he put this on me? How dare he apologize to me out of one side of his mouth and blame me for what is solely his fault out of the other side?

But I don't say anything, too furious to talk.

My silence surprises Kit and I can see he's panicking by the way he starts to sputter, "I never led her on but she came to her own conclusions. And then it happened. We slept together and I suppose she took our flirting out of context and believed it meant something more than it did. You've got to believe me, Tess, I never intended for it to go this far. It was just innocent flirting."

"Until it wasn't." Oddly, a calm has settled over me. It's as if I needed to hear the words to be set free. All I want to do now is sleep.

"I need a shower." I get up, walk to the bathroom, strip off my clothes, and stand under a hot spray, hoping to wash him and everything he's told me away.

Avery

Bennett had to take a last-minute work trip to Los Angeles, where his company is pitching a nationwide chain of furniture stores. It's a big campaign and if they get the account, it will be largely due to Bennett's jingle. For the last several days, he's been tweaking it at the piano and now it's stuck in my head, which is the objective, right?

In any event, I have the house to myself, so I invited Tess. Ever since Kit came clean about sleeping with that Annabel woman, she's been spending a lot of time in her old bedroom at my parents' house, sleeping. It's not healthy.

I baked her favorite cake. It's Norwegian and called a *Kvæfjordkake* (don't ask me to pronounce it), a combination of sponge cake, meringue and almonds. It's filled with either rum or vanilla custard and whipped cream. In this instance, I made a rum custard because I figure Tess could use the booze, and who doesn't love custard?

The first time I made it for her she ate the whole thing at one sitting. I've wanted to put it on the menu at Stones, but Dad, of course, doesn't want to rock the boat.

After going to all the trouble of making it, Tess canceled. Kit is coming to town and they "need" to talk. I don't see what there is left to talk about unless it's the details of their divorce. In my book, what he did is unforgivable. Tess has said she thinks so too and has even contacted a lawyer.

So, here's the bad thing, the thing I'm ashamed to admit about myself. I may want Tess to divorce Kit, but I fervently hope she doesn't wind up staying in San Francisco. Yes, there was a time when I dreamed that my sister and I would live next door to each other for all eternity but not anymore. I'm sure it is not intentional on her part, but when she's around I'm half the person I'm meant to be.

For instance, this morning I was cleaning out Bennett's old desk, the one he never uses, and found old pictures of him and Tess. In one of them, he was looking at her with his heart in his eyes. The sheer power of his expression, filled with so much adoration and emotion, made me lose my breath. And I wondered if he ever looked at me that way.

That's when I got out the photo albums to compare. It was the worst thing I could've done because as I thumbed through the pages and saw all the ways in which Bennett loved me—how he looked upon me with respect, kindness, affection, and even deep attraction—no matter how hard I searched or yearned to see it, not one of those pictures showed him looking at me the way he looked at Tess.

I tell myself all the time that it doesn't matter, that love grows and in time his will catch up with mine. After all, is there ever equal distribution of affection in a relationship? Isn't every marriage constantly evolving? And even if Bennett's feelings for me are less than what he feels for Tess, I love him enough for both of us.

I look at the clock on the kitchen wall, realize it's barely seven, and try to remember the last time I had a night out. Not since Bennett and I went to a pub on Geary to meet up with a few of his work friends.

On a lark, I shoot a text to my best friend Leslie to see if she wants to do anything. She's married with two toddlers and rarely has time to hang out anymore. But maybe Dave will watch the kids for a couple of hours.

She texts me back five minutes later. "No can do. Have to finish this report by Wednesday." Leslie is a real estate appraiser. We met in middle school and have been friends ever since, even though our lives have moved in different trajectories.

I consider calling Reese, another one of my childhood friends. Then remember she and her girlfriend are on an Alaskan cruise.

I'm just about to throw in the towel, put on my pjs, and settle in for a night of Netflix, when I say screw it.

Twenty minutes later, I'm sitting at the bar in Les Corniches, sipping the best martini I've ever had. The thing about being in the hospitality industry is everyone checks out everyone else's establishment, so no one looks askance at me for being alone, not that they would anyway.

I can see the lights flickering on outside on the patio and wonder if anyone has ever gotten drunk enough to fall in the pool. The liability insurance must be a fortune.

The bartender brings me a bowl of stocafi, dried cod stewed in tomato sauce. "From Chef Gains."

Shit, he's here. I didn't think he would be, figuring the last time he was in one of his kitchens was during a total eclipse of the sun.

Moreover, he's clearly keeping an eye on his dining room, keenly aware of who's here. It's fairly standard for a restaurateur of his caliber. Even at Stones, we'll write *VIP* on a ticket to signal to staff there's a celebrity or industry person in the house and to treat them with extra care. That's not to say everyone isn't treated with care but yeah, Idris Elba gets a little more.

"Please convey to Chef my appreciation," I tell the bartender.

If heaven had its own scent it would be this, I think as I sniff the fragrant smell of the dish, then taste it, deciding that not only would it be heaven's perfume but its official food. My God it's good.

The next thing I know, the bartender is replacing my empty martini glass with a glass of champagne. "Bon appétit."

"Thanks," I say as he makes two lemon drops for the couple four seats down.

But it's only the beginning. Over the next hour, the bartender brings me dish after dish. A bite-size fritter stuffed with Swiss chard, spinach and ricotta cheese that is beyond delicious, a gorgeous stuffed tomato, and a mini pan bagnat that beats my father's tuna sandwich a million to one (I'll take that truth to my grave, though).

By dessert, I'm ready to explode but wouldn't dare offend le pâtissier. Besides, I'm curious. Last time I was here I had the *Fougassette Monégasque*, which was spectacular but could've been a one-off. Tonight, it's a cherry-almond tart. I'm about to dip in when Jeremy appears. He's in chef whites, leading me to believe he's actually working in the kitchen.

He grabs the stool next to me, which only a few minutes ago was occupied by a man in his midfifties here on a business trip from Kansas, who was disappointed when I revealed I wasn't famous and was only getting VIP treatment because I'm a pastry chef at another restaurant.

"How is everything?"

I give him the so-so hand waggle and his mouth quirks.

"How often are you in the kitchen?" I'm still dubious. Maybe he puts on a chef's jacket every now and again to impress people. *I'm the guy who won the Bocuse d'Or.*

"Not as often as I'd like. But my chef de cuisine is on vacation, so I'm filling in. Where's the fiancé?" He pretends to look around me but it's obvious he knows I'm solo.

"Business trip. He's in advertising, a jingle writer actually, and they're pitching a big furniture company based in LA." I'm rambling and sure that it's more than Jeremy wants to know. "While he's gone, I decided to come check out the competition." I'm not sure he knows that I've been here before. Though I've mocked the swimming pool, it is common knowledge. Every food blogger in the city has written about Les Corniches's ridiculous pool.

"You want the tour?"

By the tour he means the kitchen, a long-honored tradition in the culinary world.

"Sure." I try to sound casual, like I'm doing him a favor, but I'm dying to see it.

"Now or after dessert?" He nudges his head at my tart.

"I could use a breather." I pat my stomach and his lips curve up.

He flags down a server to take away the tart and I almost grab it out of her hands, worried I'll never see it again.

"We'll get you a fresh slice when you're ready," he says, the mind reader that he is.

I want to tell him not to throw that one away. Such a waste. Instead, I follow him into the kitchen where there's a chorus of "Chef."

The space is immaculate, set up like a proper French kitchen brigade with twice the number of stations as Stones.

The first thing I notice is the quiet. There is no music. You'd be surprised by how many chefs don't allow music in their kitchens or if they do, they're extremely territorial about what is played. I once heard that when Anthony Bourdain ran his own kitchen, he threatened to fire anyone who played Elton John or Billy Joel.

My friend from culinary school is chef de cuisine at a three-Michelin-starred restaurant in Yountville. Every evening before dinner starts, he revs up the troops with ABBA's "Dancing Queen." But the second diners start arriving, it's music off and all focus on the food.

Dad doesn't run that kind of ship. Then again, we have no Michelin stars, not even a Bib Gourmand. Macalister Stone has never been fond of restaurant awards, or restaurant critics for that matter. The only audience he cares about is his diners.

In Jeremy's kitchen no one is talking, everyone focused on his or her task. It's actually a little creepy and antiseptic.

Jeremy is about to tour me through the pantry when he abruptly stops. "Give me a sec." Something has caught his eye. He cuts through the kitchen, stands behind the *poissonnier* and whispers loud enough for everyone to hear, "Keith, what's going on with you, buddy? You're fucking up. Throw out the shrimp and start over."

"Yes, Chef. Sorry, Chef." He dumps the shrimp into a nearby compost can.

I blanch. It's at least a hundred bucks' worth of seafood Keith just eighty-sixed. I didn't see what he did wrong and am not about to ask in a crowded kitchen. Jeremy stands over Keith, watching until even I'm shaking in my boots. Apparently satisfied, he returns to me, and we continue our walk through the pantry, where everything is labeled and lined up in neat rows as if elves with obsessive-compulsive disorder sneak in every night to organize the place.

"Is this your idea?" I turn in place, gazing at the metal racks that hold everything from flour to salt.

"What? The pantry?"

"The way everything is just so." I gesture at each ingredient-filled clear tub with a chopping motion.

Jeremy nods. "I do all my pantries this way."

"You're not normal. In fact, you need help." God help us all if he manages to take over Stones.

"Is there anything about me you approve of?" he asks with what I've come to describe as his mischievous-boy grin.

"The jury is still out." Though I almost say his *barbajuan* is magnificent. But every restaurant critic in America has already told him that, so he doesn't need to hear it from me.

After the kitchen tour, he leads me out to the patio. There's another bar out there and with the lights reflecting off the bay, it's really kind of dreamy. He motions for us to sit in the corner, away from the rest of the bar-goers, away from the pool, which by the way is empty. Not a swimmer in sight.

Every table is taken and even though it's late July, the hum of lit patio heaters mingles with the sounds of clanking silverware, lively conversation, and French pop music.

"If you need to get back to the kitchen, go do your thing." I really should leave anyway. Tomorrow's a workday and I have to be up before dawn.

The bartender magically appears with two drinks: a martini for me (someone is keeping track) and a glass of fizzy water for him.

"So where you at on Stones? You give your dad the thumbs-up yet?"

"Not yet," I say, deciding to go with honesty.

"Ah, this must've been a reconnaissance mission." Apparently Jeremy Goddamn Gains lives in a spy novel.

"Nope. Just wanted to see how the other half lives."

He chuckles.

"It's not just me, you know? My sister has a say too."

"The newscaster?" Jeremy says.

"How'd you know she's a newscaster?" Then I remember his restaurant in New York. "Let me guess, you're a huge fan."

"A fan of your sister? I've never watched her before. She's on too early. I do follow sports, though, and read the news."

"Then you're up on all the salacious details." I have no clue why I'm discussing my sister's business with him. Until a week ago, we'd never spoken. He was just Jeremy Goddamn Gains, the guy who owned a fleet of over-the-top restaurants.

He takes another sip of his fizzy water and looks at me over the rim of his glass. "Why didn't you ever leave Stones, go out on your own?"

"Because it's my family's restaurant, our legacy." I say it like isn't that obvious? But we both know it's not. There's a good many other things I could've done with my pastry degree.

"And if I take it over, what do you think I should do with it?" He's still looking at me, really looking, and it's unnerving, like he can see right through me.

"Carry on, do the thing we do, the thing that keeps folks coming back day after day."

He doesn't respond and for some reason I think he's disappointed, like I failed the test, a very important test.

"I better get going." I'm standing and reaching for my purse. "Thank you for dinner. Everything was delicious." Which is more than he said about my pie and cake, not that I'm holding a grudge or anything.

"Thanks for stopping by, Avery."

When I get home Tess is there, sitting on the lawn in the dark, except for one lousy motion sensor that flickers on when I open the car door.

"Hey," I call, then look around for my mother's old Volvo wagon or my dad's truck. "How'd you get here?"

"Uber. Can I stay the night?" There's a kind of desolation in her voice and I can tell things didn't go well with Kit.

"Of course." I usher her through the door. It's not Park Avenue but the spare room is hers as long as she needs it.

I flick on the lights and head for my bedroom for a pair of pajamas. When I come out to give them to her, she's sitting on the sofa, staring blankly into the room.

"Where's Kit?"

"I left him at the hotel. He's leaving first thing in the morning. I hate him, Avery."

"Did something happen?...I mean besides what has already happened."

"I told him I want a divorce."

I take a minute to absorb it. *Divorce*. She wasn't fooling around about the divorce attorney. I don't know why I'm surprised but I am. I guess it just feels so final.

"I'm sorry, Tess."

"Don't be." She tries to sound strong but there's anguish in her voice. So much anguish that it makes my heart fold in half. "He's a liar and a whore."

He is but I don't respond, even though I'm furious with Kit and would like to cut his balls off and shove them down his throat. But it's the last thing my sister needs to hear. She has enough hatred for him for the both of us.

"Why don't you change," I say. "And I'll cut you a piece of cake."

She perks up. My sister has never been one to sulk, perhaps because until now the worst thing that's ever happened to her was a nasty hangnail. "The kafcaca?" she says in a fake accent with lots of hocking sounds and hard *a*'s that make me think of a cat hacking up a hairball.

We both laugh until we're doubled over. And somewhere midhysterics, I remember what it used to be like before Bennett, before everything started revolving around Tess, when she was just my sister. My best friend. The lioness whose claws came out when anyone tried to hurt me.

We used to say, "Never mess with Tess, she's ruthless," which back then worked in my favor.

There was the time at CIA when I was dating a guy in the culinary program who dumped me on social media by announcing his engagement to an *Eater LA* restaurant critic. He posted a video of him down on one knee under the Hollywood sign, slipping a ring on her finger. The whole time we were dating, he never so much as mentioned there was another woman. I thought we were quasi-serious. Apparently, though, I was just someone to keep him warm on those cool Napa Valley nights while his girlfriend was busy, eating her way across Los Angeles.

I was more humiliated than brokenhearted, but Tess was livid. Five months later, when he landed a coveted job at Pizzeria Mozza, arguably one of the haughtiest pizzerias in the country, Tess started her vengeance campaign. Every day for two weeks, she had a Domino's pizza delivered to the restaurant in my ex's name. Needless to say, he was summarily fired.

Tess and I giggled over it for days, like two high school girls who'd pulled off the caper of the century.

We were always protective of each other like that. In a lot of ways, Tess was my surrogate mother, standing in for Mom, who was always at the restaurant.

"Put those on." I point at the pjs, cotton leggings and a T-shirt covered in brightly colored spatulas. "Then come in the kitchen."

I pop back in the bedroom and slip into my own loungewear, then put on a pot of decaf. In the back of the cupboard, I find a bottle of good brandy to go with the rum-infused cake.

Tess sits at the table, her feet bare. Channeling my mother, I grab a pair of slippers from my closet and throw them at her.

She can use some TLC tonight.

"Where were you?" she asks as I slide the cake from the fridge to the counter.

"A restaurant on the Embarcadero. It's Jeremy Gains's place, Les Corniches."

"Why? I thought he was public enemy number one."

"Yeah, I don't think so anymore. But I could be wrong."

She does a double take. "Is he dropping out of buying Stones?"

"No, but he's not as bad as he seems." I slice her a huge helping of cake and set the plate in front of her with a fork.

"Avery, you don't have to pretend for me. The money for the bakery... Kit...we'll figure something out even if he's no longer in the picture. You're everyone's first choice. Mom's, Dad's and it goes without saying, mine."

Just not Bennett's.

The thought wraps around my throat like a cold hand.

"What about you? What's next?" I ask, changing the subject. Or maybe I'm subconsciously being vindictive by picking at Tess's wounds. No job and soon no husband.

"I don't know yet but I need you to do something with me." She takes a bite of the cake, leans her head back, and closes her eyes. "Oh, Avery, you're magic. This is freaking magic." She points at the cake with her fork. "Really, forget Stones. We could sell the kafcaca"—she makes the guttural sound again, offending Norwegians everywhere—"on the Internet and get rich." She takes another bite. "So good. You know this is the first thing I've eaten that hasn't made me barf."

"Wow, that's some praise right there. My cake didn't make you hurl. Hopefully it doesn't give you the trots either."

We erupt in fits of laughter again.

"Seriously, I'm going to eat this whole piece. I'm not even going to feel bad about it. What are you doing this weekend?"

"Work, last minute wedding stuff, laundry. Why?"

"I need you to come with me to New York, so we can spy on Kit."

"Tess, is that really a good idea?" Because it sounds like a catastrophe waiting to happen.

"Probably not," she says around a mouthful of cake. "But it's better than planting a microchip in his penis."

"And what are you hoping to find out that you don't already know?"

"If he is still seeing her. I'm leaving him either way but I need to know how much of a liar he is for my own peace of mind."

I hardly see how that'll make a difference but I don't argue because I can see she's hanging on by a thread. If playing Nancy Drew makes her feel better I'm willing to placate her.

"How do you plan to pull this off?" Because to me spying requires some modicum of stealth and subterfuge. And Tess has neither.

"Rodney is going to lend me his nanny cams. Kit has a game Saturday evening. I thought you and I would get in early and plant them around the apartment."

"What if he doesn't go home?" I put the cake away because clearly my sister has had enough sugar—and alcohol—for the night. Both have gone to her head.

"We'll follow him."

I don't bother to ask how. This cocked up scheme of hers is ludicrous and makes me wonder about her hold on reality. I imagine us in disguises in a cab in the middle of Manhattan, yelling to the driver, "Follow that car!"

"It might be a good idea to rethink this, Tess."

She scrapes her plate clean with the edge of her fork. "But if I do it are you in?"

"Sure," I say. Because why the hell not?

* * *

By the time my alarm goes off in the morning, I've had less than four hours of sleep. Tess and I stayed up most of the night, talking, laughing and she did a good amount of crying.

She is in the next room, so I try not to make a sound as I'm getting ready, even forgoing my morning coffee ritual. I'll make a pot at the restaurant.

I leave a note, telling her to take the rest of the cake and to make sure she locks the front door. Then I remember she doesn't have a car and offer to pick her up if she needs a ride to our parents'. More than likely, though, she'll Uber.

I can barely stay awake at the restaurant and decide to be kind to myself by making the butterscotch pots de crème again today, even though it's

Thursday and I traditionally do bread pudding. But I don't have the energy to cube thirty baguettes and twenty brioche loaves, which I should've done yesterday but didn't. Anyway, everyone loves my pots de crème, so it's not worth beating myself up over. Besides, I'm making berry buckle with all the beautiful fruit Bruce brought in. Soon, the berries will be out of season, and I'll only have stone fruit to work with until pears and apples are here.

I ponder the wisdom of running to Top Me Off for a cup of coffee and decide to go with my original plan to make a pot instead. The coffee station is next to the bar and that's where I am when I hear someone banging on the door in the kitchen. I race back and it's Jeremy, holding one of Les Corniches' beautiful to-go boxes and a Blue Bottle carrier with two coffees.

I eye the coffee and may even salivate. "I should just give you a key."

"You forgot this when you left." He puts the coffees down and opens the blue foil box, presenting me with last night's cherry-almond tart.

"You came all this way at five in the morning to bring me coffee and breakfast?" I'm sort of dumbfounded—and touched.

And then he ruins it by saying, "No, I need more measurements. But help yourself."

I don't wait and grab one of the coffees and pop off the lid, taking a large sip. "Hot!" I wave my hand over my tongue.

He raises his brows. "Coffee usually is."

"You mind if I show myself into the dining room?" He has that laser measuring gadget in his hand.

"Knock yourself out."

I watch his back disappear behind the swinging doors, then turn to the box and sniff the tart. I don't bother with a fork, just lift the pastry to my mouth and take a big bite. It's delicious. Not making-me-see-stars delicious but good, especially given that it's a day old. But the *Fougassette Monégasque* was better.

I get back to my pots de crème, trying not to peek through the portholes in the doors to see exactly what Jeremy is doing. He appears laser focused on taking over Stones, even though we haven't given him an answer yet. No reason to be surprised. Jeremy Gains is no doubt a cutthroat businessman, in addition to being a lauded chef. No one gets where he is before forty without being one.

I've got my ramekins in a hot-water bath in the oven when he returns to the kitchen, takes one look at the empty to-go box and says, "You've got crumbs on your apron."

I take the bait and brush the nonexistent crumbs off my chest.

"You get what you need?" I ask, wondering what's with all the measurements.

"For now. What do you got there?" He nudges his head at my baskets of berries.

"It's for buckles," I say over my shoulder as I head to the pantry for cake flour.

"Buckles? Isn't that like something grandmothers used to bake in prewar times?"

It's a jibe to be sure but now that I've had my coffee and breakfast, I'm feeling too zen to dignify it with a rebuke. Instead, I wave my middle finger in the air.

Jeremy laughs. It's not something I expect from a Michelin-starred chef, especially given the rap on him. I remember Richie's story about Jeremy firing the chef de cuisine at Da Lucrezia for buying mushrooms at Safeway, him telling poor Keith to throw out the shrimp because the *poissonnier* had quote, "fucked them up." You may think Gordon Ramsey is all schtick because assholes make good TV. But he's kind of not. That's kind of how executive chefs the caliber of Gordon Ramsey and Jeremy Gains run their kitchens.

So the fact that a little-known pastry chef just flipped him the bird and all he did was laugh is, yeah, unexpected.

"Come on, Stone, you're better than buckles."

I'm about to whirl on him. Who the hell is he to tell me what I should be doing or how I should do it? But somewhere, hiding in my head, right there in the temporal lobe, is the truth. I'm better than buckles. I'm better than pots de crème. And I'm better than baked Alaska.

I can make a cherry-almond tart that would put the one from Les Corniches to shame.

He sees it written all over my face, the moment when I embrace the truth about myself. And that's when he surprises me the most. Because instead of reveling in the satisfaction that he's right, that he knows I'm settling, he says the one thing I'm unprepared to hear. "What are you going to do about it?"

Tess

On the morning we're supposed to leave for New York, I wake up so sick I fear I might actually be dying. I retch for what seems like hours in the bathroom my sister and I used to share. When I try to get up from the floor, I nearly lose my equilibrium as a wave of dizziness hits me hard enough to knock me over.

I press my hand to the wall and manage to make it to the sink where I wash my mouth and face and tell myself I'm okay now.

It must've been the chicken I had last night for dinner. Maybe E. coli or salmonella. Foodborne illness is more common than most people think. My parents go to extraordinary measures to sanitize the kitchen at the restaurant. One case of listeria and it's curtains.

"I'm here," Avery calls up the stairs. "I brought ginger tea, Pepto and whether you like it or not a pregnancy test. I say we do the test first and eliminate that possibility before we move on to the other remedies."

She's at the top of the stairs now, standing outside the open door of the bathroom, waving a CVS bag in the air. I'm tempted to tell her to go away. I don't want her to witness my meltdown if the stick turns pink or blue or whatever the hell happens when you pee on it and the results are positive. Because I'm pretty sure that's what's going to happen. The foodborne illness was just wishful thinking.

Another reason to hate Kit.

"You ready?" She takes the box out of the bag, comes into the bathroom, and shoves it at me.

"Can I at least do this in private?" I give her a little push and shut the door.

I stall, giving the toilet a good cleaning with Lysol, then decide to wash out the sink.

"What are you doing in there?" Avery bangs on the door. "Jesus, Tess, are you showering? If you can't pee I'll get you a drink of water."

"Please tell me you're not standing out there, waiting."

There's a stretch of silence then, "Okay, call me when you're ready."

Suddenly, I want to tell her not to leave, to come in and sit on the edge of the tub, like we used to do when we were teenagers. When she used to watch me get ready for a date or a dance. Or cry over Steve Blakely, who in an endless cycle of make-up and break-up broke my heart more times than I could count.

I hear her retreat down the hall, take a breath, and unpackage the kit. The instructions are basic enough and I follow each step as if I'm taking directions to deactivate a nuclear bomb. She only brought one test and I don't want to second-guess myself.

Finally, I pee on the stick, then wait the obligatory three minutes. I can't do it. I can't look.

"Avery!" I yell and swing the door open.

She comes trotting down the hallway. "Well?" Her face is wreathed in a giant question mark.

"I can't...You look." I move aside and let her in.

She hunkers over the sink vanity and it feels like an eternity passes while she examines the stick. I feel like throwing up all over again.

I'm ready for the worst but am still praying for food poisoning. A baby has never been in the plans, not even a little. I've got my career, or rather had it but am hoping to get it back again. Soon. And Kit's a lousy candidate for Mr. Mom. Not with baseball claiming eight months of his life a year. And that doesn't count his extracurricular activity of screwing sportscasters.

"What does it say?" I finally ask.

There's a long pause and then, "Pregnant."

I tell myself to breathe because I've been holding my breath so long, I might pass out. All at once, I'm hit with a barrage of emotions and let me tell you, elation isn't one of them. No, what I'm feeling right now is fear. So much fear that my heart is pounding in my ears. It's so loud, I check to see if Avery hears it too.

"Tess? You okay? You want to sit down?"

I let her lead me to her old bedroom, where I sink into her fake fur Pottery Barn chair that she begged my parents to get her for her fifteenth birthday. The kind of chair my kid will probably beg me for, even though it doesn't go with any of the décor in my apartment. "Are you sure?"

"Pretty sure."

"Pretty sure or definitely sure?"

"Definitely sure. But I can run out and get another test if you want me to."

What's the use? Deep down inside I suspected it all along. The heightened sense of smell, the nausea, the fatigue, the mood swings (well, those could be attributed to being married to a philandering asshole) and the general sense that something wasn't right.

It's not enough that Kit is good at everything he does, he also has to have bionic swimmers that could breach my Fort Knox of a diaphragm. Life isn't fair.

"What are you going to do?" Avery asks.

"I don't know...Shit, Avery, what would you do?"

"I wouldn't make a decision now, right on the spot. I'd take some time to think about it, to think about what you want to do...what you want to tell Kit, because unfortunately he has a stake in this too."

"Yeah, I guess," I say, though staying calm and coming up with a plan has never been my strong suit. If it was I wouldn't be sitting here today, unemployed.

"Come on." Avery gives me her hand and pulls me out of the chair. "Let's go downstairs and I'll make you something to eat."

"I can't even think about food." I hold her gaze because I know it's coming. "Don't."

"Don't what?"

"Don't you dare say I'm eating for two now."

"I won't but at least have some of that tea I brought. You're probably dehydrated."

Avery makes herself busy in the kitchen while I sit at my parents' little breakfast table, staring out the window at my mother's thriving ferns. They're the only thing I know that likes the fog.

"Try this." Avery hands me a cup of tea that smells like a cross between ginger and mud. I hold my nose and take a sip. Strangely enough, I like the flavor.

"I'm supposed to be past my optimal childbearing age." I lay my head down on the table, still trying to understand how this happened. Still trying to figure out what I should do.

"Tess, you're thirty-six not sixty."

"Even so, this is probably my last chance. After Kit, I'm done with men. Maybe not forever because I still believe in love. Look at Mom and Dad. And you and Bennett." Avery flinches and I wonder what I said wrong. But that's my sister for you, prickly as a cactus. "Anyway," I continue, "by the time I trust a man again my eggs will be cooked. And despite Kit being a cheater and a liar, he has good genes. Strong, healthy, smart."

"What are you saying, Tess?"

Ten minutes ago, before a plastic stick turned my world upside down, I would've said I'm not mother material, no way, no how. And I still don't know if I am or if I can even do this without screwing it up. But my heart is telling me I have to try, or later, down the line, I'll regret it.

"What I'm saying is we're having a baby."

* * *

It's Saturday and I'm bored to tears. Everyone is at the restaurant, except Avery, who took yesterday and today off for our spying expedition in New York.

Well, that's off. I would never survive the six-hour flight. At least Avery's tea seems to be helping with the morning sickness, which by the way, should be renamed all-day sickness.

Twenty times I've picked up the phone to tell Kit, "Hey, asshole, you're going to be a father" and have thought better of it. Not the best way to break the news.

Instead, I call Avery.

"Hey, how are you feeling today?"

"I don't think there's anything left in me to puke up, so I guess better. The tea you brought helps. Sorry I had you take the day off for nothing."

"No big deal. I was due a day off anyway."

"At least you and Bennett can have the whole weekend now. What'll you do?"

"Bennett's in San Jose, helping his dad clean out the garage."

"You want to do something?" I feel like the walls are closing in on me here and could use a distraction.

"Uh, I may go out to look at wedding dresses," Avery says.

"You don't have one yet?" Even before Kit and I got engaged, I'd picked out a wedding gown. It was in the window of Bella's Bridal Boutique on Fifth Avenue, a wispy slip dress with a plunging back made of the softest silk crepe. It reminded me of the dress Carolyn Bessette-Kennedy wore when she married John John and from the minute I saw it I knew I had to have it.

"Nope," she says.

Avery was never a clotheshorse or even remotely interested in fashion. Last I looked, her entire wardrobe consisted of jeans, T-shirts, and the occasional peasant skirt. But waiting until the eleventh hour to buy a wedding dress is bizarre in my book. In anyone's book.

A long stretch of silence passes between us, then I say, "Why don't we go shopping, then? We can call Mom and have her take a break from the restaurant and meet us at that bridal shop on Maiden Lane." Given the state of my marriage and my unwelcome news, sitting in a bridal shop sounds like Dante's Inferno. But this is a time-honored tradition between sisters and if I leave Avery to her own devices there is no telling what she'll walk down the aisle in.

"That's okay," she says quickly, too quickly.

"You don't want me to come?"

"It's not a big deal, Tess. I might just get something at Nordstrom, something I can wear again."

"I could go with you to the mall, too, Avery."

"I'll go with Mom and Leslie on Monday."

I don't have the wherewithal to argue with her about it, not today when my already shaky world is spinning on its head. But it's obvious for whatever reason she doesn't want me to come.

It seems we've slipped back into Avery holding me at a distance again. I thought we were making progress, that we were nearly back to being best friends. Or at least friends. These last couple of weeks it felt as if we were getting somewhere. Talking and laughing and even confiding, like we used to do. She even went to all the trouble of baking me the kafcaca or whatever it's called.

"I don't know why you're pushing me away," I say.

"Really, Tess." She pauses, starts again, then stops, and finally says, "Think about it. Think about why I might not want you to come to buy a wedding gown for my marriage to your ex-boyfriend."

I swallow hard because I hadn't thought of that. Probably because it's ridiculous. "Seriously, Avery. That was more than four years ago. Ancient history."

Avery sighs. "Look, I shouldn't have said that. I'm not casting aspersions. It's just awkward for me in the same way it would've been awkward for you if Bennett had gone to your and Kit's wedding."

"It wouldn't have been awkward for me. That was yours and Bennett's decision not mine. I wanted him there. I wanted him there because you love him and I love you."

"Or did you want him there to add to your fan club?"

"What?" I can't believe she's saying these things to me.

"I didn't mean that." Avery is trying to sound contrite, but I finally understand what's crawled up her ass as far as I'm concerned.

"Yes you did. You know what, Avery, I don't need this right now. I've got enough crap going on in my life without your petty jealousies. I've got to go." Before she can say anything, I hang up.

I finish my tea, which is now lukewarm, feeling even worse than I did from the morning sickness, realizing that all along my sister has been holding a grudge over something that's totally out of my control. I'm no threat to her and Bennett. If she can't see that, there's nothing I can do about it.

I climb the stairs to shower and dress in something other than a pair of old sweats, convinced that between yesterday and today things can't get any worse. Then Elsa my agent calls.

Avery

Three days later, I get my wedding gown in an East Bay strip mall at a David's Bridal. It's an off-the-rack strapless A-line in lace. It's more formal than my usual style but it fits like it was custom made for me. Mom and Leslie love it and it didn't break the bank. A win-win.

We part ways with Leslie in the parking lot and rush back to work because we left after the lunch service and Mom needs to be back for dinner. Traffic is crazy driving over the bridge, everyone in the world appears to be going to San Francisco.

"Avery, honey, how come you're so quiet? It's a beautiful dress. I would think you'd be bouncing in your seat with excitement."

"I am," I say and I wholeheartedly mean it. The dress is lovely and I am lucky to have found something off the rack that doesn't need alterations. "The dress is perfect. But Mom, can I ask you a question that doesn't have anything to do with my wedding? Why didn't you and Dad come to me first about the restaurant?"

"There was nothing to come to you about. We weren't looking to sell. Jeremy Gains sought us out. No one was more surprised by his offer than your dad and me.

"Avery, honey, we'd love nothing more than to put Stones in your able hands, you know that, right? But for us, the house and the restaurant are all we have. Over the years, your father and I have been able to sock away a little bit of savings but it would never be enough to retire on. The restaurant provides us a good living, even enough for a vacation home, but it means working the rest of our lives unless we sell."

"I know and I'm not asking for a handout, Mom. I just wish you and Dad would've come to me if you wanted out." What I really want to say is that I'd like people to stop treating me like I'm invisible, like I'm unworthy.

We're sitting at the interchange otherwise known as the maze (for good reason) where the interstate splits into three freeways, stopped still, waiting to inch closer to the metering lights. At one time, Bennett and I considered house hunting in Berkeley or Oakland where we could get more bang for our buck. Seeing this, we made a good choice to stay put.

Mom gives me a sideways glance from the driver's seat and sighs. "It's a hard life, Avery. I'm not saying I don't love the restaurant but it took a lot out of us, including your father's health. I don't want that for you."

"Do you think it'll be any different if I work for someone else?"

"Yes," she says without hesitation. "You won't have to worry about finding replacements at the last minute for employees who don't show up, the skyrocketing price of food, bad reviews on Yelp that threaten your reputation, or keeping the lights on day in and day out. You can have regular days off and do the things that normal families do. We only want the best for you, Avery. That's all."

"I know."

There's a long silence as Mom navigates traffic. But I can hear her debating what she's going to say next.

"You're so talented, Avery. I'm not sure we've done you any favors by keeping you at the restaurant."

"What's that supposed mean?" I ask but know exactly what it means. I'm simply being defensive because in essence she's saying I've wasted my career on the family business.

"We've been terribly selfish where you're concerned. That's what it means. Your father can be difficult and sometimes it's easier to bend to his will than to fight for yourself." She slants me another sideways glance. "I want you to fight for yourself, Avery."

She pats my leg. "And you need to let your sister in more. It's not her fault that Bennett was with her first. He's marrying you, not Tess."

"She told you I didn't want her to come wedding dress shopping with us, didn't she?"

"She's your sister, Avery. She wanted to be included and I can't blame her for being upset that you intentionally left her out. She married Kit and is pregnant with his child. The only person clinging to her and Bennett's history is you. Let it go, sweetheart."

I'm not sure it's true that I'm the only one clinging to their history. This is the thing I've wondered for a long time but have always known it was fruitless to ask. Does Bennett love me because it's the closest he can come to her? To Tess.

But I don't share that with my mother because it goes back to her comment about fighting for myself. Here's the thing, fair or not, it's easier to fight with Tess.

"For once I just wanted this to be about me," I say because it's the truth, just not the whole truth. "And whenever Tess is in the room it's always about her."

"Then you need to make it about you, Avery."

As if it's that simple.

"She's not even here." Tess has been in New York since Sunday. None of us knows what's going on, only that she went there to break the news about the baby to Kit.

"She would've stayed if you'd only asked."

I won't win this one, that much I know. It's Mom's job to be Switzerland, even if she is taking Tess's side, yet believes it's for the good of both Tess and me.

Traffic opens up as soon as we pass the interchange for the MacArthur and Nimitz freeways. Once we're through the toll plaza and on the bridge it's smooth sailing.

"I'll take the dress home with me," Mom says. "That way you can surprise Bennett on the big day."

When we get to Stones, she hangs it in the office. There's been a bunch of car smash-and-grabs in the neighborhood and without a real trunk in Mom's wagon, the dress screams, "Steal me."

When I get to the kitchen, Jeremy's there, talking to Dad. The man is like a bad penny. You would think he'd be in New York or Vegas, tending to his own restaurants.

"How was the dress shopping?" Dad asks.

I give him a thumbs-up and he goes back to his conversation with Jeremy. I only catch snippets of what they're talking about but they appear to be debating the pros of grey sea salt versus pink Himalayan. My dad says both are bullshit and shoves a box of Morton kosher salt in Jeremy's hand.

"A quarter of the price and I defy you to tell me the difference."

Jeremy catches my eye and winks. He appears to be enjoying himself. And despite himself, so does Dad. Today, he's got the Kinks on, a stark contrast to Jeremy's kitchen, where all you hear is the sound of line cooks hard at work.

Technically, I'm here for another hour. But in anticipation of dress shopping, I got my baking done early. Everyone is accounted for today, therefore I'm not needed on the line. And for the first time in like ever, Mom's not shorthanded in the dining room.

I could sneak off and surprise Bennett by being home early. Or I could meet him somewhere for dinner that isn't Stones.

I pop into the office and call him at work.

"Hey good looking, what you got cooking? You have any luck with a dress?"

"I'm looking at it right now," I say and reach out to make sure the clear plastic suiter is zipped, so I don't smell like the restaurant on my big day. "I'm busting out of here early. You want to meet for dinner? We could go for Chinese or Sushi, or Mexican. Your choice."

"Mexican sounds good. How about that place by your parents'? What's it called?"

"Nopalito. I could go for that. Give me twenty minutes."

I hang up, turn around and nearly walk into Jeremy.

"Sorry." He puts his hand up. "Your dad sent me back for some paperwork. I didn't know anyone was in here."

All I hear is *paperwork*. "Tell me what you're looking for and I'll find it for you." I can't imagine my father letting Jeremy rifle through Dad's poor excuse for a filing system. "People have been known to disappear in here, it's a bit like the Bermuda Triangle."

Jeremy reaches around me and picks a manila envelope with his name scribbled across it off the desk and shakes it at me.

"What is it?" It's none of my business but I can't help myself.

"The restaurant's financial statements and a list of equipment and inventory." He lifts his brows. "Anything else you want to know?"

I don't say anything, realizing it's happening. Mom and Dad know I'll bless the sale because what choice do I have? It's not like I'd force my parents into indentured servitude.

Jeremy glances around the office, probably redecorating it in his head and planning out where he'll display his Bocuse d'Or trophy. His eyes fix on my wedding gown. "Nice dress."

I remember the blonde he was sitting with at the Ferry Building the other day and the long line of women he's rumored to have dated, including a celebrity twenty years his senior. I wonder if he'll parade his harem through Stones when he's the new owner.

"Thanks," I say. "I guess you're invited by virtue of the fact that it'll be your place."

"Nope. Your dad is waiting until after your wedding to make his decision. You've still got time to talk him out of it, Stone."

I shrug. "You know it's yours," I say, hanging my apron on a hook as I move toward the door. "See you around, Chef."

"See you around, Avery."

* * *

I arrive at the restaurant before Bennett does and put our names on a list. There's a long line to get into the tiny restaurant but it's worth the wait.

To kill time, I cruise the aisles of Falletti, a specialty food store next to the restaurant. The bakery counter is bare, only a few cupcakes, cookies and one white chocolate cake left. But it's the end of the day.

It makes me think about my future, about bakery versus pastry chef. I could get another restaurant gig, though good ones are hard to come by. The smaller places contract out their desserts and the higher-end restaurants like Les Corniches either already have someone or are looking for a name, someone with major bona fides or bestselling cookbooks on their resume. I have neither.

A bakery would feel like a demotion unless it was mine. And for that I would need a location, equipment, employees and lots of money. The bank of Kit Reid is now closed and even if it was open, I've made up my mind that I don't want to go that route. I suppose I can do something small, like special-order pastries and wedding cakes, and rent out a commissary kitchen but it would take a while until I built up enough business to make a living at it.

My phone buzzes with a text that our table is ready and I walk over to the restaurant to see Bennett is there, leaning against the wall, looking at his phone. He breaks into a smile at the sight of me.

"This is nice." He sweeps me into a hug and kisses the top of my head. "Are we celebrating the dress or something else?"

"The dress," I say because there is no something else. Unless you count that we're getting married soon because that alone should be the something else worth celebrating. Except I don't see it, which in and of itself should be a sign. But I'm good at ignoring signs, including the one that said Jeremy Gains would be taking over my family's restaurant from the get-go.

The hostess leads us to our table. Like I said, it's a tiny place. Pretty in its own rustic way. And the food is outstanding, elevated and thoughtful. Mom and Dad love to do takeout from here on their rare days away from Stones.

"Margarita?" Bennett is perusing the menu, which by now he should know by heart. There's a crease between his brows as he concentrates on the list of *bebidas*. I love that crease, it always reminds me of when he's at the piano, working on one of his jingles.

Originally, he'd dreamed of composing movie and television scores. He studied at USC's Thornton School of Music and hoped to follow in the footsteps of Jerry Goldsmith and Danny Elfman. But you know how that goes. It's a tough business to crack.

One day, he was screwing around on the piano in one of his labs, writing little promotional ditties about the class as a joke when his professor heard him and helped get him a summer internship at the AMP Agency. It turned out he had a knack for writing catchy songs for commercials and the rest is history.

"Definitely," I say. "How was your day?"

"Good. We got that account we pitched in LA. That made the bosses happy and when they're happy I'm happy. How 'bout you?"

"I need that margarita first."

"That bad, huh?" He flags down a server and puts in our drink orders.

"I'm going to tell my parents to go ahead with the sale."

Bennett tilts his head to the side and takes my hand "It's the right thing, Av, even if it hurts."

"I know."

Our margaritas come and I take a buttressing sip, letting the cold tequila and lime juice trickle down the back of my throat.

"Tess was on board from the start," I say. "Chef Gains was at the restaurant today and let it slip that my parents won't even consider selling until after our wedding. Tess is in New York, breaking the news to Kit. I'll find a good time to talk to her and tell her my decision."

He nods. "So even with the baby, you think Tess will leave Kit?"

I sort of wish I'd never told him Tess was pregnant. In my own warped way, I did it out of spite. "Tess is pregnant," I announced the day she and I were supposed to go to New York. It was over dinner at our breakfast table on Forty-Fourth Avenue. And then I watched him to see if I saw even a flicker of regret or melancholy for what could've been for him and Tess.

There was nothing obvious, just the typical dude head bob, the same kind he'd give if I'd just told him we were going out with friends, which of course I found suspicious.

Over the next several days, I replayed the scene in my head, reexamining every angle of it. How it should've been exactly the kind of news a woman shares with her fiancé about her family and about how I did it for all the wrong reasons.

Even now, when he's asked a perfectly legitimate question, I want to read into it, make it about him and Tess, when I know it's not.

"I think so," I say. "I don't think she'll ever be able to move on from what Kit did. And if she can't forgive him, I don't think she should. It's not a good way to bring a child into the world."

The server returns to take our order and we let the conversation of Tess go. We're back to the restaurant.

"You don't think there's a way you could swing the restaurant? Maybe find investors." Bennett asks when the server leaves.

"Even if I accepted Kit's money I wouldn't have enough. And I don't know the kind of people who invest in restaurants." Believe you me, I've thought long and hard about it. Because taking over Stones makes more sense than opening a bakery. I'd be keeping the restaurant in the family.

"Go to a bank and take out a loan. Sell the building for operating costs on the condition that the new owner leases it back to you for Stones."

In the scheme of things, the building is probably the restaurant's most valuable asset. That being said, my parents still owe a lot of money on the old bank. Selling it probably wouldn't be enough of a windfall to cover all my bases. Not even close. And if I did sell it, there is no guarantee a buyer would extend a long-term lease to Stones at a price I could afford. By the time I found a new place for the restaurant and paid for the buildout with equipment, I'd be broke.

"A loan? Ha. Even if a bank gave me one—and that's a big if—it could take months to jump through all the financial hoops to qualify." I lean closer across the table. "And here's the thing, I'm no restaurateur. I can barely balance my bank account. What if I drove the place into the ground? What kind of legacy would that be?"

"Not a good one," Bennett says and although it's the wrong answer it's what I love about him. He's honest. At least when it comes to matters that have nothing to do with the heart.

Tess

"This is stupid," I tell Kit as I choke up on the bat.

"That's good," he says, turning my hips just so. "Spread your legs a little wider and this time lean into it."

"I can't believe we're doing this." That's the thing about Kit, his persuasion skills are like a superpower.

He's the last person on earth I should be spending time with, yet here I am at a place called Champions in Brooklyn near Red Hook. It's a fitness center with outdoor batting cages. About twenty kids are lined up at the cage next to ours. Someone named Frankie D is having a birthday party. It's a cruel picture of my future life.

A girl in pigtails with freckles on her face and a big yellow mustard stain on her Bobby Sox jersey has wandered over from the group and is staring into our cage, eating a hotdog.

"Hey, aren't you Kit Reid?"

If it were me I'd lie. *"Hey, kid, what do you have rocks for brains? You think Kit Reid would spend his day off hanging out at some janky, low-rent batting cages?"*

But my husband, who could easily pull it off because he's a world-class liar, says, "Yep. Where'd you get that hotdog?"

"Over there." She waves her hand, also covered in mustard, in the direction of the birthday party in progress. "I'll get you one for an autograph."

"Okay," Kit says and I roll my eyes.

She scampers off and Kit goes back to coaching me. I still don't know how he roped me into this. As I mentioned before, not really a fan of baseball. And...not really a fan of Kit Reid.

I only came across the country to tell him I'm pregnant face-to-face. Instead of discussing how we're going to raise a child postdivorce, we're here. He bribed me with dinner at Ci Siamo, one of the hottest restaurants in Manhattan. But now dinner is starting to look like a raw deal.

Freckles returns with at least twelve kids in tow, waving an anemic hotdog in the air, which she pushes through the cage at him. He hands it to me, and I nearly keel over from the smell of relish and mustard, which in my pregnant state is giving off hints of rotting garbage and vinegar. How nice that the Pied Piper of Brooklyn took the time to dress the dog for him.

Kit opens the cage, steps out and takes a softball from Freckles to sign. The other kids stand there slack-jawed. One yells, "It's really him." And suddenly all of them are shoving things at him to autograph, including what looks like some kid's retainer.

Kit takes about twenty minutes to sign everything and talk to the kids. A few want selfies and to make TikToks with him. Some of the parents have begun gathering around us and one of the dads is doing that thing where he slaps Kit on the back every few minutes and laughs loudly like they're old friends.

No one seems to notice me; it's as if I don't exist. There was a time when I would've gotten as much attention, at least from the adults, as Kit. Funny, how quickly people forget.

Kit is gracious and generous and charming, lavishing attention on each kid. And I'm a little in awe at how genuine he is. And that's when I know it. I know what a good father he'll be and intuitively I know our child will love him more than he or she loves me. And I can feel my heart cracking in two.

The kids and their parents drift off, leaving Kit and me alone. Kit takes the hotdog I'm still holding and shoves half of it in his mouth. He holds the other half out to me.

I shake my head, he shrugs, and eats the rest of it.

"You're disgusting."

His lips curve up and he hooks me around the waist, lifting me off the ground. "We're having a baby, baby."

"Shh, someone might hear us. We're not supposed to tell anyone until twelve weeks."

"Your family knows."

"That's different," I say but I know he's already told Jonas and that we'll wind up telling his parents, too.

He presses me against the cage, cups my face with the palms of his hands and goes in for a kiss but I push him away.

"Don't."

"Come on, Tess."

"This," my hand automatically rests on my stomach, "doesn't change anything. I told you that. So don't push it, Kit."

He holds up both hands. "I'm not pushing, I promise. I just thought we could have a nice day."

And despite not liking baseball or batting cages or grubby kids with hotdog breath, I am having a nice day, even though I don't want to. Even though it feels like the whole world, my world, is caving in around me.

"Let's go home, then I'll take you to Ci Siamo." He drapes his arm over my shoulder and for a second it feels the way it used to, and I wish more than anything we could stop time and stay this way forever.

But by the time we get in the car, I'm crying, loud racking sobs. "What am I going to do, Kit?"

He pulls me against him and strokes my hair. "Breathe, Tess, just breathe. We'll figure it all out, I promise."

"My career is over. Everything I've worked for gone...just gone." I reach in the glove box looking for tissues or napkins. For a man who treats our apartment like a college dorm room, leaving his clothes on the floor and his dirty dishes in the sink, his car is immaculate. All I find in the glovebox is the Tesla manual and, of all things, a jockstrap. "Is this clean?" He nods and I wipe my nose on it, a new low even for me.

"Your career isn't over, Tess. You just have to bide some time in the minor leagues. It's temporary, babe."

I look at him like I want to rip his face off. "Seriously, that's what you've got? A fucking sports metaphor?"

He does the one thing I don't want him to do, he takes my hand and holds it, lacing his fingers through mine. "NBC isn't the only network, Tess. Any of those other networks would be lucky to have you."

My eyes fall to my stomach. "As soon as I'm big as a cow none of them will want me. Hell, they don't want me now."

"What do you want me to say, Tess? Look, everything is happening fast. You found out you're pregnant and then you got some bad news from Elsa. It's a lot at once. I get that."

He thinks he gets it, but he doesn't get anything. How can he? He isn't the one losing. Nope, all of Kit Reid's dreams are coming true.

"There are some silver linings here," Kit says. "She's dropping her lawsuit." He doesn't dare say Annabel's name because we both know I don't want to see it on his lips, ever, but he smiles proudly, like he single-handedly saved the day. I mean it, he actually thinks getting her to drop the suit makes him a candidate for knighthood.

Again, I want to rip his face off. It doesn't help that I'm having wild mood swings, one minute dreaming about running him off the road to the next where I love him uncontrollably.

"Let's go home," he says. "You'll feel better after a hot shower."

He's trying, he's really trying. And I give him credit for that. But if he thinks a hot shower is all I need to make me feel better, we're sunk.

* * *

"I didn't know how to tell you, Boo." Rodney reaches across the table and takes my hand.

"She's an excellent choice, really. Bilingual, gorgeous, nice. God, you know how rare it is for people to be nice in this industry?"

"That's why I'm mean as a snake," Rodney says. "Poor Eva Sanchez. The girl's gonna get eaten alive."

"No, she won't. She may be young, she may be green but she's smart as a whip. My money's on her. You'll see, she'll be the last man standing. I'd be happy for her if I wasn't so damn jealous and angry. You should've told me, Rodney. It would've been better to hear it from you, my friend, than from Elsa."

There are two people at the neighboring table staring and whispering about us. I've forgotten what it's like to sit in a restaurant in midtown and be ogled by admirers. How I secretly used to eat it up and not so secretly miss it.

Rodney starts to say something and I signal to him to keep his voice down. "Big ears next door," I whisper.

"We should've gone to the diner near the station. It's like a ghost town."

"Yeah, there's a reason for that." The place is disgusting.

Rodney mouths, "Don't be mad at me."

"I'm not because you're paying for lunch."

He gives me his best Ron Burgundy airhead look and some of my disappointment in him for not telling me that Eva Sanchez got the network job meant for me melts away. And now I wish I could break my twelve-week rule and tell him about the baby. I don't of course because of neighboring big ears and I don't want to be another headline on Page Six.

"What am I going to do, Rodney?"

"Truth time?"

"Yes," though I don't know if I'm ready to hear it.

"Take a year, write a book, come back with a bang."

"A book?" I may be a journalist but I'm not a writer, not a long-form writer anyway. "Like a tell-all?"

"Hell no. You go Katie Couric on us and you'll never work again in this town. I was thinking more like Kathie Lee Gifford's *I Can't Believe I Said That!*"

I bust out laughing. "You made that up, didn't you?"

"Girl, you never read the book? It's a classic."

I'm on my phone, searching the title because I still don't believe him. "Holy shit. Who knew?" I'll read it because now I'm wildly curious but I'm not writing a book. Besides not being much of a writer, I don't have the stomach for a memoir, my memoir. Like the song goes, "Nobody loves you when you're down and out."

"Basically, what you're saying is you think I'm unhireable for the foreseeable future."

He cocks his head to the side and there's sadness in his eyes. "I'm sorry, Tess."

"Hey," my voice cracks, "at least you're honest."

After lunch with Rodney, I walk home, looking in the shop windows, wondering how my marriage went bad, how I lost my job and found myself pregnant in one fell swoop. Like an earthquake, I never saw it coming.

Kit's gone until Thursday and frankly I can use the space to consider my options. Unfortunately, none of them good. He begged me to wait for him to return, to talk, and I acquiesced, though I'm done with him calling the shots.

Marriage counseling is a crock, at least for us. How do you fix a complete collapse of trust?

I take my time, strolling Fifth Avenue. It's too hot and sticky to walk the nearly five miles home but I'm so lost in my own thoughts that the three-digit temperature hardly registers. At least I dressed appropriately in a sleeveless shirt, baggy linen pants, and sandals. No makeup. Now I blend in with everyone else.

The sidewalk is crowded with pedestrians and half the time it's like pushing against the current to make it to the next block. I consider stopping for pizza or ice cream or a soft pretzel. It seems like all I ever do now is eat and throw up.

I pass Bella's Bridal Boutique and take a peek in the window, thinking of Avery. The dress on the right would look stunning on her. The snug mermaid style would emphasize her figure. I slip inside as much to suck up the free air conditioning as to inquire about the lead time on the dress. Mom said she already bought one and sent me a picture. Truthfully, it isn't anything special and if I'd been there I would've done my best to steer her to something else. Something with more wow factor.

"Can I help you?"

It's not the same woman who helped me with my dress but that was three years ago. "I was wondering about the dress in the window...the mermaid one."

"It's lovely isn't it? Would you like to try it on?"

"Oh, it's not for me. My sister is getting married in a few weeks and I'd love to gift her that dress."

"A few weeks?...We couldn't possibly meet that deadline. Madam's dresses are all custom made."

"Yes, I had mine made here." I flip my sunglasses to the top of my head but it's clear the salesperson doesn't recognize me. "Giselle did such a beautiful job that I just thought I'd...well it doesn't hurt to ask, now does it?"

The woman gives me a lukewarm smile, letting me know she has zero intention of selling me the dress in the window. For a second, I consider pulling *I'm the wife of Kit Reid*. Cheesy but I'm used to getting my way. The only thing that stops me is the prospect that even if I do throw out Kit's name it won't get me anywhere. My ego simply can't take any more rejection.

Besides, Avery wouldn't thank me for it. She's made it crystal clear she doesn't want me to have any part in her dress.

I leave the store and head straight to the nearest ice cream shop, where I wait in line for twenty minutes and get three scoops of chocolate peanut butter cup. Losing my waistline is a forgone conclusion, why not enjoy it?

I cross over to Central Park and find a park bench where I can enjoy my six million calories in peace. There's a woman there, her face shoved in a book. *Anna Karenina*. I wonder if it's a sign to throw myself in front of a train. Nah, death by ice cream is better.

"Tess? Tess Stone?" She closes the book and looks straight at me.

Shit, the one time I don't want to be recognized, I'm recognized. Shoveling ice cream into my mouth, no less.

"Hi," I say around a full bite, planning to find another park bench as soon as I can extricate myself without being rude. Then I realize I know her. "Stephanie?"

"I can't believe this. I don't know a soul in this city and I run into you."

"Are you still at KNTV?" We overlapped there. She was in advertising while I was a reporter. The station, based in San Jose, kept a floor in the Flood Building in San Francisco for some of its advertising staff. It's where she worked and she'd let me borrow a corner of her office whenever I had a story in the city.

"No. I'm at WNEN in Stamford now. Are you still at *Good Morning New York*?"

Apparently, word hadn't spread through the advertising ranks of broadcast news, even as close as Connecticut. "No," is all I say.

"I always knew you were destined for big things. Where are you now? Network?"

I toss the rest of my ice cream in the trash can near our bench, the taste of it starting to sour in my stomach. "Actually, I was fired and am now unemployed," I say. "It's on YouTube if you want to Google it."

"Oh...wow...I don't know what to say."

"You don't have to say anything. So what brings you to Manhattan?" It seems like a long way to come to read a book.

"My husband works for Aetna and the company is having its annual meeting in Manhattan. I rode in with him. Later, after his meeting, we have tickets to a show and plan to stay the night at a lovely boutique hotel near the park. I figured I'd catch up on my reading." She holds up her book.

"It's a nice day for it," I say. "Congratulations on WNEN. I have to get going but it was nice running into you," I say and sort of mean it. Under better circumstances I would've been thrilled. I'd always liked her and had even made it a habit to grab drinks or lunch with her on the days I found myself covering the news in San Francisco.

"You too. Do you have a card or anything? I'd love for us to keep in touch."

I rifle through my purse, find an old business card, and write my cell phone number on the back. Just to be polite I ask for hers and plug it into my phone.

I take a cab the rest of the way home, deciding that my initial decision to walk was overly ambitious. Howard is standing sentry at the door and helps me out of the taxi. I can tell right away something is wrong. I'm either being served with another lawsuit (just my luck) or Jonas has tried to sneak past Howard (again), or someone has tried to break into our apartment (someone not Jonas).

"What is it Howard?"

"There's a woman here to see you. I told her you weren't home but she insisted on waiting."

I'm not expecting any visitors and I'm getting a vibe from Howard that this one isn't someone I'm going to want to see. That's the thing about doormen in New York, they know more than they let on. And the good ones have your back.

"Do you know who she is, Howard?"

His gaze drops to the sidewalk. "Yes, ma'am."

I don't have to ask because I already know. I also know this isn't going to end well.

"It's okay," I say and walk past him into the lobby to find Annabel standing against the wall.

Her hair is tied back and she doesn't have on a stitch of makeup. She's in exercise pants and a tank top and if I didn't know better I'd assume she came straight from the gym. Yet, even without all her television armor, she's beautiful. Like cover model beautiful. It takes everything I have to remain civil and not scratch her eyes out.

"What can I do for you, Annabel?"

She gazes around the lobby, then back at me. "Can we have this conversation somewhere more private?"

If she thinks I'm going to bring her up to our apartment she's crazy. I've seen *Fatal Attraction* at least three times.

"Nope." I pretend to look at my watch. "I've got to be somewhere, so say whatever it is you came to say."

She pushes off the wall, coming only a few inches from me. "It's about Kit. You sure you want everyone to hear this?"

I don't but there is no way I'm letting her sully my apartment, even though for all I know she's been inside many times while I've been away.

"I'm sorry," she says and her eyes fill. And me being a skeptic wonders what her game is. She didn't come here to clear her conscience, that I'm sure about. Sorry is just her entrée in.

"Then I guess we're all good here." I start to walk away.

"I'm not the kind of person who does something like that."

I whirl around. "By "that" you mean sleeping with another woman's husband?"

Howard is hovering in the background by the door, pretending to be inordinately interested in something outside. At this point, I don't care who hears. My dirty laundry has already been aired in public by me and preserved for posterity by YouTube.

"I want you to know that I'm not a bad person, that I don't sleep with married men," Annabel says.

"And yet you did. And then you sued me, in essence telling the world I was a psychotic drama queen who made the whole thing up."

"You tried to ruin my career."

"No, you did that all by yourself. But the last I looked, I am the one out of a job and you're at ESPN."

She sniffles and a single tear rolls down her cheek...And the Oscar goes to Annabel Lane. "He never stopped pursuing me, he was relentless."

"Are you saying he forced you?"

"No, of course not. I'm as culpable as he is. I don't know what he's told you, but you should know he's as guilty as I am. It may have started out innocent but he's the one who..." She shakes her head. "It doesn't really matter because in the end, he chose you. You win. Congratulations."

"I win? Congratulations? Is breaking someone's heart a contest to you? Is this what you came here to tell me? Are you really that clueless? You know what, Annabel? He's all yours."

It only takes me seventeen minutes to ride the elevator up, pack my things, and call an Uber to the airport.

Avery

Tess and I are in the attic for "spring cleaning," even though it's summer. What's really happening is we're culling thirty-six years of history in case my parents wind up putting the house on the market. My mother is pushing to move to Tahoe full time and I'm betting she gets her way.

"You want this?" I hold up a baby blanket that belonged to either Tess or me. It's a patchwork of vintage pink chenille with big yellow and white flowers. I think my mother's friend, Toni, made it. "It would be pretty for the baby."

Tess lifts her head out of an old photo album she's been looking through for the last twenty minutes. Except I haven't seen her turn the page once. Ever since she came home, she's been far away. It's either pregnancy haze or depression. I don't know which one because neither of us has made an effort to talk. She's angry with me for not inviting her on my wedding gown hunt and I'm angry with her for...everything.

She studies the blanket for a second and reaches out to run her hand over the soft fabric. "Yeah, I'll take it."

I fold it and put it in the to-keep pile.

"There's a lot of crap up here." She shuts the album and stacks it on the to-keep pile closest to her.

"Who knew Mom and Dad were hoarders?" It's actually pretty organized for a storage attic. All the boxes are labeled and stacked neatly on shelves. I'm pretty sure hoarders don't do that.

If anything, Mom and Dad are sentimentalists. And yet, the two places—this house and the restaurant—that hold all the Stone memories will soon be gone.

I guess one of the things about parents is you expect them to stay exactly the way you want to remember them, even though everything else is changing around them.

"You want this?" Tess holds up my junior prom dress, a Jessica McClintock number with enough ruffles to make fifteen bed skirts.

"I think you should have it."

We both laugh, the first sign of camaraderie since she returned home from her days away.

"How did I ever pick out anything this hideous?"

"If you'd had my help you wouldn't have." She stares at me pointedly and we both know we're no longer talking about prom dresses.

"If you didn't always have to be the center of attention I would've," I say, regretting it as soon as it slips out of my mouth, even though it's the God's honest truth.

"Fuck you, Avery. I don't need this right now." She gets up and stomps down the ladder, leaving me alone to sort through four hundred square feet of the Stones. Four hundred square feet of our family.

I continue the task of making keep and toss piles, figuring if there is something Tess wants, she can dig it out of the garbage. After an hour, guilt gnaws at me and I go in search of her, not to apologize because I'm not sorry but to call a truce. My wedding is only a month away and I'd like for us to at least be on speaking terms.

I find her in the kitchen with Bennett, hugging. She's crying and I immediately recognize that he's consoling her, nothing more, but it doesn't stop that sickening feeling in the pit of my stomach.

He instantly pulls away, even though he's done nothing outwardly wrong, which leaves me to wonder whether he's guilty of things I cannot see.

"Hey," I say, trying not to let on how affected I am because it feels petty but most of all humiliating.

"Tess is having a bad day," Bennett says, stating the obvious. But of course, he's only telling me so I'll know the hug was innocent, which only makes it worse.

I'm not proud of this but it's when I kind of lose it. "Well, since you guys are so close you can finish sorting through the attic because I'm out of here." I storm off to my car and drive away.

Okay, not my finest hour.

And by the time I blindly hit Masonic, I realize I have no idea where I'm going. I don't mean I'm that kind of lost, I know these streets like I know the back of my hand. But I don't know where I'm headed.

Of all places I wind up at Les Corniches. I take one of the many vacant stools at the bar. It's too early for dinner and too late for lunch. Despite the place being mostly empty, the bartender takes his sweet-ass time taking my order.

"What can I get you?" he asks, seeming perturbed that I'm interrupting his downtime. Probably his Tinder time.

"Chef Gains. Is he here?"

"That depends on who's asking."

"Tell him Avery Stone is here to see him."

The bartender slips away and a few minutes later Jeremy appears. This time, he's traded in his chef whites for a suit, European if I had to guess.

"Don't you have ten restaurants? Why are you always here?" I'm raring for a fight and he seems like the perfect target.

"I own the place, what's your excuse?" He eyes my ancient, dust-covered overalls and starts to touch my head.

"What are you doing?" I pull away.

"You have a cobweb in your hair."

I reach up and with my fingers comb it out. Suddenly, I feel ridiculous coming here like this. It's not just that I'm coated in attic yuck but I'm spinning out of control. He must sense this because he takes me by the elbow and leads me down a long corridor behind the dining room, adjacent to the kitchen.

At first, I think he's about to throw me out of the restaurant. A perfect ending to a shitty day. Instead, he pulls me into a large dark-paneled office with a desk covered in menus. And there it is, his Bocuse d'Or trophy on display just like I always knew it would be.

This is definitely not my father's office. It looks more like a gentleman's study. There is even a soft leather map on the wall with pins to denote each city where Jeremy has a restaurant and framed photographs of him with other chefs, including Thomas Keller and Jöel Robuchon.

Judging by the pillow and blanket in a heap on the brown Chesterfield sofa and a pair of men's slippers tucked under a chair on the cowhide rug, it appears Jeremy sleeps here sometimes.

There is a whole wall of shelving filled with dishware, flatware, glassware and linens from each one of his ten restaurants. The reason I know this is because each setting is meticulously labeled. Spread out on the coffee table are blueprints of a kitchen and dining room. When I glance closer, I see the word "Stones" written across the top of the elevations.

"We're not even dead yet and you're already remodeling." I don't know why I'm surprised. For weeks he's been coming in and out, taking measurements. That and he told me he was making tweaks. I may not be an architect but the plans show way more than *tweaks.*

"Avery, I've got an investor dinner in twenty minutes. If you've got something to say talk."

He has me because I have everything and nothing to say. I don't even know why I came here, why this man, of all people, seems to draw me to him. He's about to take away the one piece of security I have, the one thing that loves me as much as I love it. The one place that is safe.

"I don't know what to do." It's out of my mouth before I can pull it back.

"About what?"

And there it is. I don't know what to do about anything. The restaurant, Bennett, Tess, the rest of my life.

"I don't know," I say and my eyes fall to my white Keds, which are also filthy. "I'm lost."

There's a long stretch of awkward silence. Then I rise and say, "And you're not a therapist, Chef. Sorry to have barged in here the way I did. I'll see myself out."

"Avery," he says. "You're not lost, you're simply trying to find your way. There's a difference, you know?"

I nod, even though no, I don't know what the difference is. But staying here any longer is more mortification than I can take.

"Hey," he says as I'm about to leave. "A chef, a very famous chef, once told me to only focus on the joy. Without the joy, he said, there's no soul. And you know what? It's become my mantra."

He motions for me to take the wingback chair. "Take your chocolate layer cake, for instance. It's nothing particularly original, nothing that any pastry chef worth his salt couldn't replicate. Yet, I taste the joy in every bite. So much joy that for the past two years, I've been eating that cake, sending my assistant to Stones three times a week to get me a slice because it's become an addiction.

"Now, your berry pie is competent," he continues. "The all-butter crust very nice. No one is ever going to say that's a bad pie, or even a mediocre pie. There are even people, finicky people, who will tell you it ranks in the top ten. Ranking in the top ten is a big accomplishment. There are chefs, good chefs, chefs making a fine living, who will never rank in the top one hundred, let alone the top ten. That's the truth, that's the reality of the kitchen.

"But, Avery, I don't taste an ounce of joy in your berry pie. I taste skill, I taste good ingredients, I even taste fledgling ambition. But not a drop of joy."

He holds my gaze, trying to see if I get it, if I get the significance of what he's trying to tell me. "Find the joy, Avery, and you'll find your soul."

Long after I leave, I ponder the meaning of joy but I keep coming back to one thing: Jeremy Goddamn Gains is addicted to my chocolate cake. If that's not joy I don't know what is.

     * * *

It's eight o'clock when Bennett gets home. Even though it's not dark yet, it feels late, like I've been going for days without sleep.

"You over your snit?" Bennett asks. He sounds annoyed, which isn't like him. He's usually the most easygoing person I know.

"She drives me crazy." We both understand I'm talking about Tess.

"Your sister's having a tough time. Maybe cut her a little slack," he says, rushing past me to our bedroom. A few minutes later, I hear the shower running.

I wander into the bathroom—we have a no-knocking policy—and ask, "Did you guys finish the attic?"

"Yes. Tess put all the things she thought you'd want to keep in your old bedroom." He's standing under the showerhead, washing his hair with my shampoo. Unlike me, he grabs whatever is closest. "Anything you don't claim by next week is getting chucked, according to your mom. Thanks for sticking me with the job. It's definitely how I wanted to spend my Sunday."

"Sorry." And I am. Cleaning the attic wasn't his responsibility. "It's just everything is always about her."

He turns off the water and slides the glass door open. I hand him a towel. "You need to get over it."

He's right of course. If I think things are spinning out of control for me I can only imagine what Tess is going through. I still have a job, at least for now. And I'm about to marry the love of my life while Tess is headed for divorce two months pregnant.

Even in the pity department, she wins.

Okay, that's low even for me. I chide myself for being an unsympathetic, self-entitled bitch. I promise myself to do better.

"Are you hungry?"

"I ate at your folks'." He moves into the bedroom to dress and is giving me the silent treatment.

"So you're not talking to me now?"

"What do you want to talk about, Avery? Because I'm sick of talking about Tess." There is an edge to his voice, an edge I don't like, an edge that is more defensive than it is tired. An edge that gives me that sick feeling in the pit of my stomach again.

To make it go away I say the one thing Tess can't give him that I can.

"I love you, Bennett" and I wrap my arms around him.

Tess

"Elsa, you have to find me something," I say over the phone as I stare at myself in the full-length mirror hanging on the back of my old bedroom door. Although I'm not showing yet, it's only a matter of time before my belly swells up like a balloon. In other words, I won't be terribly appealing to television executives.

"I'm trying, Tess. I'm doing everything I can. But you're a little toxic right now." Elsa lets out a loud sigh, like this is all very taxing for her. "At least the lawsuit's gone. That was making everything worse. It was like a constant reminder of what you'd done."

What I'd done.

I keep from snorting, thankful that Elsa can't see me flipping her the bird through the phone on the opposite coast.

"I heard CBS was looking for a reporter, someone to cover Florida." I want to anchor not report and I don't want to leave New York. But I'll work my way back if I'm forced to. It's not like I have a better chance hanging out in my childhood bedroom, eating Doritos. Because until Elsa returned my call that was exactly what I was doing.

"I'll send them your tape," she says as if she doesn't think it will go anywhere.

"That would be great." I try to keep the sarcasm out of my voice but fail miserably. Either Elsa doesn't care or she doesn't notice. I'm betting on the first.

My phone clicks with an incoming call. I glance at caller ID. Kit. Again. Ever since his concubine paid me a visit and I hightailed it out of Manhattan, he won't leave me alone. I let it go to voice mail as I've been doing since I left New York. Of course, it's only putting off the inevitable.

We're having a baby; at some point I'll have to talk to my child's father. But not any time in the near future. Not if I can help it.

"Is that all?" Elsa asks, making it clear she wants to be done with this conversation and done with me.

"Just get me a job." I click off not feeling optimistic.

It's only noon and I've already completed my to-do list. Earlier, Mom came with me to my first prenatal doctor's appointment before skipping off to work. The big takeaway is that, yes, I'm really pregnant, no, I don't have syphilis (with Kit you can never tell), I should stay away from cat litter boxes, and my due date is March 29. I scheduled an ultrasound two weeks from now, even though I'm not sure where I'll be. Here, New York, Miami, or, knowing my luck, some tiny station in Lodi, covering the state barbecue championship.

The doorbell rings and I consider ignoring it. Probably just a salesperson or a Jehovah's Witness. But then I remember a real estate agent is supposed to be dropping by and dash downstairs.

It's not an agent, it's Kit, who's supposed to be in St. Louis today. My pulse quickens. As angry as I am, seeing him makes my treacherous heart swell and my eyes fill. I try to tell myself it's pregnancy hormones and start to slam the door in his face.

He palms the door before I can get it closed and with little effort keeps it from shutting. "I came to take you to our first doctor's appointment."

"As usual, you're a day late and a dollar short." I try to close the door again but it won't budge with him holding it open.

"Did I miss it?" His face falls and for a fraction of a second, I feel sorry for him.

"It was two hours ago. What are you doing here, Kit? You have a game."

He looks exhausted. There are dark circles around his eyes and his usually clean-shaven face is covered in whiskers. His mouth is drawn in a hard line, making him look ten years older.

"I thought it was at one." He shakes his head. "I just flew six hours. Can I at least come in?"

I move aside, making way for him. He drops his duffel on the floor and pulls me in for a hug but I push him away.

"You don't get to waltz in here and pretend that everything is the same." I turn away from him and go in the kitchen. "Do you want something to eat or drink?"

He follows me and straddles one of the breakfast table chairs like it's a horse. "What did they say at the doctor's?"

"That I'm pregnant."

"Come on, Tess."

"Nothing. It's just a routine appointment. I told you that."

"When's the baby due?"

"March 29."

"Wow." He breaks into a grin. "Everyone is healthy, then?"

"I'm healthy, no thanks to you and your walking-chlamydia girlfriend. But it's too soon to know about the baby, so don't go announcing it to the media."

"I told my parents," he says with a hint of guilt.

"Of course you did." I want to punch him in his left arm, his dominant arm.

"Why should your parents know and not mine?"

He does have a point there. "Because for all intents and purposes, I'm living here. It's a little hard to keep it a secret when I'm retching all morning long."

In all honesty, him telling his parents is the last thing on my grievance list. I pull out the ham Mom made the other night and start to make him a sandwich just to keep busy. He gets up and pours himself a glass of water.

"You don't have to be living here," he says. "You can come home. How are we supposed to work this out if you're here?"

"What makes you think we're working this out?"

"Because we were until Crazytown showed up."

"No, you thought we were because you're delusional." I put his sandwich on a plate and shove it at him. "Let me ask you something, Kit. What would you do if you were in my position, if the tables were turned and I was the one who cheated on you? Let's make this good. I cheated with Kris Bryant." Arguably the hottest player in baseball, not including Kit, and a former San Francisco Giant, even if it was for only fifteen minutes.

Kit squints his eyes. "No, we're not playing this and stay away from Kris Bryant."

"See! Just us talking about it makes you mad. Imagine if it was true, Kris Bryant and me. Are you willing to just forgive and forget? Are you, Kit?"

He doesn't say anything.

"Eat your sandwich." I pour him a glass of milk and set it on the table. He's the only adult I know who still drinks milk.

He sits down and takes a bite of the sandwich. I take the seat across from him, my back to the window that faces the garden.

"What about your game?" I finally ask.

He checks his watch, the one I bought him for our second anniversary. "I chartered a flight out at two-thirty. If all goes to schedule I can still make it in time for batting practice."

"This was crazy, Kit."

He puts his sandwich down and scowls at me. "My baby too, Tess. You seem to be forgetting that. No matter how much I screwed up, this is still our baby together." His hand moves to my stomach. I feel the heat of it there and don't push him away this time. "The woman is crazy, Tess. She's distorting what happened. I flirted with her and I won't lie, I wanted her. But this wasn't some big love story, like she's making it out to be."

I wanted her. The words cut me like a knife.

"She didn't describe it like that. She said you were relentless in your pursuit of her. Is she wrong? Is she lying?"

He doesn't say anything at first and I have my answer.

"She pursued me too. This wasn't one sided, Tess."

"And that's supposed to make me feel better?" We're going round in circles with this and we're no further along than we were when I first found out.

"No, of course not." He looks away but not fast enough to keep me from seeing there are tears in his eyes. "We were making headway until she showed up, spewing her bullshit. I want to make this work, Tess."

"No, that's not true. We were not making headway. It's just what you want to believe. I was and still am unbelievably hurt and angry. Honestly, I don't know how we come back from this, Kit."

"Don't say that. We come back from it because we love each other. We're having a kid for God's sake, Tess."

"That's not a reason to stay together." Though I'm not entirely sure about that. I grew up healthy and happy in a two-parent home. That's not to say that other children don't grow up healthy and happy with a single parent. But don't I at least owe my child to try with Kit?

Then again, I also want my kid to grow up not taking shit from anyone. I want him or her to grow up with enough self-respect to know when to leave. How do I teach those things if I don't live by them?

It's a conundrum I don't plan to solve today. Or tomorrow. I'm too damned tired.

"Does that mean you're going to leave me?" Kit asks and I can see the utter despair in his eyes. It's the first time I've seen my husband afraid, truly afraid, and the sick thing about it is I like it.

Avery

It's our first cookout of summer, which is pretty sad because it's already August. One could argue that summer in San Francisco doesn't really start until August, so we're right on schedule.

Bennett, whose cooking experience is limited to anything you can put in a microwave, is manning the grill. I made the hamburger patties, using my dad's recipe, and marinated enough chicken to feed the entire Richmond District.

The barbecue is doubling as a wedding shower. Technically, Leslie's throwing the shower. But her upstairs bathtub sprung a leak and flooded her whole house, so we decided to have it here.

Leslie and her husband came over earlier and decked out our small backyard with balloons and streamers. Mom bought a cake from Irene's, a bakery in the Haight famous for its booze-infused pastry. I volunteered to make it but was told in no uncertain terms that the bride doesn't make her own shower cake, even though I'm making the one for the wedding.

Tess is here early to allegedly help with the messy work of setup but she's dressed like she's the guest of honor at a tea at the Ritz Carlton in a halter dress and skyscraper-high heels. I don't know who she's trying to impress. It's just a small group of friends and family, including Javi, Carlos, Wen, Cybil and Mandy from the restaurant.

Mom and Dad show up thirty minutes after Tess. Besides the cake, they come bearing my mother's famous Portuguese salad, my father's equally famous potato salad, two cases of champagne and bags of ice. I point them to the two picnic tables that are already sagging with food.

The sun has decided to grace us with her presence (a rarity in the avenues) and a sea breeze wafts through the yard, filling the air with a hint of brine. I can't remember a day this lovely in a long time and see it as a good omen. Mother Nature has seen fit to bless this party.

People start showing up around noon and Bennett puts the first round of burgers and chicken breasts on the barbecue, showing off his moves by flipping patties in the air with a spatula. My dad, unimpressed, shoos Bennett away from the grill and takes over.

"Put your hands together," Bennett raps. "Chef Stone is in the house."

There's a round of applause and my dad shakes his head as if we're all crazy. I find a corner and watch him as he stands over the grill, distributing the coals to create different cooking zones. The chicken goes to the right where it's hottest, the burgers in the center and the corn on the cob on the left where it's only about 350 degrees. It's like watching performance art, his motions are so fluid, so confident.

I can't help but ask myself what it'll be like for him in retirement with no people to feed and no kitchen to man. I think about what Jeremy said about joy. My father puts it in every dish he makes and in every soul he nurtures. His food may not be fancy or complicated but it's every bit a part of him.

I envy him for having it all figured out and at the same time grieve for him giving it up. Because deep down in my heart I know he doesn't want to sell the restaurant. It's what he needs to do to please my mother but it's not what he wants to do.

Out of the corner of my eye I see Tess and Bennett talking. They're standing close but still a respectable distance. She hasn't talked to Kit in days while they take "space" from each other. I wonder if my sister had to do it all over again would she have stayed with Bennett? He's not a famous ballplayer who makes a seven-figure salary like Kit but he's not a cheater. At least not the physical kind. Wasn't it Jimmy Carter who said he had committed adultery in his heart? How many times since Tess has been back has Bennett committed adultery in his heart?

"What are you doing over here all by yourself?" My mother brings me a plate.

"Nothing, just watching Dad. You think leaving the restaurant will be hard for him?"

Mom lets out a long sigh. "It'll be harder for him to stay. He's been doing it a long time, Avery. He's tired."

"Why Nevada, Mom?" It seems like so much change all at once.

"When you see it, you'll know why. Now come on, it's your bridal shower. Mingle."

I stuff a quarter of my burger in my mouth and follow my mother to the other side of the yard where there's a cluster of people from Bennett's ad agency. I'm not that well acquainted with any of them. Besides the occasional pub gatherings, we don't see them all that much. Working in the hospitality industry is murder on the old social life.

I'm repeatedly hugged and the women ask me questions about the wedding. *"Do you have your dress?" "I couldn't find your registry." "Where are you guys going on your honeymoon?"* They all love Bennett and can't stop talking about him, about his jingles, and how fun he is.

I slide my glance over to where he and Tess were standing and note that Bennett is gone. Leslie has taken his place. She and my sister are laughing about something and I find myself drifting from the AMP group toward Leslie and my sister only to be waylaid by Javi.

"Happy shower." He hands me a gift wrapped in butcher paper. "It's a chef's knife." He nudges his head toward the kitchen. "Yours suck."

"They're Bennett's." I never got a fancy set in culinary school because I was in pastry. "Thank you, Javi. It's very thoughtful of you and probably the only wedding gift I'll actually use. How are you holding up?" This is the first time I've discussed the sale of the restaurant with him. I've been so wrapped up in my own drama I haven't stopped to ask Javi how he's handling all the changes coming down the pike.

"I'm out."

I rear back in surprise. "What...why?"

"These tired bones need a break and your mom and dad have been kind enough to offer me a cut when the sale is final." He kisses the top of my head. "I'm going to miss you, kid. But I'm too old to be on my feet every day."

"Are you doing this because of Jeremy?" I imagine Javi would stay on if it was anyone else at the helm and not an exacting restaurateur who doesn't even allow music in the kitchen.

"He's offering me a nice package to remain at the restaurant. But it's time to move on," he says without really answering my question. "Change is good, Avery. Embrace it, baby girl. I'm getting me a couple of chicken wings before they're all gone." He walks toward the grill, toward my dad, his best friend of thirty years, and a sense of loss washes over me in waves and I feel as if I'm drowning.

My chest squeezes so tightly that I'm finding it difficult to breathe and I'm suddenly dizzy. I recognize the symptoms enough to know I'm having a panic attack. It's not my first one. Five years ago, when Bennett first met Tess, I had to be rushed to the emergency room because I thought I was having an asthma attack when I don't even have asthma. It felt exactly like this.

I grab onto a lawn chair to stabilize myself and close my eyes. When I open them again, Tess is there.

"Avery, what's wrong?"

The last thing I want at our wedding shower is to become a spectacle but I can't seem to get any words out. I lock eyes with Tess and silently plead for her to be discreet. It seems like an odd time to be worried about discretion, given that catching my breath should be the top priority, but I guess I'm panicking over the panic attack.

She hooks her arm around my waist and navigates me into the house, where she leaves me safely on the sofa to get me a glass of water.

"What happened?"

"I was talking to Javi and all of a sudden I couldn't breathe and it felt like my chest was in a vise grip. I think I was having a panic attack."

Tess joins me on the couch. The party is still going on outside as if nothing has happened for which I'm grateful. Everyone seems to be having a nice time. Through the French doors I can see Carlos and his wife dancing to Bennett's iPod mix and Dad still working the grill.

"Is it nerves over the wedding?" Tess asks.

What it comes down to is it's everything. The restaurant, the future trajectory of my life, which includes the wedding. Mom and Dad moving away to some hellhole gated community in the snow. Javier leaving and Jeremy Goddamn Gains moving in.

"Javi was talking about retiring from the restaurant and...I guess I lost it. Too much change at once."

"Yeah, I know the feeling." She eyes my untouched glass of water. "Drink."

I do as she says even though I don't see how a few sips of water is going to cure my panic attack. Where's the science on that? But it's nice sitting here with Tess, even though it was only a short time ago that I was openly hostile to her for showing up early to help set up with no intention of actually helping.

"Take some deep breaths," she instructs, like suddenly she's a doctor.

But I do it anyway, leaning into the method I learned during my one foray into yoga. The nearby community center was offering free classes, so I spent butt loads of cash on a mat and a bunch of exercise outfits I never wore. They are stuffed in the back of my drawers somewhere. I gave the mat to my mom to use while she's gardening.

Unlike the water, the breathing exercises do indeed help. I wouldn't say I'm completely over it but I can probably go back outside and join the party without suffocating to death.

"Feeling better?" Tess asks and for a second, she sounds almost exactly like Mom.

"I think so. Should we go back out before everyone misses us?"

"Give it a couple more minutes. Then we'll walk out together with another one of Mom's salads, like we were in here making it."

It sounds like a plan, a good plan.

I flash on middle school when Tess was in the eighth grade, two years ahead of me. I'd accidentally broken Mom's Sascha Brastoff ceramic bowl. I was jumping on the couch, caught my foot in my pants hem, and fell, landing on the bowl in the center of the coffee table. It broke clean in half like the way my father cuts a cantaloupe into two perfect orbs.

Tess, being the sneakier of the two of us, painstakingly Gorilla-glued it back together at the dining room table. Without inspecting it too closely, you'd never see the microcrack that ran vertically down the middle of the bowl. If Mom ever noticed it she never said a word.

Today, Tess is her eighth-grade self. She is the Tess I love most.

"Ready?"

I nod and just before we head out of the French doors, she grabs one of Mom's tomato salads from the fridge and presses a bottle of tequila someone brought as a gift into my hands.

"Let's roll."

* * *

I've had two more panic attacks since the cookout. One, a week after the party and the other, two days ago. They all started the same. First, like an elephant is sitting on my chest and then, like I can't breathe without taking large gulps of air. All the while my heart is racing like it's competing in the Indianapolis 500.

Both times I was at the restaurant when it happened. In neither circumstance was I doing anything stressful or taxing, nothing that would trigger anxiety. Fearing that maybe it wasn't a panic attack and instead something worse, I looked up my symptoms on the Internet. Every medical site (and some not so medical) confirmed my original diagnosis.

Basically, I'm a basket case.

But today, I'm going to sit back and enjoy the ride. My parents, Tess and I are taking a road trip to the new house my parents are buying.

We stop at a Starbucks in Incline Village to use the bathroom. It's only ten minutes to Mom and Dad's gated community but Tess can't make it. We've already visited four other Starbucks along route 80 for her to pee.

This time, I get a grande dark roast. It's the least I can do given how many times we've used the coffee chain's restroom. Dad waits in the car, like he always does. I decide to get him a coffee too. It's his first Sunday away from the restaurant in as long as I can remember. I think the last time was for his and Mom's fortieth anniversary. And the time he got sick.

The plan is to stay the night since the restaurant is closed tomorrow. Even though construction on the house isn't completed yet, part of the incentive package includes three complimentary weekends in one of the development's guest condos.

I'd hoped Bennett could get Monday off and come with us but he and his team have a presentation that he can't miss.

I hand Dad his coffee through the driver's window and get into the back seat of my Mom's old Volvo. I'm surprised the car made the trip and didn't just belch and die going up Donner Pass. Tess is working on them to get an all-wheel drive for the snowy winters.

I still don't understand why they picked this place. We don't ski or boat. Last I looked, my parents don't even hike unless you count walking to Bi-Rite for ice cream. And their idea of gambling is buying the occasional lottery ticket.

"The girls almost done in there?" Dad is getting impatient to get to the new house.

"I think so but there was a line."

"What do you think of this place?" he asks, drumming his fingers on the steering wheel.

Except for the traffic and the display of new Range Rovers and billion-dollar real estate, it's gorgeous. Dotted with regal pines, Lake Tahoe and the Sierra Nevada is enough to take your breath away.

And in the winter, when the mountains and trees are covered in snow it's like a Christmas card. But it's a place for the families of the kids I didn't like in school. The kids whose parents took them to Aspen for winter break and Cabo San Lucas in the summer. The kids who didn't live in the Haight and had weekend homes in wine country.

"Impressive," I say dryly.

My father laughs. "Come on, kiddo, it's not so bad."

"It's beautiful but it doesn't seem like your kind of place. It was Mom's idea wasn't it?"

"Nope, it was all mine."

I don't believe him but don't want to be a killjoy. Today is my parents' day, not mine.

Mom and Tess come out of Starbucks with iced coffees and what I'm sure are day-old muffins made in a factory somewhere. It reminds me of the rare times we used to go camping up in Shasta County, when Dad would talk Javi and the boys into holding down the restaurant for a day or two. When we'd pack a tent and sleeping bags and eat fast food. I loved those trips.

Tess and I would put on our bathing suits, slather ourselves in baby oil, and lie on the top of the station wagon until we turned golden brown, then cool off in Battle Creek. Once we even panned for gold, Tess swearing that she'd hit the mother lode when she mistook a piece of glass from an old beer bottle for a nugget.

Those trips were the extent of our outdoor adventures. Though my mother was raised in the bucolic Central Valley, our people gravitated toward the grit of city life. That's why this whole moving to the mountains strikes me as odd.

"What a gorgeous day." Mom hands me one of the muffins and I try not to turn up my nose at it.

"Gorgeous. It's like a hundred degrees," Tess says, being even less of a good sport than I am. "Turn on the AC, Dad."

"Everyone buckled up and ready to go?" He noses the Volvo onto the road before we can answer.

Next thing I know, we're climbing above Lake Tahoe into the trees. Both my ears pop and I open and close my mouth a few times to unclog them so I can hear, though no one is talking. We're all staring out our respective windows at the view. The blue green of the water, the endless pines, the majestic mountains. It's pretty awe inspiring. But you won't hear me uttering the words unless someone pries it out of me with a crowbar.

I glance over at Tess and she's staring out into the distance, her mouth slightly agape. It's not like it's our first trip to Tahoe. We've stayed at friends' cabins here, come up to eat at our former line cook's new restaurant, and spent weekends in one of the luxury hotels. The place is a rite of passage for any Northern Californian.

Perhaps because it's Mom and Dad's future home we're seeing it, really seeing it, for the first time. I have to admit I can understand the appeal now. It's that beautiful.

"I bet bears will get into your garbage," Tess says apropos of nothing.

"Everything in the development is bear proof," Dad says and I can't tell if he's stating fact or being flippant.

For the next few minutes, Dad follows a windy road that switches back through the mountains until we're level with the lake again. We drive past two huge stone pillars with "Bear Creek Tahoe" engraved in bronze on each side, up to a guard stand where a woman in a camp shirt with the Bear Creek Tahoe logo makes us sign in before lifting the gate. Kind of formal but whatever.

"Look over there." Mom points at a gorgeous lodge at the edge of the lake. "It's an original Julia Morgan built in the 1920s. In the summer, the residents use it as a communal beach house and in the winter it's base camp for the ski resorts. There's a shuttle every couple of hours."

It's on the tip of my tongue to remind her that she doesn't ski but why yuck her yum. This is clearly my parents' version of living the dream. And from what I've seen so far, I can't blame them. It's extremely tasteful for what amounts to an upscale tract development at the foot of Lake Tahoe, one of the state's crown jewels.

"That over there is the clubhouse." Mom points again. "Mac, park, so the girls can walk around and see it."

Dad slides into one of the abundant parking spaces and we get out of the car. The clubhouse is a modern version of the Julia Morgan lodge, only twenty times larger with a lounge area that looks like a grand living room with a stone fireplace, grand piano, and lots of leather seating. There's a restaurant, café and bar with soaring views of the mountains, a party hall that can hold up to four hundred people, a couple of meeting rooms, a gym, and a spa.

"Wow, this is pretty slamming." Even Tess is impressed.

Outside is a recreational fantasy. A huge pool with cabanas, a hot tub the size of Bennett's and my backyard, a game room, tennis and pickleball courts, and on the south end of the clubhouse, bocci ball, firepits, and picnic tables.

"When will you guys ever use this stuff?" Tess asks, giving voice to my own thoughts. Though the amenities are righteous, it's not the kind of place I picture the Stones.

Yet, in defense of my parents' decision to move to the middle of nowhere, I say, "Dad will golf." Wending its way through the property is an eighteen-hole golf course. Golfing, when he can find the time, is the one thing my father likes to do besides cooking.

"The amenities are one of the reasons we picked it," Dad says. "The other reason was to get away from you two." He puts both of us in a headlock, each arm wrapped around our necks, like he used to when we were kids.

"Stop it, Mac." Mom elbows him in the ribs. "The amenities are a bribe to get you here. This place is better than a resort and we want all of you to come as often as possible."

It is just as good as a resort, no question about it. I'm not sure I'm the resort type, though. Four years ago, I'd say Tess wasn't either. Even though she's always been a diva, she was a down-to-earth city diva. But marrying a major league baseball player, moving to Manhattan and being a top-rated anchorwoman (before she got canned, of course) has made her even glossier than she used to be. So who knows now?

Her lips are drawn in a thin line and her expression is sour as she takes in Mom and Dad's new bougie Mecca. There is nothing here not to like. For the life of me I can't understand why she's so visibly disapproving.

That's when I get it. She hates this move even more than I do, and I hate it a lot.

It's not the place or the circumstances, or even the distance. It's the idea that the one thing that always remained constant will never be the same again. That our predictable parents might actually change, too.

"Let's see the house," Mom says, and I have to say I can't remember the last time I saw her this happy. Her glow is like a neon light. Even Dad seems enthusiastic, which is as rare as a leap year.

We trudge back to the car and get in, even though our bodies rebel after the four-hour drive. Dad takes us on a pine-lined street, past contemporary homes with lots of steel and glass and weathered wood. Architectural in a cookie-cutter way.

"This is it," Mom says as Dad pulls into the driveway and cuts the engine.

There's a porta potty on the sidewalk in front of the house and construction materials covered in blue tarps. But the house looks well on its way to being finished, at least from the outside.

Like the others, it's contemporary but this one is more like a typical Tahoe A-frame style with a pitched roof, wooden decks and stone accents.

"It's beautiful," I say and nudge Tess, who stands near the porta potty, staring up at the large picture windows, to say something too.

"It's so different from the house on Baker Street." She moves to another spot, so she can see it from a different angle. "It's fancy."

"We're fancy people," Dad says, leading the way to the front door.

"Since when?" I follow, anxious for the first time to see it, to see this new life my parents are taking on, shedding their old one like winter coats.

There's still a lot that needs to be done. The walls aren't painted, none of the trim is in, and boxes of fixtures and cabinets are pushed against one wall, waiting to be installed.

Light pours through the interior, an open floor plan unlike the warren of rooms in the house on Baker Street. Here, the kitchen, living room and dining room are one giant space. While it's all beautiful, giant glass windows, new wooden floors, impressive iron ceiling trusses, huge stone fireplace, it's the kitchen range that makes my jaw drop.

"Holy smokes, whose idea was this?" Because the forty-eight-inch Wolf is not my father's Kenmore. It is even nicer than the Vulcans at the restaurant.

Mom throws her head back, taking with it a cascade of dark curls, and laughs. "I insisted. If anyone deserves a stove like this it's your father."

No greater truth has ever been told. A million great meals will be made in and on this range that is not my father's Kenmore.

"I wish the hood was in." My mother turns her gaze to the collection of boxes. "It's a real showstopper."

I go in the kitchen to inspect it closer, opening the oven doors and playing with the burners. Then I sneak a peek at my father, who is grinning like a madman. He'll never admit it but he likes this range. He may even love it.

I don't know why but I start to cry. I turn my head, pretending to be fixated on the Wolf, so no one will see the tears in my eyes. Who are these people and what have they done with my parents?

* * *

Dad loads the car with our duffel and overnight bags. Tess is the only one with a suitcase, her idea of traveling light. The morning is cool and crisp but if today is anything like yesterday, temperatures should climb to the nineties by noon. By that time, we'll be well on our way back to the fog.

After we settled in at the condo, we made use of the pool, the hot tub and the sauna, like kids at an all-you-can-eat dessert buffet that closes in an hour. Tess and I even played a game of bocci ball, not because we like bocci ball but it seemed a shame to let it go to waste. Then we ate in the clubhouse restaurant, which was better than I imagined but still ho-hum.

Before going to bed, we sat out on the deck, looking at the stars and the way the moon glowed over the mountains, listening to my mother's contented sighs. Tess and I shared a room and slept side by side in the twin beds that were made up straight out of a Ralph Lauren catalog.

"Can you get over this place?" Tess whispered in the dark.

"It's weird, right? Not the place but that Mom and Dad are moving here."

I drifted off to sleep thinking how did we get here? How did we get to a life without the restaurant, without the house on Baker Street, without the world I'd lived in for thirty-four years?

"We ready to hit the road?" Dad asks, slamming the tailgate closed.

"Tess is peeing again. Then we can go," Mom says. She's wearing a long tiered skirt, a dozen silver bangles on her arm and has lost ten years since we left San Francisco a day ago.

Even Dad seems relaxed or at least not as tightly wound as he characteristically is. It must be the mountain air.

Tess comes out of the condo. "Did anyone see my sunglasses?"

I stare at her as if she's lost her mind. "They're on the top of your head."

Her hand immediately goes to where a pair of Ray-Ban Jackie O knockoffs are perched and pushes them down over her eyes. "Well, shit."

Dad shakes his head. "Let's get a move on, family."

We scoot into the car and head down the mountain, our short-lived vacation soon to be a distant memory.

Mom turns in her seat. "Would you and Bennett like to take one of the complimentary condo stays as a honeymoon?"

We're planning to eventually go to Hawaii but haven't gotten our shit together to actually plan it. "Maybe," I say. "I don't want to take it away from you guys, especially when you may need to be here to make decisions on the construction."

"Your father and I can always stay at Dave and Carol's cabin. We would love for you to take it."

The wedding is only two weeks away and the last thing on my mind is our honeymoon, though it should probably be the first thing. I brush the thought away as I'm wont to do lately with any questions that are inconvenient. I'll think about it tomorrow, except I've been telling myself that ever since Bennett proposed.

"I'll see what Bennett wants to do," I tell my mother. "Thank you for the offer."

"I meant what I said about hoping you girls consider the new house your second home."

Tess is awfully quiet. I poke her to make sure she's even awake. Or alive.

"Ow! What the hell's wrong with you?" Tess pokes me back.

"Do I need to pull the car over and hit you both?" Dad pipes up from the front. It's an old refrain, one that harkens to when Tess and I were two pissed-off adolescents, fighting in the back of the car on the way to dance lessons or soccer practice. Nothing shut us up faster than those twelve words.

Tess stifles a laugh, remembering it too. And for a second, we hold each other's gaze and we're those sisters again, the pissed-off adolescents who used to fight in the car but in all ways loved each other. I'm the first to look away and the moment is gone.

We drive in silence, staring out at the view until we hit Interstate 80. That's when Tess has to use the bathroom. In Auburn, Dad takes the Lincoln Way exit, which dumps us out in Old Town, a cute commercial district that plays up its Gold Rush roots.

Mom and Tess pop into one of the restaurants while Dad and I go in search of drinks. It's got to be a hundred degrees and the Volvo's air conditioner ain't what it used to be. I'm as parched as the desert.

There are lots of people milling around, peering in the old brick and wooden buildings that house everything from hat shops and houseware stores to a brew pub and enoteca. We find a tiny grocery store and stock up on waters for the rest of the ride home. That is if Tess can hold her bladder that long.

"Adorable town," I say to Dad who rocks his hand from side to side and shrugs. "I know, you have to uphold your curmudgeon status at all costs."

He winks and we walk back to the car with our bottled waters. Tess and Mom join us, Beatriz holding a bag of old-fashioned candies she bought at a novelty shop. Tess tosses Dad a gift box with little red hearts.

"What's this?" He opens the box and pulls out a pair of socks featuring a guy in an apron and a spatula with a caption that reads, "I'll feed all you fuckers."

He raises one bushy salt-and-pepper brow and chuckles. "Nice. You ready to get back on the road?"

Once again, Tess and I slide into the back seat. Dad cranks up the Grateful Dead and takes the on-ramp onto I-80. Strip malls, big box stores, apartment buildings, hovering at the edge of the interstate, interspersed by stretches of brown pastureland dotted with cows blur past us.

Two hours later, we cross the Carquinez Bridge and are back in the Bay Area. Only forty miles from home. That's when Bennett calls. But I rush him off the phone because I want to savor the remaining minutes we have left together.

This trip is about us, about the Stones and the way we were before weddings and babies and cheating husbands. Before selling our restaurant to a Michelin-starred chef and before Tess and I fell apart from each other. For just a little longer I want it to be the way it used to be when it was just us.

"That was quick." My mother turns around to look at me. "Is he disappointed he couldn't come with us?"

"Probably. But he'd be more disappointed not to have a job."

"Oh, you mean like me." Here it comes, Tess the perpetual victim.

"You do know that not all conversations revolve around you?" And just like that the tension between us is once again palpable. We can't even go twenty-four hours.

"Screw you, Avery."

"Go to hell, Tess."

Dad glares at us in his rearview mirror. "It's hard to believe the two of you are in your thirties."

I'm about to apologize because he's right—we sound like aggrieved teenagers—when Dad swerves into another lane. The motorist next to us leans on his horn before narrowly escaping being sideswiped.

"Mac," my mother screams. "Mac!"

Our Volvo slides across two more lanes. Tess shrieks. Mom tries to take control of the car by climbing over Dad, who is slumped over the steering wheel.

The screeching blare of car horns pulls me out of my stupor and that's when I realize we're careening out of control. As we speed toward the guardrail, I grab the back of the driver's seat, holding on for dear life. Tess is still screaming, clutching her stomach, preparing for impact.

Baby, Dad, Mom, Tess. Oh my God, we're all going to die.

"Wake up, Mac. Mac!" Mom is yelling. Even with all the chaos, I've never heard my mother more panicked, more out of her mind with fear.

While everything is moving at warp speed, it feels like slow motion, like I'm in the midst of a bad dream, the one where you drive off a cliff into the ocean and wake up before you plunge to your death.

Except I don't wake up from the nightmare—or the sound of sirens.

Tess

The three of us are sitting in the ICU waiting room at San Francisco General, trying to piece together the last few hours. Mom's got a mild concussion and Avery a dislocated shoulder. I'm fine. The baby's fine. Thank God.

Dad is the one we're worried about.

The last thing I remember is Avery and I arguing in the back of the car and Dad hollering at us to stop acting like two-year-olds. Then, without warning, in what amounted to a fraction of a second, Dad goes limp and we're lurching across the freeway at seventy miles an hour.

Thank God for Good Samaritans, one of them a cardiologist who called 911 and went with Dad to the emergency room via ambulance.

The waiting room is cold and I wish I had a jacket on or at least a long pair of pants instead of shorts and a T-shirt. Mom is as pale as the white walls and I'm worried about her. I'm worried about all of us.

A doctor, a middle-aged man wearing scrubs and a skull cap and who for some insane reason reminds me of John McEnroe the tennis player, comes in the room and Mom is up before he can even inquire whether we're Macalister Stone's family.

"Is he okay?" The words come out broken.

Avery and I rise to our feet and the three of us hold hands, praying for the best but expecting the worst.

"Are you the Stones?"

I nod, afraid to hear what comes next.

"I'm Dr. Patrick Conner," he says to Mom. "Your husband suffered a myocardial infarction, a heart attack, Mrs. Stone. If it wasn't for Doctor Brown, the cardiologist on the scene, we'd be having a different discussion right now. Fortunately, we were able to perform a percutaneous coronary intervention where we found a blockage in his left anterior descending artery. We inserted a stent, which should keep the artery open for now. But there was quite a bit of damage and at some point, your husband may need bypass surgery."

"But he'll recover?" I say.

Dr. Conner turns from my mother to me. "He'll recover. It won't be overnight, he'll need plenty of rest and a change in diet and lifestyle, but as long as we can keep an eye on him, he should be okay."

"I'd like to see him," my mother says.

"He's still in recovery but as soon as he's out, I'll have a nurse come get you. Only one person at a time, okay?" He looks from Mom to me to Avery and then at his watch. "And not too long. He needs his rest and after what you all went through so do you."

Bennett comes through the door, looking as if he ran the entire way from work. He's out of breath and frazzled. "Sorry, I was away from my phone and just got the message." He embraces Avery who flinches because of her shoulder and he quickly lets her go. "Sorry, sorry. How's Mac?"

"Dr. Conner was just telling us that he's going to make a full recovery," Avery says.

It's not exactly what the doctor told us. It sounds like Dad will probably need more surgery in the future and his heart will be a chronic issue if he doesn't take care of himself.

"Doctor, is his heart attack related to his high blood pressure?" I ask because we were warned last year that if he didn't make changes he'd wind up where he is now.

"It didn't help but I doubt it was the only contributor. Still, it's important he keeps up with the hypertension medication he's taking and for us to keep an eye on all of it, including his stress levels."

"He's retiring," Mom says. "We own a restaurant but we're selling it." In this she is steadfast, I can see it in the set of her jaw. No more needing anyone's blessing.

After Dad nearly died, I don't even think Avery can argue.

"Stones." John McEnroe's doppelganger smiles, showing off a mouth of pearly white teeth. "I've eaten there many times and will be sad to see it go. But a lifestyle change in a situation like this is sometimes imperative. I'll send someone out as soon as we move your husband to a room."

When the doc leaves, Avery and Mom cry. I think it's part relief and part realization that we all could've been killed. Mom says she saw Dad clutch his chest right before the car went out of control and then it was mayhem. If it wasn't for the guardrail there's no telling how catastrophic it could've been.

The Volvo is totaled but we at least will live to see another day. And thank God no one else was hurt. If it had been Sunday, when traffic is always heavy with weekenders returning to the Bay Area from the mountains, who knows what've might have happened? Though I don't think I'll ever get the shrill screech of car horns out of my head. Or the sight of us erratically crossing the freeway at high speed. The terror of it is going to stick with me for a long time.

It's hard to believe only hours ago we were celebrating my parents' new life in Tahoe, oblivious to how in only a matter of minutes everything could irrevocably change.

My phone rings and I step out to take the call. I need air anyway.

"Kit?" It's loud in the background and I'm having trouble hearing over the din.

"Hang on a sec, let me go somewhere quieter." A few seconds later, he says, "Better?"

"Yes. Is the game over?"

"Never mind the game, what happened?"

"Dad had a heart attack while we were driving home from Tahoe. Everyone is okay but Dad had to have emergency surgery."

"Ah, Jesus. I'm sorry, Tess. He's going to pull through, right?"

"Yes," I say but my voice cracks. "The doctor thinks he should be fine but may need bypass surgery later."

"And the baby...they checked to make sure the baby's okay?"

"The baby is fine. We were all very lucky, Kit."

"I'll get the next flight there."

I want him to come but at the same time know it'll complicate where we are. And things are already too goddamned complicated as it is. Yet, I don't say no, which I know I'll wind up regretting. For right now, though, I can't see past the moment and my own need.

"We'll be at the house," I say.

When I go back inside Mom is gone. It's only Avery and Bennett sitting on the waiting room chairs.

"Did she go in to see him?"

Avery nods.

"Do you think it was our fault for fighting? That we stressed him out?"

Avery hitches her shoulders, her face as white as Mom's. "I doubt it. I think he wasn't taking care of himself and pretending that he was."

"You mean like not taking his medication?"

"He took his meds," Avery says. "At least I'm pretty sure he took them. Mom watches him like a hawk. I mean like working too hard, like killing himself over the restaurant."

"Why don't you guys go home and I'll wait for Mom? We can Uber home. But there's no sense in all of us sitting here. The doctor said Dad needs his rest. Tomorrow we can take shifts."

Avery glares at me. "I'm not leaving until I see Dad. And tomorrow I'll have to run the restaurant." She punctuates that with another glare.

"Jesus, Avery. I only suggested it because you look like you're in pain. And you're supposed to be icing." I nudge my chin at her shoulder. "Freaking sue me for caring."

Bennett gets to his feet, jams his hands in his pockets, and wanders off. He's probably sick of Avery's drama. I certainly am.

Twenty minutes later, Bennett returns with coffees and a cup of decaf for me. We drink in silence, cognizant of all the things not being said, like how the hell did we get here? I think about how fragile life is, how everything can go to hell in an instant and wonder why my parents didn't sell the restaurant sooner. Why Avery is still at my throat?

Mom returns to the waiting room, looking exhausted, and even frail. In my whole life, I've never seen her this way, utterly and completely spent.

Avery, Bennett and I jump to our feet.

"How is he?" Avery asks.

"Weak." My mother's bottom lip trembles. "But he's mostly relieved that we're all okay. Avery, he wants to talk to you, he wants to make a plan for Stones. I don't want you to argue with him. I want you to agree to what he tells you. And then I don't want any more discussion about it. Do you understand what I'm saying? He's very sick and the last thing we need is for him to be worrying about the restaurant...and your hurt feelings. Do you understand?"

Avery chokes on a sob. "Yes."

"Then go." Mom rubs Avery's back and kisses her on the top of the head, before she nudges her toward the entrance to the ICU. "You're the one he trusts when it comes to the restaurant. I need you to live up to that trust."

As soon as Avery is gone, I turn to my mother. "What's going on?"

"That's between Avery and your father." She pulls me in for a hug and holds me tight. "Did you talk to Kit?"

"He's coming. He's catching the next flight out."

"That's good. It's important that he comes, no matter what happens between you two." She loops her arm through Bennett's and pulls him into our huddle. "We're all going to get through this, one way or another."

* * *

The next morning, I leave Kit lying in my childhood bed fast asleep. He looks so innocent there, his hands under his head as if he's in prayer. It reminds me of when I first fell in love with him. When I believed in him.

I stand over him, watching him breathe. After everything that has happened, he still has the power to make my heart leap.

I write him a note and leave it on the dresser, grab my purse and tiptoe out of the room. Other than the upstairs toilet running, the house is dead quiet. I pop in the bathroom, give the flush handle a jiggle and head downstairs.

Mom must still be asleep because the kitchen is empty. Good, she needs the rest. A concussion, even a mild one, is no joke.

An Uber is waiting for me at the curb and I take it to California Street. It's already eight, later than I'd planned but I overslept, exhausted from yesterday.

The alleyway door to the restaurant's kitchen is locked, so I pound on it. Javi appears a few seconds later, takes one look at me and wraps me in an embrace.

"I'm here to help," I say. "Tell me what to do."

"Can you take the front of the house?" Avery says. She's frosting cakes with one hand, the other arm, her dislocated one, is in a sling, and there's a streak of chocolate across her nose.

"You got it. What can I do in here until lunch starts?"

Avery looks at Javi and then back at me. "Can you help chop vegetables?"

Though I've never been much good with a kitchen knife, I can try. "Show me where to start."

For the next hour we work in companionable silence, Wen, Carlos, Javi doing what they do, except twice as much without Dad. He was like all three of them put together and believe you me, they're a force. Dad always said work smarter not harder. But he did both.

I never did see the appeal of the kitchen and I still don't. It's hot and messy and backbreaking. That's how different Avery and I are because she loves it. She can't live without it. This restaurant is her home more than even the house on Baker Street.

I think about my father and how like for Avery this restaurant is everything to him. And I can't help but be angry because what did it ever do for him besides take his health and give him a living that was meager compared to the hours he put in? He can't even afford to retire without liquidating, how sad is that?

When we have the work in hand, Carlos and Wen go to the alley for a smoke. Javi takes a coffee break, leaving me alone with Avery.

"What was that yesterday with Mom talking about you, Dad and the restaurant? What did she want you to agree to?"

"They're accepting Jeremy Gains's offer. I was going to give my blessing anyway." She gives a half-hearted shrug.

"What if I get Kit to invest in the restaurant instead? Then you can run it."

"It wouldn't be enough, Tess. We're no competition for the likes of Jeremy Gains's machine. He has investors from all over the world." She stops what she's doing and faces me. "I've made my peace with it. All I want is for Dad to get better."

"All I want is for you to not wind up like Dad." I look around the kitchen. It's not even ten and it feels like we've been working for eleven hours. "Have you decided what you'll do?"

"Not yet."

"You should do something that gives you back as much as you put in."

Avery cuts me a look, a hard look. But her expression is soft, like she's thinking, really thinking about what I said. It wasn't meant to be offensive but who knows anymore with her.

"What?" I throw my arms up in the air.

"That may be the smartest thing you've ever said."

Avery

Two days after the accident and my dad's heart attack, we're in the kitchen lined up like tin soldiers in chef whites. Jeremy flew in from New York this morning to take over the restaurant. He brought four of his people with him—all men of course—who I'm presuming are here to whip us into shape.

I feel like I'm back in high school at a pep rally. Jeremy's holding court, giving a rousing lecture about what it means to work at an establishment that has been serving food to generations of families for, well, generations.

I sneak a glance at Javi and he winks. Thank God he's agreed to stay on during the transition. I don't think I could do this without him, Wen and Carlos. I miss Dad being here and I hate that even though the sale isn't even in escrow yet, it already feels like the restaurant belongs to someone else. To Jeremy.

I swear his four henchmen are staring down their noses at us as if we are cafeteria workers in a prison.

Jeremy has added three new items to the menu: A mac and cheese made with orecchiette and Roquefort, roasted chicken with a bacon-chive waffle, and Wagyu beef sliders. While on the face of it there's nothing particularly avant-garde about the dishes (they actually fit in with our whole Americana vibe), Dad would hate them. I can hear him now. *What the hell is wrong with elbows and cheddar? Why are we reinventing the wheel? It's mac and cheese for Christ's sake.*

After the "pep talk" everyone scatters, taking a station. There's a subtle face-off between one of Jeremy's guys and Javi over who is second in command. All it takes is one withering glare from Jeremy for the other guy to step off.

A few minutes later, Jeremy is standing over me at my station. I don't know why it makes me nervous. I'm doing what I always do, it's like rote.

"Chef," Jeremy says and I nod my acknowledgment. "Your dad seems to be holding up fairly well, considering the circumstances."

I do a slight double take. How would he know?

"I dropped by the hospital when I got in yesterday," he says because besides being a famous restaurateur he's also clairvoyant.

This surprises me as my father is private and I wasn't aware they were friends, or at least close enough for an in-person hospital visit.

"Hopefully he'll be out soon and will be able to recuperate at home," I say. "He's complaining about the food."

Jeremy breaks into a grin. "We'll have to fix that." He changes his focus to the cream cheese frosting I'm whipping in the mixer. "Oh yeah, it's Wednesday. Carrot cake day. I almost forgot." If a voice could roll its eyes his does. "Remember what I told you about joy, Stone." He pulls my dessert schedule off the wall and tears it in half. "Bring it."

Before I can decide whether I'm furious or liberated by his words, someone pounds on the alleyway door. Javi opens it and Tess waltzes in, her blond hair windblown and her blue eyes sparkling, looking like the star of her own show.

I hold my breath, knowing exactly what kind of reaction she'll elicit from all the new men in the kitchen, including Jeremy. Especially Jeremy.

It's like with Bennett all over again.

I secretly watch him, telling myself I don't care but I do, which is its own problem. A problem I'm not ready to face yet. He turns from what he's doing to see who is coming through the kitchen, his kitchen now.

"And you are?"

"Tess Stone. You must be Chef Gains." She sashays toward him, her hand extended.

"Nice to meet you." Jeremy shakes her hand but appears distracted by something one of his cooks is doing. "If you're not here to work please get the hell out of my kitchen."

Tess draws back, stunned that Jeremy would talk to her like that. "I came to help with the front of the house. Mom's at the hospital today."

Jeremy has already turned his back on Tess and is onto something else. "Great," he mutters. "You know where the dining room is. Try not to get underfoot and be useful by showing Paul around." Paul is the only one of the men Jeremy brought who is not in chef whites. I assume he's our new manager.

On her way to the dining room, Tess passes by me and whispers in a voice the whole kitchen can hear, "I can see why you think he's a dick."

"I heard that," Jeremy yells from the pantry. "And you're wrong. She loves me, she just doesn't know it yet."

I can feel my face turning fifty shades of red.

As we get closer to lunch the kitchen turns more frenetic. Jeremy's cooks have mad skills but Carlos, Wen and I are tripping over them. We're not used to having this many people in the kitchen at one time. And except for the swish of a knife or the thump of a pan, it's so quiet I can hear Javi breathing from across the room. No Grateful Dead or Rolling Stones today.

"Ten minutes," Jeremy barks.

My dad never had to remind us of the time, our internal clocks did it for us. But his men pick up the pace. Even Wen and Carlos, usually laid-back even in crunch time, have more pep in their step It's the first time any of us have worked with a Michelin chef and I'd be lying if I said it wasn't exciting.

Paul sticks his head in the kitchen. "We're opening the doors."

As pumped as I am, it strikes me that Dad may never cook here again. My mind goes to Saturday, the last time we were in the kitchen together. The Beatles were singing about traveling on the one after 909 and Dad was shucking clams for cioppino. And then Monday everything went haywire.

There's no time to dwell on my melancholy, though. Orders are starting to come in.

"Let's not get in the weeds," Jeremy calls and for the next two hours we're on fire.

We do more tickets than I can remember in recent history. It makes me wonder if word is out about Jeremy, though I haven't seen anything in the press.

And as much as I hate to admit it, his mac and cheese, chicken and gourmet waffles, and sliders are a huge hit. We got more orders for those three items than anything else on the menu. We'll see how they do for dinner.

Tess comes back to the kitchen to let us know the rush is over. There should be a steady trickle until dinner but for now we're getting a breather. Dinner is another story. If the news is truly out about Jeremy we can expect a full house.

"Oh my feet are killing me." Tess sits on an old barstool that Dad stuck in a corner of the kitchen years ago, takes off her three-inch heels and starts rubbing her soles. "I don't know how you all do it."

"Does this look like a podiatrist's office?" Jeremy says. "You want a break, take it in the office or take it outside. My kitchen isn't for lounging."

I look at him to see if he's joking but he's dead serious.

I grab Tess a bottle of water from the cooler and shoot Jeremy a scowl. I come close to telling the jackass my sister is pregnant but Tess wouldn't appreciate that. "I'm taking a break with my sister."

We go to my dad's cramped office, and I push Tess down in our father's chair. I hop up on the desk.

"The guy's got a stick up his ass, doesn't he?" Tess says.

"You think? That's why he owns ten famous restaurants and has Michelin stars stamped across his forehead."

"You can't stay here, Avery. What are you going to do?"

I've been asking myself the same thing, vacillating between whether to go out on my own or stick it out here to see what happens. I love the energy of a restaurant and don't know if working at a bakery would give me the same rush. And there is a part of me that believes I can learn a thing or two from Jeremy. In the meantime, I could put out a few feelers.

"What's going on with you and Kit?" I ask, wondering if the baby and Kit rushing here after the accident has given her second thoughts about the divorce.

She tosses her shoulders. "He has to leave soon."

"How do you feel about that?" The question I'm really asking is can you guys work it out, is your marriage salvageable?

"I don't know. I might be stupid enough to believe he'll never do it again." She turns her head away and stares at the wall. "I have to find a job before the baby comes."

If she stays with Kit she never has to work again—at least moneywise. But the women in this family work. We're self-reliant. We're industrious. Still, what I think Tess is really saying is she's leaving Kit. Even if her head doesn't know it yet, it's what her heart is telling her.

"Any prospects?"

"Not a goddamn one. My agent doesn't even take my calls anymore."

"I'm sorry, Tess." And for the first time in forever I hug her, holding her like I used to do when I was six and she was eight. When she was my world. "No matter what happens, we're all there for you."

"Avery, what if I suck at this?"

"At what?" I'm not sure if she's talking about being on her own or being a journalist.

"At being a mother. Besides the fact that my life is a mess, I'm not exactly maternal material. Your baby, your child, the fruit of your loins, is supposed to come first, supposed to be the one person you put your life on the line for, even die for. But this is the thing—and I'm not proud for saying it—I love me best."

I throw my head back and laugh because it's the most honest thing I've heard her say and Tess has always been honest. Even when we were kids, the closest she ever came to lying was by omitting the truth, like Gorilla gluing my mother's Sascha Brastoff bowl together, which isn't dishonesty as much as it is fixing something that is broken.

"Stop laughing," Tess swats my arm. "It's the truth."

It's funny that she's convinced that I'm laughing because I don't believe her. It's proof of just how much Tess loves herself. But the wonderfully contradictory thing about Tess is while she loves herself best, she's still capable of loving others with significant ferocity.

"You will be a wonderful mother," I assure her.

"I don't know." She leans back in my father's office chair. "You want to know a secret? One of the reasons I loved Kit so much is because I was positive he loved me more than I loved him."

The words bubble out of my mouth before I can stop them. "Bennett loved you more than you loved him and yet you dumped him."

"That was different." She waves me off. "I was moving away, starting a new life. And his life was here."

Yet, I know that's not the real reason. The real reason is Bennett didn't measure up to Tess's ideals. He isn't rich or famous. He isn't wildly ambitious. It makes me sad for her because Bennett never would've cheated on her. There probably isn't a man alive who would love her more.

It always hurts to think about it but not as much as when she says, "Besides, Bennett loves you more than he ever loved me" because we both know it's not true. No one can compete with Tess's sparkle, especially in Bennett's eyes.

* * *

On Thursday I try something new. It's the mille-feuille that I've wanted to add to the menu for ages, but Dad thought it was too excessive.

I get to the restaurant even earlier than usual to make the puff pastry dough. Most bakers use commercial-bought because the dough is a pain in the butt. But I don't have to ask to know that Jeremy Goddamn Gains rolls homemade. The guy probably makes his own ketchup for all ten of his restaurants. But to be honest, I enjoy making the dough from scratch anyway. It soothes me in the same way tinkering at the piano is like meditation for Bennett.

I'm using up the last of the season's peaches and have already mixed up a citrus cream with basil for a bright, fragrant punch. Dad's CDs are stacked in a neat pile on a shelf over the sink. I find *American Beauty* and slip it into the player. Soon, "Box of Rain" fills the kitchen and it makes me yearn for my father until I feel it in my chest, like a piece of my anatomy is missing.

By the time "Ripple" comes on, my pastry dough is ready for chilling and I'm swatting at my teary eyes. That's when Jeremy shows up. I brush my face against my shoulder, wiping away my tears, pretending it's sweat.

"Morning, Chef," he says.

"Morning." I roll my dough into discs, wrap them with cellophane and balance a stack of cooking sheets on my way to the cooler.

"What do you have there?" he asks, pointing his chin at the pans in my hands as I open the fridge with my knee.

"Puff pastry dough. I'm making mille-feuille."

If he's surprised he doesn't let on. Nor does he comment that mille-feuille is French, not American, which I'll admit gave me pause while I laid in bed last night going through a list of desserts in my head. But it's what I want to make today.

He puts on a chef's jacket emblazoned with his name. I guess it's in case he comes down with a case of amnesia. Then, he starts making lists with a black Sharpie. Dad never made lists.

Without looking up, he says, "How's the wedding plans coming?"

He doesn't strike me as the kind of chef who makes idle chitchat in the kitchen—or ever—so the question surprises me.

"They're coming along fine."

"Fine?" He raises his head from his list and looks at me, really looks.

"My dad just had a heart attack and almost died. You're taking over our family's legacy. And frankly I don't know what I'm doing here. So, I'm not exactly thinking about my wedding."

"Don't know what you're doing here as in you're out of your depth?" He cocks his brows. "Or you don't want to be here? If it's the latter..." He swings his head in the direction of the door.

Jeremy doesn't pull any punches.

"Yes to both," I say. "But until you actually own this place, I outrank you."

"I wouldn't go that far," he says, amused. "So what's up with your sister?"

Here it comes. He'll want to know if she and Kit are divorcing and when she'll be ready to date again, so he can swoop right in. It's a familiar refrain. So familiar it makes me want to throw up.

But he surprises me when he says, "Please tell me she's not planning to stay on and I don't have to fire her."

I snort. "Tess considers working here, especially with you, the seventh circle of hell, so you don't have to worry. She's only here temporarily to help." And then as an afterthought I add, "But you'd be damned lucky to have her working the front of the house full time. She grew up in this restaurant. Our diners have known her since she was knee-high and they adore her." I'm defensive on her behalf. She is my sister after all. "What's your problem with her anyway?" From where I'm sitting it was generous of her, especially because the restaurant is only days away from belonging to Jeremy, who she doesn't owe a thing.

"You want to know my problem with her? My problem is she told Paul to fuck off when he made several suggestions about streamlining how we run the pass, which will get the dishes out faster, so the food isn't served lukewarm. Apparently a problem here. And when I talked to her about cleaning up her attitude she told me to fuck off. Employees don't generally tell me to fuck off, not unless they're shooting for unemployment."

I laugh to myself, visualizing my sister telling off the almighty Jeremy Gains. Yes, Tess is a prima donna. But this is the thing, I can say that about my sister. He can't. Not now. Not when I'm just starting to get her back.

"Look, you need to realize we're still adjusting to our family restaurant changing ownership and to you—"

He holds up his hands to stop me. "Yeah, yeah, I get the gist. Do me a favor, let her know we'll muddle along without her."

I shake my head. He must be the only man on earth who isn't enamored by her charms and for some reason that makes me like him less.

Or me more.

I return to preparing the filling for my mille-feuille and he goes back to his list making. A few minutes later, he turns off the CD player.

"Hey, I was listening to that."

"Not anymore."

"Why instruct a person to find joy if you're only going to suck it out of the room?"

He chuckles. "You're funny, Stone."

Now there's only quiet and I'm finding it difficult to concentrate on my peaches. You know what? Screw the peaches, I'll use them in something else. I go to the pantry and root around for the apples, deciding this mille-feuille is my ode to nouveau American. I start a cinnamon balsamic reduction and at the last minute toss in my diced apples. I want the fruit soft but not too soft. As a test, I bake a small piece of the puff pastry until it's golden brown. When it's cool, I slice it in three equal parts and slather each piece with my pastry cream, stack the layers and top it with my apple mixture.

I've been tasting as I go but want the full effect, so I cut a sliver and pop it in my mouth. It's so good I want more.

Before I can eat another piece, Jeremy is there, helping himself to a sample. I watch him, self-conscious, trying to read his face. He swallows, then dips a spoon into my bowl of pastry cream and slides it into his mouth.

"More citrus. But I'm feeling the joy, Stone. I'm definitely feeling the joy."

And so am I, realizing it's been a long time since I've felt it. Really felt it. And yet, my grasp on this newfound joy is fleeting. Somewhere deep down inside I know that. I know to keep it I have to make things right with Tess, with Bennett, and even with my parents. But most of all I have to make things right with myself.

Tess

Dad came home today and Kit left. His emergency time off is over and he has a game tomorrow against the Mets. He asked me to come back to New York and I reiterated that I want a divorce.

I can't see how we recover from this. As much as I want to try for the sake of our baby, for the sake of us being a family, I don't know how to forgive him and move forward. And as much as it scares me to have a child on my own, being disappointed by him again scares me more.

So, this is it. The end of what I'd hoped would be a beautiful love story.

I plan to stick around until my sister's wedding, then return to Manhattan to pack my stuff and figure out a new living situation. None of it will be easy without a job. But I can't sponge off my parents forever and soon they'll be leaving here, moving to their retirement home up in the trees.

It's strange to think of some other family living here, sleeping in our old bedrooms and cooking in our kitchen. As much as it makes me nostalgic and even sad to see this drafty Victorian sold, I hope it is as loved by the next family as it was by us.

I'm getting dressed to go out with Lori, my public relations friend. She has some ideas of how I can rehabilitate myself in the court of public opinion. I'm about to put on makeup when my phone rings. It's an area code I don't recognize and I decide to let it go to voice mail, but something tells me to answer it.

"Tess?"

The voice on the other end of the phone sounds vaguely familiar but I can't place it. "Yes."

"It's Stephanie. Stephanie Clark, your former KNTV colleague."

"Oh, hey Stephanie. How's Connecticut treating you?"

"It's great. We're really enjoying it here. The station has been a bit of a challenge but I've slowly been making changes."

Changes? "Are you head of advertising?" When she was at KNTV she was a salesperson. As I recall she had some fairly large accounts but maybe she's moved up the ladder at WNEN.

"I'm actually the general manager here."

"Wow! Good for you, Stephanie." I had no idea. General manager is the top rung of the ladder. She's in charge of the entire station, including the newsroom.

"That's why I'm calling," she says. "I'm sure by now you've landed something in a big market. But...if you're still looking we have an opening for the six and eleven o'clock anchor slot. We're not New York or San Francisco but we're doing great things here in Stamford and you'd only be a couple of hours from the city," she trails off, knowing as well as I do that it would be a huge demotion.

Salty tears trickle down my cheeks, leaving a burning sensation on my skin. I should be flattered and thankful—she's the only person on God's green earth offering me a shot at steady employment and redemption—but all I feel is defeated, like I'm starting over again. Like I'm going backward instead of forward.

"Thank you, Stephanie, for thinking of me," I manage to sputter, trying to pull myself together so I don't come off rude and unappreciative, especially because she's going out on a limb for me. By now she's seen my epic meltdown at WNBC and knows the whole sordid story, I don't delude myself otherwise. And yet, here she is, willing to take a chance on me. "I'll talk to my agent and have her get you a tape."

"Tell her to send it to my news director," Stephanie says. "I'll make sure she looks for it. I hope we get to work together. It really is a good place, Tess. Maybe not what you're used to pay- and perk-wise but here you'll be treated well and our viewers will love you."

"I appreciate it, Stephanie."

By the time I end the call, I'm shaking from racking sobs. This can't be good for the baby, yet I can't seem to stop crying. The downfall of Tess Stone is now utterly complete. As Kit would say, I'm being sent back to the minors. You can't write this shit, no siree.

"Tess, honey, are you okay?" My mother taps on my bedroom door, jarring me.

"I'm fine," I say, choking on a sob.

It's her cue to walk in and find me sitting on the bed in my underwear, a total mess. "What's wrong?"

"I got a job offer. Or at least an offer to apply for a job."

"That's good, right?" My mother sits next to me on the bed and wipes my tearstained face with her hand. "Honey?"

"It's the kind of job I would've gotten five or six years ago. Not now." Correction: Now it's the only job I'm apparently qualified for. "It's beneath me."

"What kind of job is it?"

"Anchoring the news at a small station in Connecticut." I grab a tissue from the nightstand and blow my nose.

"That sounds like a big job to me."

"I was supposed to go to network, Mom. I was supposed to be the next Gayle King and now my only prospect is somewhere where...no one outside that tiny market will even know who I am. I'll be a nobody."

"You'll always be a somebody to me and your father. To Avery. To Kit."

I start crying all over again. "I wasn't enough for Kit even when I was a somebody. And Avery barely tolerates me."

"That's not true. Avery loves you. Avery will always love you. And as for Kit maybe he's not enough for you. You ever think about that?" She gives me her mother-knows-best look. "Tessy, a job doesn't define you. The number of people watching you on television doesn't define you. What defines you is here." She presses her palm against my heart. "It's what's inside. It's doing something that makes you happy no matter how many people are watching. It's like your father. He loves cooking and he loves feeding people. It never mattered to him that he didn't get glowing reviews or James Beard recognition. None of that mattered as long as he got to do what he loved. If you love being a journalist you should consider this job. And remember, Tess, it's not the end of the line. It's only the beginning." She pats my leg. "Get dressed and come downstairs. I made caldo verde. It's good for the soul."

I'm supposed to meet Lori in forty minutes. But I dash her off a text that I'm running late because my soul needs soup.

* * *

The next day I'm at the restaurant, sitting at the bar, waiting for Avery. Her idea of including me in prewedding activities is to make me her official wedding cake tester. Only Avery would bake her own wedding cake, though in truth no one will make a better one. Yes, I am biased. But in this case, it's simply a fact.

She's been playing around with recipes for days, staying after work to fine-tune the wet-to-dry ingredient ratio of her batter and experiment with a bunch of fillings. I'm surprised Jeremy lets her use "his" kitchen as a laboratory for her extracurricular baking, though technically the restaurant still belongs to my parents until escrow closes.

I nurse a glass of cranberry juice, pretending it's a Negroni, and eye my neighbor's lobster galette. Apparently we serve seafood galettes now. Elegant. It smells wonderful, which means I must be getting over my first-trimester aversion to all things fishy.

Last night, I woke up in a cold sweat after having a dream that I gave birth to triplets on the *Good Morning New York* set and Annabel was my doula. Psychologists everywhere would have a field day with that one.

I still haven't called Elsa to tell her about the job in Connecticut. There's a chance—a good chance—I never will, even though I'm jobless, pregnant, and about to be single. It's a testament to my pride—or to my snootiness. Neither will pay the rent. Still, I'm holding out for something better.

I look up to see Jeremy staring down his nose at me and immediately raise my arms in the classic surrender position. "Don't worry I'm not here to work just to drink." I hold up my glass of juice in a mock salute.

He shakes his head and goes back to the kitchen.

I'm starting to fear my sister fell in the mixer, when she appears with four plates balanced on her arms, each one containing five small squares of cake. And in that moment, I know I'm going to eat them all.

"Ready?" Avery asks.

"It's a shitty job but someone's got to do it. Where do I start?"

"Anywhere you want. I need you to rank them from one to twenty."

"One or twenty being best?"

"One is best. Twenty is worst."

Before I can take my first bite Beelzebub is back.

"Take it into the office, please."

Jeez, it's a family restaurant, not Jean-Georges. Before I can tell Jeremy to shove it, Avery grabs all four plates and leads the way to my father's old office.

To my surprise, Jeremy grabs one of the stacked chairs from the storage closet, drags it up to the desk, then leaves only to return with a fistful of forks.

Avery and I exchange glances and she shrugs.

Without invitation, Jeremy takes a bite out of the red velvet square on the first plate. "Dry. Boring."

I don't have to taste it to be outraged on my sister's behalf. "Avery doesn't do boring. Ever." I take one of the forks and dip in, then let the rich taste of it melt on my tongue. Okay, it's a little dry. "It's delicious, Avery."

Jeremy is on to his second square, a yellow cake with what looks like either lemon filling or custard. "Better."

His one-word critiques are obnoxious.

I taste. He's right, it is better, moister with a zingy finish. Even though I'm a chocoholic, I'd pick this one. "I agree," I say but there are eighteen more to go.

Jeremy is motoring through them, giving his opinions like he's Betty Crocker's smarter brother. My sister is taking copious notes and doesn't seem the least bit perturbed by his brusque attitude. If I didn't know better I'd think they were a match made in heaven.

All this over cake. Cake that no one other than my sister is going to give a second thought about. Even her worst attempt is better than any wedding cake I've ever eaten. And I've eaten a lot of wedding cake in my time, let me tell you.

The two of them should relax instead of treating this like it's as important as achieving world peace.

"I'm partial to the eighth one." It's a génoise cake with a fresh-strawberry-and-cream filling. Not only is it light and delicate but it feels very weddingish to me.

Well, knock me over with a feather, Jeremy is nodding in agreement. "It's good, even though a cliché," he says. "Pair it with the green tea sponge and the dark chocolate ganache for something less expected."

While the green tea was tasty it's a little out there.

"You think?" Avery appears as dubious as I am.

"I don't think, I know." Jeremy heads to the door. "My work here is done."

"Arrogant much?" I mutter as soon as he's gone.

Avery is too absorbed in retasting the green tea cake to hear me. "You know, I think he's right."

This is the most enthusiastic I've seen her as far as wedding planning goes. Even at her shower, she appeared one step removed. It was as if she'd gone MIA, instead of enjoying a party in her honor. Since that day, I've often wondered if her panic attack was as much about getting married as it was about the sale of the restaurant.

"How come Bennett didn't come?" Even with our crazy schedules, Kit and I moved everything around so we could pick our wedding cake flavors together at a beautiful little mom-and-pop bakery a few blocks from our apartment that had gotten a nice write-up in the *Times*. Kit was really into it, weighing our own personal taste with that of our families', so everyone would be happy. It was really sweet.

"Cake is my department," Avery says and it strikes me as a tad detached. Yes, she's a baker. We all get that. But the cake should reflect both their choices, not Avery's and Jeremy's.

"He didn't want to come?"

"If you're so worried about Bennett maybe you should've married him," she snaps.

I jerk back. "Avery, I was just asking."

There's a long pause and just when I think she's going to go off on me again, she says, "I'm sorry. That was uncalled for."

You think? "I wish you weren't so touchy. I feel like I'm walking on eggshells around you. It never used to be that way between us."

"I know. It's not you, it's me."

I drill her with a look. "You know how many times I've used that line before?"

We both bust up laughing.

"Seriously, Avery, we have to work out whatever it is you resent about me because I need you. I need you now more than ever. If it's about Bennett and me, then you have to lay it to rest. We're sisters, we can't have a man, your future husband, come between us."

Avery gets up and shuts the door. "I don't know how to," she says in a near whisper. "Believe me, I've tried." There's so much pain in that sentence that it cuts through her voice with the sharpness of a razor blade.

"Why? Because of Bennett. Because of me."

She gives an imperceptible nod, and I can see anguish written across her face. The kind of anguish that makes me know my sister is on shaky ground.

"There's nothing between us, Avery. Bennett loves you. You. Not me."

"I'm not so sure about that," she says. "But the truth doesn't matter. All that matters is how I feel."

"How do you feel?"

"That I love Bennett more than he loves me. I used to think it was enough to have him love me at all."

"But not anymore?"

She shakes her head. "You said it best when you were talking about the restaurant, about how I should do something that gives me back as much as I put in."

"But what if you're imagining it? What if Bennett loves you every bit as much as you love him?"

She pauses, then says, "I guess it doesn't matter whether I'm wrong, whether it's all in my head. All that matters is how I feel, and how I feel is full of doubt, like I'm in a one-sided love affair. I know Bennett cares for me, even loves me. But our feelings for each other aren't equal. Perhaps it's never equal in a relationship." She shrugs. "Even you said, Kit loved you more than you loved him."

"Yeah, well, look how well that turned out." I roll my eyes.

"Tess, I don't think Kit had an affair because he lost his love for you. I think he had an affair because he's a self-indulgent child, which is a problem in and of itself. But for what it's worth, I think he loves you more than life itself. I can see it in the way he looks at you and in the way he jumps on a plane and drops everything to be with you. I'm not saying you shouldn't leave him, all I'm saying is you're loved."

I reach for her hand and give it a squeeze. "Thank you for that."

"Thank you." She sniffles and wipes her nose. "Thank you for being a good sister, even when I'm not."

Now we're getting at the crux of the matter. "Why are you always angry with me, Avery? And it can't just be about Bennett."

She's quiet for a long time and I can't tell whether she's contemplating the question or blowing me off.

"I used to think it was," she finally says. "But I'm not so sure anymore."

"Are you mad at me for leaving, for moving to New York?"

"No, you were living your dream, Tess. I would never be angry with you for that." She takes a minute and in a quiet voice says, "I think I was mad at you because I wasn't living my dream. I guess I resented you for being everything I couldn't. And it wasn't fair."

"Oh, Avery. Don't you see? You have it all. Talent beyond anyone's wildest dreams and a man who would do anything for you. What I wouldn't do to have what you have."

Avery dabs at her eyes. "I think we're having a moment."

I laugh. "Does this mean we're good again?" I ask.

"Working at it." She leans over me and kisses the top of my head and somehow, I know we're back. Not quite solid yet but we're headed in the right direction.

Avery

When I think of all I could've lost it scares me down to my marrow. Even days after the accident, the need to speak to my father, just to hear his ornery voice, is all consuming.

Tess's and Mom's voices too.

I find myself calling several times a day and then dropping by after work, bringing food from the restaurant as an excuse, even though I don't need one.

Escrow closes on the restaurant the Monday after the wedding, though it's only a formality. For all intents and purposes Jeremy is the owner now. I never thought I'd see the day when Dad wasn't running the kitchen and someone else would take his place.

It's devasting, strange and oddly exhilarating all at the same time. Too many emotions for me to unpack right now. Instead, I'm taking it all in, watching Jeremy and learning whatever I can. My exact plans are still up in the air, though I've been pleasantly surprised at the restaurant. Jeremy has given me carte blanche to take the pastry department in any direction that pleases me. It's both daunting and freeing.

We're still, however, fighting over music in the kitchen, the last vestige of my father's legacy.

This morning, it's just the two of us. I'm making a chocolate mousse pavlova and Jeremy is focused on the week's menus. It's funny that he does them in the kitchen instead of the office.

"Closing in on the big day, huh?"

"Yep," I say and without warning feel something icy crawl up my back.

Jeremy is talking but I can't hear him over the pounding in my ears. The panic attack is back and it's all I can do to catch my breath and remain standing. My knuckles are white from clutching the edge of the table. The only thing I'm cognizant of is mousse trickling out of the bowl onto the floor.

"Hey. Avery! Avery!"

I feel a pair of warm hands on my shoulders and the next thing I know I'm sitting in a chair, Jeremy kneeling in front of me. Besides being mortified, my chest hurts and my vision is fuzzy.

"You okay?"

"I think so," I say but I'm not. I'm the furthest thing from okay.

"What happened?"

I can lie, tell him I'm coming down with the flu but he won't buy it. He's too observant for that. "It was a panic attack."

He tilts his head to the side. "Why?"

There's so much jammed in that one-word question that it startles me because I know why. I've always known why. And, yet, I don't want to have to verbalize it. Because if I do, I'll lose it. And the last person I want to lose it in front of is Jeremy Goddamn Gains.

"It's not the restaurant," is all I say.

He nods, his eyes filled with knowledge. Too much knowledge and it makes me wonder if it's that obvious. If Bennett and I are that obvious.

"Don't do it then," he says quietly, like there are others in the kitchen when it's only just the two of us. "It's your choice, Avery."

He's right. It's always been my choice and I chose the easy road instead of demanding more for myself, instead of realizing that it was never Tess. That it was me.

I nod, my eyes now a watery mess. On second thought, I don't care if Jeremy sees me cry. In the scheme of things, it ranks pretty low on my list for what I have to do next.

* * *

Bennett is in bed, awake, when I get home. It's been a long day. Two line cooks failed to show and I wound up staying late to help with the dinner service. Afterward, I stayed to close out and have a drink with Jeremy.

I suppose part of me was putting off the inevitable, afraid I'm about to make the biggest mistake in the world. Life-altering decisions are rife with second-guessing myself. But deep down inside I know it's for the best. We both deserve more than we're getting. And I need to stop pretending I'm okay with being Bennett's best friend instead of the love of his life.

"How did it go?" Bennett turns on his side, watching me get ready for bed.

I forgo my nightly bath ritual and crawl in next to him. "Okay. Word has spread about Jeremy and we've got a whole new set of diners. The kind of diners who put a notch on their bedpost every time they eat at a famous chef's restaurant. I hope they don't displace our regulars."

"They'll be new regulars," he says with the same wide-eyed optimism that made me fall in love with him in the first place.

"Maybe," I say but I'm not thinking about the restaurant now. I'm thinking about how to tell him, how to make this right. "Bennett, we need to call off the wedding."

At first, he looks at me like I'm joking, then seems to comprehend that I'm dead serious. "You mean to give your dad time until he's a hundred percent?"

"No." I shake my head, my eyes pooling, my heart breaking.

Bennett sits up. "Avery? What are you talking about?"

"I don't want to be second choice anymore."

"Ah, Jesus, we're back to that." He scrubs his hand through his already bed-mussed hair and my chest aches. "I love you, Avery. Don't do this. Don't make problems that don't exist."

I take his hand, trying to come up with the best way to explain it, the best way for him to see this is the right decision for both of us. That what hurts today will save us tomorrow.

"Don't say anything," I tell him, touching my finger to his lips. "But be completely honest with yourself. Was I your second choice?"

He starts to talk and I raise my hand to stop him. "Answer the question to yourself, Bennett. Be honest with yourself. That's all I'm asking."

"I don't want to do this, Avery. I feel like this is a test. And I don't want to be tested."

"Why?" I gently stroke his cheek. "Because in your heart you know what I'm saying is the truth?"

He doesn't speak for a long time. And I can see he's deliberating on how to undo this. How to keep us on track. "This is a ridiculous exercise," he says at long last. "Yes, you were my second choice. But that doesn't mean I don't love you. That doesn't mean we can't have a wonderful life together or that..."

"What? Or that what?"

"That I don't love you as much as I love...loved...Tess."

"Which one is it, Bennett? Love or loved?" I ask without anger because I already know, have always known. And today, for the first time, it only hurts a little. Mostly, though, I hurt for him. No one should ever settle for his second choice.

"We both deserve more," I say and squeeze his hand. "We both deserve to be in a relationship where the love is equal."

"Did you ever stop to consider whether that may be impossible? Maybe love is infinite, something you can't measure?"

"All I know is what I feel in here." I touch his hand to my heart.

"And you don't feel it from me?" His hazel eyes are sad but in them is also a confession, a flicker of truth. "Because it's there, Avery. It's always been there. From the very first time I saw you at Stones."

"And yet, you chose Tess."

He is quiet, his eyes no longer meeting mine. "And yet I chose Tess."

"I don't doubt you care for me, Bennett. I never did."

"But it's not enough," he says in a voice so low I lean closer just to hear him.

"Not anymore," I say. "And it shouldn't be for you either."

He pulls me close to him, like we belong. The way we'd convinced ourselves that we did when we never really fit at all. I lie in his arms, remembering the thrill of our first time, how willing I'd been to accept him after Tess crushed him. How I'd convinced myself that with time he would realize that he should've picked me first.

"Are you sure this isn't a case of cold feet?" he asks. "Tomorrow you'll wake up and realize we were meant to be."

I shake my head and he nods, realizing it's futile to argue.

"What are we going to do?" he asks.

"Sleep."

"Are you sad?"

"I am," I say. But surprisingly not as much as I thought I would be. I brush a lock of hair away from his eye. "How about you?"

"I'm still hoping to convince you that this is just a case of cold feet." He brushes a light kiss against my lips.

"And if you can't?"

He closes his eyes. "Then I'll be sad."

I can hear the sorrow in his voice. But there is something else there, too. Something that sounds a little like relief.

Tess

I finally told Elsa about the job opening in Connecticut, figuring I had nothing to lose but my pride–and a huge cut in pay. I fly out tomorrow for an interview the next day. Stephanie's assistant booked me a room at a Residence Inn and said the station would spring for a cab.

When WNBC recruited me, they put me up at the Ritz-Carlton, Central Park and sent a driver.

Oh, the times they are a-changin'.

It'll be fine, I keep telling myself. The most important thing is steady employment because even more than the paycheck I need health insurance. Prenatal care ain't cheap. And Kit can't keep me on his plan if we're no longer married. Furthermore, I can't keep lying around without purpose or I'll go crazy.

I search through the closet that still holds some of my high school clothes. All my good suits are back in New York and my flight is to Westchester County. Here, it's slim pickings as far as professional wear but I'll make it work.

I stack neat piles of the things I'm packing on the bed. It's only a four-day trip, including travel, so I don't need much. But it's better to be overprepared than under. I dash to the laundry room to get a load of underwear out of the dryer and make it halfway back when my phone rings. I drop the basket on the bed and lunge for the call before it goes to voice mail.

"Hello."

Just when I think no one is on the line, a woman says, "Is this Tess Reid?"

"It's Tess Stone. Can I help you?"

"This is Barbara White from the Yankees. There's been an accident. Kit was hit in the head with a ball while he was up to bat. He's on his way to New York-Presbyterian and asked us to call you."

"Oh my God, is he okay?"

"The team doctor thinks it's a concussion. He was out for a few seconds but was talking when they loaded him into the ambulance."

The average velocity of a fastball in major league baseball is 92 miles per hour. I can't remember who the Yankees are playing today but some of the teams have closers who can pitch as fast as 100 miles per hour. The impact can kill a person.

"Can I talk to him?" My whole body is shaking.

"They took him straight from the field. I doubt he has a phone. But I can try the team doctor. I'll see if there's a way for him to call you back and patch you in with Kit. But Ms. Reid...I mean Ms. Stone...I'm not sure Dr. Luckett is even with him."

"Okay, I'm leaving right now to catch a flight out. I'm in California and I don't know how long it'll take. So please have someone call me with an update on his condition."

I throw my carefully folded piles into my suitcase and dump my entire basket of laundry in there too. I'm just about to zip the bag but you know what? Screw it. Luggage will only slow me down.

I call an Uber and on the way to San Francisco International I use my phone to buy a ticket to LaGuardia, which is only six miles from the hospital. For all I know he'll be released by the time I get there but I have to go. I have to make sure he's okay.

The flight boards in forty-five minutes. I've never cut it so close and it's rush hour. Even though it's a reverse commute, there's still plenty of traffic on the road, people heading home to the Peninsula or the South Bay. I nervously drum my fingers on the back seat.

"You in a rush?" the driver asks.

"Yes, my husband is a New York Yankee and he got hit by a ball."

"Shit, Kit Reid?"

"Yes, how did you know?"

"Lady, it's all over the news. He got clocked in the face by Justin Verlander. Got taken out on a stretcher. What time is your flight?"

I check my watch. "We board in thirty minutes."

"Hang on, time for some evasive measures." He exits the freeway, takes a few sharp turns and winds up on the frontage road, where there's a lot less traffic.

"I hope he's okay." He sneaks a peek at me in his rearview mirror.

"Me too. I'm kind of freaking out a little. Did it look bad?"

"I didn't see it, just heard it on KCBS." He taps the radio on his console. "But it sounded serious. Dude got a standing ovation when they took him out on the stretcher. He's the first baseman, right?"

"Yes," I say, checking my phone in case I missed a text from Kit or someone from the team. "They're supposed to contact me before I board." I deliberate on whether to hit redial on the woman who called me, though she didn't seem to know much. Probably just an assistant in the front office.

"I'm sure he'll be okay. He was wearing a helmet, right?"

If he was up to bat he was and that's what the woman had said. "I think so."

"Don't worry, I'll get you there on time."

"Thank you."

The driver's shortcut shaves off a good chunk of time as we are only a few miles from the airport. I remind myself to give him an extra big tip. He drops me off in front of Terminal 2 and I hop out before the car comes to a complete stop.

"Good luck and tell your husband to get well soon," he calls after me as I sprint across the sidewalk to the gate.

Twenty minutes later, I'm sitting in business class (the only seat available). As the crew prepares us for takeoff, a call comes in with a 212 area code. I'm just about to answer it when an officious flight attendant admonishes me that all electronics must be turned off.

I try to explain that my husband's at death's door (hopefully a gross exaggeration), but she, along with the other passengers in business class, glowers at me, and tells me to turn off my phone. Instead, I surreptitiously text the caller that my plane is about to take off, to please e-mail me an update on Kit's condition and that I'll be in communication as soon as I can sign onto the airline's Wi-Fi. Then I quickly turn off my phone before Ms. Bossy Pants catches me in the act and has security remove me from the plane and I miss my one chance to get to Kit tonight.

Once we're in the air and electronics are allowed, I check my e-mail. *Nada.* So I scroll for news, hoping to learn more about Kit's condition. Other than the original incident report—Kit Reid was hit in the face or head (depending on which story I read), was rushed to the hospital, yada, yada, yada—there are no updates. I spend the entirety of the flight conjuring the worst. Kit's paralyzed from the neck down. He's got permanent brain damage. He's in a coma. For as many times in the last two months I've wished for his face to fall off, I didn't mean it. I was angry, betrayed, hurt. I'm still angry, betrayed and hurt. But with all my heart I want Kit to come through this.

I'm not a religious person but find myself praying for Kit, for me, for our baby.

Six hours later, I'm running through LaGuardia like a madwoman, literally pushing people out of my way to catch a cab. There's a line at the taxi stand and I'm tempted to pull the I'm-the- wife-of-Kit Reid card but settle for the end of the queue. I use the time to call Kit's number and of course get his damn voice mail. Next, I try Jonas but he doesn't answer either. Then I hit redial on Barbara White's number only to get a Yankees' front office recording.

Once I'm in the cab, I look up New York-Presbyterian and ask for Kit Reid. I get the ER duty nurse instead.

"I'm trying to find my husband," I explain. "He's Kit Reid. I'm on my way to the hospital but I want to make sure he's still there."

"I'm sorry, I can't give out patient information."

"I'm his wife," I say, about to lose my shit.

"We'll have to see some identification."

"Does that mean he's still there?"

There's silence on the other end of the line. My guess is every media organization in the free world is trying to find out Kit's condition and she's abiding by HIPAA laws, not to mention that the Yankees' front office wants to control the story and she's been given strict orders about talking to the press. I wonder how many unscrupulous reporters have called, pretending to be Kit's wife or relative.

I get it, I get it. But it doesn't mean I'm not frustrated as hell.

"Okay," I say. "I just flew in from California, haven't been able to get ahold of anyone from the team and will be there in a few minutes. Where should I go?"

"Go to the information desk. They'll handle it from there."

My stress level by this time is through the stratosphere. The cabdriver drops me in front of the ER where there's no one at the information desk. I'm about to start pounding on the wall, screaming bloody murder, when someone comes out from behind two swinging doors.

"I'm looking for my husband," I say. "Can someone please help me."

It turns out he's a janitor, but he must see the abject fear in my face because he goes in search of someone in charge. I'm redirected to the main hospital where I find myself standing in front of a new information desk. There are two people ahead of me and I'm now officially furious.

Why don't the Yankees have a liaison to make this easier? Why am I on my own here?

When it's finally my turn, the information desk jockey is an eighty-year-old volunteer, who is hard of hearing and moves as slow as ketchup. In frustration, I shove my ID in front of him but because I don't share Kit's last name, he has to call someone. Who? I have no idea. So here I am again, waiting while my husband is probably bleeding out somewhere.

Finally, after what seems like an hour, a woman in a suit, clearly a hospital administrator, meets me at the information desk. She must see that I'm a hair trigger from going off because she pulls me aside and quietly asks to see my identification, anything that proves I'm Kit Reid's wife.

"Sorry, I didn't bring my marriage certificate." Sarcasm isn't helping but at this point it's all I've got. "Look, I just flew across the country. I've been in the air for six hours without any information other than my husband was hit by a ball and taken by ambulance here. I don't know how injured he is and I'm freaking out. Take me to him this instant or I'll call my lawyer."

"Ma'am, this isn't helping." She pins me with a stern look as if that'll cow me into submission. Well, she's got another thing coming because this ain't my first rodeo. "We just need to prove you are who you say you are."

I pull my phone out of my purse, Google Kit and my name, bringing up a flood of pictures of us together, including the wedding photo of us that ran in the *Times*, and shove the screen in her face. "Are you satisfied now?"

She actually has the audacity to study the photos next to my face. Sure I don't have on makeup, my roots are showing and my hair needs a trim but even a person with cataracts can see it's me.

"You've got to be kidding."

She hands me back my phone and motions for me to follow her. It appears we're finally getting somewhere.

We get on an elevator and when she's sure no one is within hearing range she says, "Please understand that your husband is a public figure and it's our duty to protect his privacy. We've had no end of inquiries from the press and fans about his condition, including a few who have tried ruses to get information."

My mind immediately goes to Annabel. I wonder if I'll find her loitering in the halls.

"How is he?" I gird myself for bad news, otherwise he wouldn't still be here. And the hospital staff wouldn't be so secretive about his condition. If he was fine the Yankees would've sent out a press release by now.

"I'll let the doctors discuss that with you."

That's when I know it's even worse than I think.

I'm not paying attention to what floor we're on when the elevator stops and the door slides open. I don't even know what ward we're in. I just dutifully follow the woman in the suit to a small, private and empty waiting room.

"Someone will be out shortly to speak with you."

"Can't I see him?"

"That'll be up to his doctor. It shouldn't be too long," she says and leaves me there alone.

The only solace I take in the empty waiting room is that Annabel isn't here, waiting too. It seems like hospitals are now my home away from home.

I check my phone. The only messages are from my mom and Avery, wanting to know how Kit is. I write back that I'm still waiting for word from the doctor. No sense in sharing my fears with them until I know for sure.

It's the second time in a week I'm in a hospital with my heart in my mouth.

To keep busy, I flip through the pages of a *People* magazine. It's a year old and the pages are finger worn. The room itself is also on the worn side. Dingy yellow walls and what are supposed to be cheerful pictures of flowers that only help drive home that this is a sad place, that no number of daisies or tulips is going to change that.

The ring of my phone rends the silence, startling me at first. I wonder if I'm even allowed to have it turned on. At San Francisco General there were signs in the OR that cell phones were supposed to be turned off. I check the screen and instantly recognize Jonas's number.

"Hi," I say, unusually happy to hear Kit's brother's voice.

"You rang, Lurch?"

Clearly, he hasn't heard yet, which given that it was news even in San Francisco seems odd. Kit's parents are on a cruise. They go every summer. This year it's a trip to the Bahamas, so I doubt they know. But Jonas...

"Kit was hit by a pitch and is in the hospital," I say, getting straight to the point.

"What? When?"

"At least seven hours ago. Where are you?"

"Ensenada."

I shake my head. The guy doesn't have enough money for bus fare but somehow he's in Mexico, probably on a sandy beach with a couple of blondes, drinking margaritas.

"Shit, Tess. How is he? Let me talk to him."

"I haven't seen him yet. I just got to the hospital. I'm waiting for a doctor to tell me what's going on. Someone from the Yankees called me earlier but since then not even crickets. I'd hoped you knew something."

"No. Jesus, should I come home?"

"I don't know. Jonas, someone just came in. I've got to go."

"Call me as soon as you get the 411."

"I will."

"Ms. Stone?"

"Yes." I get to my feet. Unlike Dad's John McEnroe in scrubs, this man is in khakis, a golf shirt and loafers, and looks like he still gets carded at bars. Not until he introduces himself as Dr. Glassier do I even think he's a physician.

"Kit's resting," he says. "He has mild TBI."

I skip over the "mild" part and immediately jump to TBI. Traumatic brain injury. "Oh my God. Is he going to be all right?"

"We think so. We're keeping him overnight for observation. But with rest and medication, he should make a full recovery, though it's unlikely he'll finish out the rest of the season."

As if I care about the rest of the baseball season. The only thing I care about is Kit.

My relief must be palpable because Dr. Glassier reaches out to take my arm and says, "You want to say hello? He's been asking about you every ten minutes or so. Says you were flying in from San Francisco and that he was worried it wasn't good for the pregnancy." Doogie Howser gives me a quick once-over.

I shake my head but a rush of warmth swamps me.

He leads me out of the waiting room into the hallway and takes me to Kit's room. My husband is in bed, his face black and blue, resting against a wall of pillows.

"Look who I found," Dr. Glassier says.

Kit's battered face lights up at the sight of me and I start to cry.

"Ah, baby, come here."

The next thing I know I'm on the bed in his arms. By the time it dawns on me that I should ask if it's okay for me to hug Kit, Dr. Glassier is gone.

"Am I hurting you?" I ask, reluctant to let him go.

"Are you kidding? You're exactly what I need to get better."

"Damnit, Kit, you scared the hell out of me. Why didn't you answer your phone?"

"Don't have it. Someone from the team is supposed to bring it by." He curls around me, pulling me against his chest. "I miss you."

"Yeah? The next time you want to see me let's not do it in a hospital."

"You got it." He kisses the back of my head and rubs his hand over my belly. "How's this guy?"

"You gave us both a scare but the baby is fine. And FYI, there's a fifty percent chance this guy is a girl."

"You think?" He tugs me onto my back and hovers over me, grinning and playing the dumb jock when he's anything but.

I lightly swat his arm. "Between you and my dad, I've aged ten years."

"You don't look a day over twenty-one."

I flip onto my other side so I can look at him. Really look. I trace the edge of his bruise with my finger. "I hate Justin Verlander."

His lips curve and even with his face messed up he's so beautiful I want to kiss him. "Ah, he's not so bad."

"Was he trying to walk you?"

"Nah, he was trying to strike me out and the ball got away from him. It happens." Kit shrugs.

"Well, he better send you flowers."

"I was hoping for a steak." Again with that smile that always manages to go straight to my heart. "I get to go home tomorrow. I'll need someone to look after me." He gives me a puppy dog look with those blue eyes of his and I melt. "You coming home?"

"Nope, I've got a job interview." It's not until the day after tomorrow but Kit has made me vulnerable. If I go home with him tomorrow I'm liable to never leave.

"The one in Stamford, right?"

"Uh-huh."

"You'll kill it," he says and I can hear the sleep in his voice.

"I should go. You're supposed to rest."

"Stay. I rest better with you here, in my arms." It's a cheesy line but the thing is I know Kit means it. And I know he loves me. On some level throughout the whole Annabel fiasco, I've always known it.

But the question still remains: Does he love me enough?

Avery

Bennett moved out today but before he did, we sent out eighty-five "forget the date" e-mails, canceling our wedding. I thought it would be humiliating and even devastating but it turned out to be the thing that made us laugh again, Bennett and me.

Afterward, we packaged up all the gifts from the shower and left them out for the UPS guy to return to sender.

It wasn't until Bennett left, a duffel bag containing the last of his things slung over his shoulder, that a wave of melancholy swamped me. Not because I regret my decision—I don't—but because now I have to live up to it.

Dad is waiting for me with his famous grilled cheese when I get to the house on Baker Street. I told him I needed comfort food when what I really need is him.

"How you doing, kiddo?" He opens his arms and I walk into them, like I did that first time when Bennett fell for Tess instead of me.

"I'm okay, just needed my dad."

"We all need someone we can lean on," he sings in his best Mick Jagger voice and just like that I'm transported to the kitchen at Stones, Dad playing "Let it Bleed" while chopping meat for beef stew.

And I'm bawling so hard I can't catch my breath.

"Ah, honey, don't cry." My father has never been good around weepy females, especially me.

"I'm not," I say, wiping my face on his shirt. "It's just that everything is...different now."

"Different is good, Avery Bear. Different can be exciting. Bennett is a good man, he's just not good for you."

I wiggle out of his embrace. "Did you always think that?"

He hitches his shoulders, trying to brush it off but I won't let him. "Dad?"

"It wasn't for me to say. My little girl had to figure it out for herself."

"I thought you and Mom loved Bennett."

"We do. But you and him...Avery, he was the wrong person for you. It wasn't the right chemistry."

"What if I never find the right one, the right chemistry?" I say, throwing his own words back at him. But I'm not just talking about Bennett anymore. I'm talking about all of it. The restaurant, my career, the future.

"You'll get there. Or maybe you're already there and you just don't know it yet."

"You mean Stones?"

He nods. "Stones and other things."

"What other things?"

He shrugs but there's a smile playing on his lips. "Not for me to say."

"Stop saying that." But I know what he's saying or rather who he's saying it about. "You're wrong about Jeremy."

"If you say so." He winks.

I shake my head like he's crazy. "What about you? Are you going to miss it?"

"The restaurant? Every day for the rest of my life. But like I said, different is good. And in my case different may just save my life—and keep your mother from leaving me." He points to my grilled cheese. "Stop asking questions and eat your sandwich."

I take a big bite and around a full mouth ask, "Will you miss this house?"

"Just the stove," he says but I know he's lying.

* * *

Afterward, I go to Stones. It's my day off but I figure I'll sit up at the bar and raise a drink to single life and to love, the kind of love that gives as good as it gets.

It's crowded but I still find an empty stool. Cybil is bartending tonight and despite the rush, makes me a martini without me even having to ask.

"You look like you can use it," she says. "Can you believe this place?" She gazes out over the throngs of diners and the line of people waiting by the hostess stand. "Word is definitely out about Jeremy Goddamn Gains. I'm not gonna lie; the tips are way better under his helm."

"But the music sucks." It's some kind of techno crap.

"I didn't pick it. Paul did," someone says in my ear.

I turn to find Jeremy next to me. "How do you do that?"

"What?"

"Always know when I'm at one of your bars."

"It's a gift." He holds my gaze. "Come into my office."

I follow him, taking my martini with me.

He sits in the chair behind the desk like he owns the place, which I guess he actually does. Escrow at this point is just a formality. He gestures for me to take the chair on the other side of the desk.

There have been small changes here. For one thing, my dad's framed family photos are gone, including the one of my grandfather at the old restaurant when it was on the Embarcadero.

Mom came in last week and wrapped them up and took them away. In their place is a picture of Jeremy with the late Jöel Robuchon, different from the one at Les Corniches. He must've really loved the guy.

There is a new wall of shelves, which makes the room much tighter than it was before and it was pretty tight to begin with. On the shelves is an array of dishware. Unlike at Les Corniches, they're not organized by restaurant.

"What's this?" I wave at the shelves.

"Stoneware."

"I can see that. What's it for?"

"Stones. Which one do you like? I haven't chosen yet."

I doubt he called me in here to pick out china patterns. And it hurts. My father has been gone less than a minute and Jeremy is already making changes.

"What's wrong with what we already have?" It was good solid white Tuxton from the restaurant supply store. Inexpensive but classic.

"I want to liven things up."

I get up to take a closer look. Right off the bat, I can tell everything on the shelf is expensive, some even Heath, which my parents have at home but consider too pricey for the restaurant.

I pick up one of the white Heath bowls, beautiful in its spare and timeless design.

"That's what we use at Les Corniches but in blue."

Of course it is. Heath probably named the line after the restaurant.

I put the bowl down, immediately thinking about Bennett and me. How we never registered for china, or anything for that matter. We figured we had everything we needed.

I wonder if it was an early sign that we were never really invested. Couples don't register because of need, they register because they're starting a life together and want to make their house a home that reflects them as a unit. Our home was a mishmash of things I'd collected from the restaurant and my parents' house. Other than Bennett's piano, it was all me.

"Is that your pick?" Jeremy points to the Heath.

"Yeah," I say, though I don't know why he's asking. It's his restaurant now, I'm just an employee here. "Why not?"

"It's mine too." He gives me a small smile. "Take a seat."

I prefer to stand, getting the feeling this can't be good, though it would take a hell of a nerve to fire me even before he gets the deed to the place. Then again, he's Jeremy Goddamn Gains. "Just spit it out."

"Do you need time off?" He gets up and sits on the edge of the desk. "I find work is the best thing when everything goes sideways but I would understand if you wanted to take a few days or even a week. Anything over a week, though, and you're on your own, Stone." He grins to show he's joking, which makes me kind of half laugh, half cry.

"Why are you being so nice to me?" I swat at my eyes, trying to keep the tears at bay.

He gives a half-hearted shrug. "Don't get the wrong impression. It's not as if I like you or anything, I'm just feeling charitable today." This time, his expression is so kind I turn away, so he doesn't see me weeping like a baby.

"Thank you, Chef," I manage to say somewhat coherently. "I'll think about it."

Before my hand reaches for the knob, he says, "Avery, I've got a proposition for you when you're ready."

"What's that?" I look up, turn around, and lock eyes with him.

He shoves a box of tissues at me. "It can wait."

I take the chair he offered to me earlier, not letting him off the hook. Another time I would've said he holds my future in his hands. But the one thing I've learned in these last few weeks is that it's my hands and my hands alone that hold my future.

Still, I'm wildly curious about this proposition.

"Shoot," I say.

"I'd like to partner with you in Stones."

I try to parse his words. What exactly in this context does partner mean? "Like co-own?" I ask, fearing that I'm being terribly presumptuous but what am I supposed to infer from the word "partner?" "I don't have any capital if that's what you mean." My entire savings is twenty thousand dollars, which Bennett and I intended to use toward a down payment on a house someday. As far as the restaurant it's peanuts. It wouldn't even cover the new Heath ceramic ware.

"Yes, you do," he says, holding my gaze. "Not money. I have wealthy investors for that. You've got two things I want. The first one is your name."

"Avery?" I ask stupidly.

He shakes his head. "Stone. It's a ridiculous name for a restaurant if there aren't any, don't you think?" He arches his brows.

"Then change it."

"I told you before the name is why I'm buying the restaurant in the first place. You know how hard it is to build a reputation in the restaurant industry that brings the same diners back day in and day out, night after night?"

"You have your own name...your own reputation." Which is world famous, I don't have to add because he already knows it.

"Yep. Now can you imagine what happens when you meld two big names, two big reputations together?"

"Me? It's my grandfather and father who built this restaurant. And my mother. Not me."

Jeremy's brown-eyed gaze locks on me. "Yep, they built it. And there's no better front of the house than your mom. If I could hire her I would. But this is the thing, Avery. Your dad is a good chef. Solid. Consistent. He knows just the right way to keep diners coming back, which is a real skill. You, on the other hand, are a great chef. I only do great."

I don't know whether to be insulted that Jeremy Gains thinks of my father as only a good chef or to be elated that he just called me a great one. It's more than a little overwhelming.

"How would this work?" I ask because I'm trying to visualize Jeremy and me as partners. The funny thing about it is I can. From day one, there's been this zing between us. In this strange way, he made me see my full potential, my worth. All his damn talk about joy.

Tess is partly responsible, too. All her damn talk about getting back as much as I give.

"Fifty-fifty is how it'll work," Jeremy says. "I'll still be the boss of course." He breaks into an arrogant grin, which I'm just starting to learn is a crock. A façade.

"What I'd like us to do is hire a chef de cuisine to take over the kitchen, so I can run my other ten restaurants," he continues. "You'll be in charge, though. And that's all there is to it. Are you in?"

"Fifty-fifty and I don't put in a dime?" I'm still waiting for the catch.

"If we ever sell, we pay off our investors and I get back my initial investment. So pretty much you get bupkes. But in all seriousness, if we come out ahead after everyone gets their cut, you get a split of the profit. In the meantime, you get a nice salary, nicer than what you're making now and the opportunity to take on future ventures with me, which is an opportunity in and of itself." Again with the damn smirk-like smile. "This will all be in writing, and I suggest you get a lawyer to look it over."

"You said there were two reasons you wanted to partner. What's the other one?"

"Anyone ever tell you you're greedy, Stone?"

"What's the other one?" I fold my arms over my chest.

"We make a good team."

"How do you know?" We'd been working together for a sum total of fourteen days. That is nothing to go on.

"Because I didn't get to where I am without knowing things. And I've got a feeling about you."

Suddenly, I wonder if we're even talking about the same thing.

Jeremy barks out a laugh. "You okay? You look like you're in shock."

"Because I am."

"Well, what's it going to be? Because I can have the papers drawn up in a couple of days. Or not. It's up to you."

What he's really offering me is a future, a way to take my career to the next level. A future I hadn't even known I wanted until now. Just weeks ago, I'd been content to work in my family's restaurant, making pies and pots de crème and calling them pudding.

Saturday I was supposed to walk down the aisle with the wrong man. Then I made the right, albeit difficult, decision to call it off, to love myself more than I loved Bennett.

I smile to myself, realizing life has an interesting way of working itself out.

"Don't get the wrong impression," I say, imitating his own words, unable to hide the smile spreading across my face. "It's not as if I like you or anything. But yes! I say yes."

Tess

Today would've been Avery's wedding. Instead of letting the day go to waste, we're throwing a party at the restaurant anyway. A big to-do with an open bar, DJ, flowers, and food (duh).

We're killing two birds with one stone, so to speak. Mom and Dad's farewell to the restaurant and to the life they're leaving behind for a new one, and a celebration, congratulating Avery and Jeremy on their new partnership in Stones.

If you ask me, which no one is, there's more between those two than business. Perhaps it's too soon after Bennett but even a person on the other side of the continent can feel the sparks flying between those two.

It's wonderful to see my sister happy. The best part—because it's all about me—is she and I are good again. We're back to talking on the phone every day and finishing each other's sentences.

I'm moving to Connecticut now. I just put the first and last month's rent down on a small house in Stamford with the cutest backyard. When the baby is old enough, I plan to get her or him (we find out the baby's gender next week) one of those play sets with a swing and a slide and teeter-totter.

Yes, I took the job. It's not network or even New York but the people seem collegial and someday I can hopefully work my way back to the majors, as Kit would say.

It's all good. And I'm not just telling myself that, I believe it. Besides, humility builds character. Though if you'd told me that two months ago, I would've laughed my ass off.

"Here, babe, it's nonalcoholic." Kit hands me a Shirley Temple with a cherry on top. I wouldn't call the cherry a metaphor for my life but I'm getting there. The big takeaway from all the bad stuff that has happened is that I can still count the good stuff.

Dad's on the road to recovery. Kit's recovered, but in an abundance of caution is on the DL for the rest of the season and is helping me get the nursery ready in the new place. I've got my sister back. I'm having a baby. And I'm no longer unemployed. All things considered, winning!

As for Kit and me, well, that's complicated. I'm not taking him back but I'm not shutting the door on him either. We're having a child together and I owe it to all of us to keep him in my life, even if it's at arm's length. Who knows? Maybe there's hope for our love story yet. Only time will tell.

He's keeping the Park Avenue apartment but is considering renting a place near mine in Stamford during the offseason, so he can be close to the baby. It seems like a sound plan.

"I brought you this, but it looks like you already have one. It's there when you need it, Boo." Rodney puts another Shirley Temple down on the table as Kit heads off for appetizers. Rodney flew in just for the party, which is beyond sweet.

I kiss him on the cheek. "Thank you for being such a good friend."

"Let's not get maudlin. I'll chalk it up to the baby hormones." He slings his arm around my shoulder. "Okay, are you ready for this?" His eyes are gleaming, a telltale sign he's got gossip.

"Lay it on me."

"Annabel Ho Lane is engaged. Guess to whom?"

"Derek Jeter," I say, playing along. Otherwise, Rodney will keep me guessing until my delivery day.

"She wishes, girl. No, Dallas Gray."

I do a double take. "Our old weather guy? The one who went to KTLA?"

"One and the same. She's moving to Hell LA and word is ESPN wants her to cover the Lakers."

"Basketball? Maybe I should warn LeBron's wife. But seriously, that happened fast."

"Not so fast," Rodney says. "According to the gossip mill, the two of them have been on and off for years."

"You know what, Rod, I wish them all the happiness in the world."

Rodney looks at me and busts out laughing. "Liar."

"I almost had you, though."

"Not even for a second." Rodney's gaze turns to Avery, who's across the dining room, standing next to her four-tier wedding confection. She made it anyway and turned it into a retirement cake for my parents. "How's sissy doing?"

"Better than I would've expected. To tell you the truth, I think she's relieved. Bennett too, honestly. They just weren't meant to be."

"Looks like she's got a new fan." He nudges his chin in the direction of Jeremy, who can't take his eyes off Avery.

"I was thinking the same thing."

"What are the two of you conspiring about over here?" Kit is back from stuffing his face at the crudo fish bar.

"Nothing," both Rodney and I say at the same time.

And before Kit can press, my father is standing at the bar, tapping a glass with a spoon.

"Can I have everyone's attention?" He clears his throat, preparing to make a speech. In my entire life, I can't remember Dad ever saying more than a few words at any event where it was required of him. Even at my wedding, his toast was short and sweet.

For a second, Dad looks flustered, but Mom takes his hand. "Welp, it's been a damn good run. Thanks for coming." He starts to sit down and the crowd, a combination of Avery's pals, restaurant industry folks and my parents' best friends, egg him on with "Speech, speech!"

He throws his hands up in the air. "That was it, folks."

Everyone laughs and my mom jabs my dad to continue.

"All right, all right. You want a long boring speech; I'll give you one. This place has been part of my life...part of our lives...for three generations. It started with my father, who worked here until the day he died. Then Beatriz and I took over. We moved it to the Financial District and made a few changes." Dad looks around the old bank building and smiles. "And for a lot of years it was home. Our home and we hope your home away from home. But all good things must come to an end. And as hard as it is to let go, we know the restaurant is in good hands.

"Jeremy...Avery." He motions for both of them to join my parents. "Jeremy and Avery, but mostly Avery, is going to take Stones to the next level, make the place reputable, maybe even add a few stars to the name." Dad winks, eliciting a roomful of chuckles. He kisses the top of Avery's head. "Kiddo, a father has never been prouder. You too, Tess. You know she won an Emmy, don't you?" He pulls me into the fold and Jeremy slips away, leaving just the four of us, the four Stones, standing at the head of the dining room with the people we love most. "You girls are the light of our lives."

His eyes mist and so do mine, knowing how difficult this must be for him. How difficult it is for all of us. Three generations. Even more than the house on Baker Street, the restaurant was the place that always brought us together.

"So enough with the speech. I'm going to leave you with this." Dad raises his glass. "To good friends, good food, good times, and new beginnings. Thanks for being part of this adventure and I hope you'll stick around for the next one." He lifts Mom in the air and kisses her, then pulls Avery and me in for a group hug.

I'm overcome by emotion. To think how close Dad came to not being here with us...To think this is the last time we'll all be together in Stones....

Jeremy encourages the guests to take their seats for dinner. He's serving all my father's signature dishes.

Kit, Rodney and I are at the same table as Avery and she's saved me the chair next to her.

Even though we're surrounded by family and friends, for the rest of the night it's just the two of us. Just Avery and I, taking it all in, the restaurant my grandfather built, and my father remade, the one Avery will carry into the future.

"Are you scared?" I whisper.

"A little bit. Okay, a lot." She glances down at my stomach. "Are you?"

I nod because I'm petrified. "Will you come to Connecticut when I have the baby?" It's a big ask now that she's part owner of Stones. But more than anyone else, I need her.

"I wouldn't miss it for the world." She lays her head on my shoulder. "I love you, Tess."

"I love you too. But promise me something."

"What?" Avery asks.

"Promise me you won't leave me again."

She looks surprised. "I never left you."

"It felt like you did."

Her expression turns to acknowledgment. "I guess in a way I did. I won't ever again, promise. And, Tess, I'm sorry."

"Kit once said I was hard to love. Is it true? Be honest."

"You're not hard to love, Tess. What was hard was learning to love myself. You, more than anyone, helped me do that."

"Are you sure?"

"I've never been surer in my life." She leans over and hugs me and that's when I know everything is going to be all right.

Epilogue
Avery

It's been eighteen months since Jeremy and I took over Stones and today we're celebrating Beatriz and Mac's. Yes, we named our new café after my parents. It was Jeremy's idea.

The location isn't too far from Stones, but the scope is completely different. The menu consists mostly of soups, salads (lots of my mom's Portuguese recipes) and sandwiches, including my dad's famous grilled cheese. But the heavy emphasis is on desserts, kind of a cross between a tearoom and a bistro. And it's totally my baby.

Everyone is here for the soft opening. Mom and Dad drove down from Tahoe and even Tess flew in from Connecticut with baby Ava. I can't get enough of my new niece. And Tess is positively glowing with motherhood, which took us all a little by surprise.

"Don't make the toast until Kit arrives," she whispers in my ear. "He really wants to be here for it."

"How soon?" I don't want to keep our investors waiting but Kit is flying in all the way from Florida, where he has spring training.

"He landed fifteen minutes ago and has a car waiting for him."

Tess says she's done with Kit, yet he lives in a house next door to her in Stamford, is over at her place in the offseason every time I call, continues to vacation with her on the Cape, and still shows up to all our family gatherings.

To me, the most telling part is my sister never actually filed for divorce and isn't seeing anyone. As far as I can tell, neither is Kit. He's just seeing Tess and Ava. Constantly.

This last year and half, he's been at Tess's beck and call and has shared in everything from diaper changing to early morning feedings. He and Ava are so smitten with each other that I have to strong-arm him just to pry my niece out of his hands.

There's no question, at least in my mind, that he's still in love with Tess. He follows her around with his heart in his eyes. I think the prospect of losing her changed everything for him.

For Tess's part, motherhood has dulled her need to be the center of attention. She's content now to let everyone else around her shine while she sits it out in the shadows. Same with Kit, to be truthful. The object of their affection is Ava and no longer themselves.

This is all to say if they're working it out, they have my blessing. Not that they need it.

Bennett is here too. No matter what, he'll always be part of the Stone clan. He came with the new woman in his life, Janell, who I just happen to be crazy about. She's also a jingle writer and the two of them are talking about starting their own marketing firm. I'm pretty sure Bennett is head over heels in love with her, judging by the way his eyes light up whenever she enters a room.

He's also back to being a regular at Stones again, taking up the same place at the bar where I first met him. When I know he's coming in, I'll make a few pots de crème especially for him.

"What are we waiting for?" Jeremy slips his arm around my waist, pulls me off to the side, and kisses me behind my ear.

"Kit. He's almost here."

"Okay. I'll tell the staff to keep the refills coming on the bubbly. How are you holding up?" He flashes his mischievous-boy smile.

"Good," I say and shove my left hand in my pocket to hide my new engagement ring, which I don't want to upstage the opening.

One night, the rascal waited until Les Corniches closed and everyone went home, talked me into a skinny-dip in the ridiculous swimming pool, got down on one knee in the shallow end and asked me to marry him. Let's just say I look at the pool in a whole different light nowadays.

"I want to wait to tell everyone about our engagement until it's only our families. Just us."

"Works for me." His lips touch mine. But before we can finish the kiss, Kit arrives, creating a stir.

I look over at Tess and she rolls her eyes. Kit may not be a Giant or an Athletic but he's still a crowd-pleaser. He waves to me from across the room, a huge grin splitting his face.

"Looks like we can get this show on the road," Jeremy says. "Nervous?"

"Nope." I'm filled with confidence, maybe for the first time in my life.

The concept for Beatriz and Mac's was my idea and it's already received a ton of press, including being called one of the "most anticipated openings" of the year. Part of the attention and accolades is due to Jeremy's name, of course. But I'm getting a fair amount of recognition too. Last month, *Eater* named me one of the top pastry chefs to watch and the Food Network asked me to be a judge on *Winner Cake All*.

Jeremy is urging me to do the show, but I've politely declined. Jeremy may have helped me up my game, but make no mistake about it, I'm still Macalister Stone's daughter. The food is supposed to be center stage, not the chef.

"Do you think Beatriz and Mac's will live up to the hype?" I whisper to Jeremy, because at the end of the day, I just want it to be a comfortable and delicious place for diners without the fanfare of awards and glowing write-ups.

"Are you kidding? It'll exceed the hype." He wraps his arms around me. "Avery Goddamn Stone is a genius. Anyone ever tell you that?"

On our second date, I broke down and told him about the nickname we'd given him. Wouldn't you know, he freaking loved it. He even had it embroidered on his chef's jacket. Jeremy Goddamn Gains.

"Let's do this, so we can get to the important stuff." He winks and I go up on tiptoes to give him another kiss.

"As soon as it's over we'll tell everyone," I say and a tingle goes up my spine. I can't wait to be Jeremy's wife. And I can't wait for the whole world to know it.

Jeremy grabs a fork and taps on his champagne flute to hush the crowd. When no one listens, Bennett lets out an earsplitting whistle, which does the trick.

"I'd like to thank everyone for coming today," Jeremy starts.

Dad shouts, "Hey, free food, we wouldn't miss it for the world."

Mom pokes Dad in the arm and everyone laughs.

"All right, I'll keep this short and turn the floor over to my partner in crime here." Jeremy puts his arm around me, pulls me next to him, and my stomach does flip-flops. The man has the power to make me giddy with love. "Beatriz and Mac's is the brainchild of this beautiful woman. Word on the street is she's a pretty good pastry chef, too. In any event, we wanted to do something different, something casual that would not only honor Ma and Pop Stone but be a place where there's no shame in having dessert as your main course. We appreciate all your support and your trust in us. Ladies and gentlemen, I give you the woman of the hour, Ms. Avery Stone."

There's a lot of applause and words of encouragement from the Stones' crew, including Wen, Carlos, Mandy, Cybil, and Javi, who's loving retirement.

I wasn't expecting to speak and am momentarily flummoxed over what to say but go with my heart. "First, I want to thank my family. Mom, Dad, Tess, Kit and baby Ava, who if you haven't already guessed, is named after me." I beam as Ava reaches for me and I snatch her out of Kit's arms.

"Beatriz and Mac's is a dream come true for me. It's not fancy or cutting edge like Jeremy's other restaurants or as classic as Stones but it's me, simple with a dash of different."

I look around at what Jeremy and I created, the cozy stone fireplace, the big, tufted chairs, the bookcases, the wooden farm tables, and the glass Viennese dessert counter showcasing a multitude of pastries, cakes, tarts and cookies. It's the kind of place moms and daughters will come for tea or special birthday parties, the kind of place friends will hit after a movie or a play, the kind of place where no one feels awkward about cuddling up with a book and dessert for hours at a time.

"We hope the café becomes a time-honored tradition in the Bay Area and a fresh canvas for baking and creating." I turn to Jeremy and raise my glass. "This is my love letter to you."

There's more shouting and howls, and even some catcalls.

Jeremy pulls me in for a hug and I whisper in his ear, "You once told me if I found joy, I'd find myself and that's when I found you."

Printed in the United States
by Baker & Taylor Publisher Services